the third generation

To Agnes,
Best Wishes

LARRY BUTTRAM

Larry Buttram

1-11-07

www.larrybuttram.com

Published in the United States by:

New Virginia Publications

9185 Matthew Dr.

Manassas Park, Va. 20111

SAN 256-0453

First Printing - July, 2007

Book Cover and Layout by Allison Media

www.allisonmedia.com

ISBN 978-0-9755030-7-2

ISBN 0-9755030-7-2

LCCN 2007925342

www.LarryButtram.com

PROLOGUE

Charlotte Waters finished loading the boxes in the truck, then sat in the living room waiting for her father. Since her mother died six years earlier, it had been just her and him. And, although he'd tried to do a good job raising her, she realized being a full time parent was not what he was cut out for. But somehow she'd made it through her high school years, and was now trying to decide what to do with the rest of her life. Presently she was trying to decide if she should tell her father that he was going to be late for work.

"Daddy, you know it's almost nine o'clock?" she yelled.

Her father soon appeared in the doorway, buckling his suspenders.

"Reckon Mr. Range ain't gonna fire me after twenty-five-years. Ain't nobody ever in the store afore ten o'clock anyway. Ya got ya things loaded in the truck?"

"Yep."

"Now, ya know ya got to be careful makin' your deliveries on these back roads. Lots a scoundrels and low lifes around nowadays."

"I know, Daddy, but nobody's hurt an Avon Lady yet. There's something in the handbook that don't allow it."

He looked at her and smiled.

"Okay, girl. Just be careful."

The two left the house and walked to the driveway. Charlotte looked in the truck bed, checked her boxes of Avon cosmetics once more, then climbed into the passenger side. Her father sat behind the wheel, started the engine, and drove off.

They were soon at Range's hardware store. Clyde Waters pulled the truck to a stop, then exited leaving the door open for his daughter. Charlotte hurried around the truck, gave her father a quick kiss, and climbed inside.

"Remember ta be back here ta pick me up at five," he said.

"Ain't I always here on time, Daddy?" she answered.

Charlotte looked down Main Street, then pulled the truck from the curb and headed out of town. By eleven-thirty she had completed the delivery of her Avon products. With that out of the way, she could now do what she had been looking forward to for days. The area became more sparsely populated as she drove out of town. She continued down the highway until she came to a familiar gravel road, and followed it until it became a narrow dirt road. With the truck windows open, she could smell the intoxicating aroma of the nearby honeysuckles. She pulled the truck to a stop in front of a small, one story house. Mrs. Royce, one of her high school teachers, had asked her to feed her cat while she and her husband were out of town. Removing the key from her purse, she unlocked the door and went inside, where she was quickly greeted by Miss Jingles. After feeding the cat and refilling its water dish, she took the litter box outdoors and dumped it. After refilling the box, she returned to the living room and seated herself where she had a view of the road. Her wait was not long. A truck soon appeared and parked next to hers. A young man got out and walked hurriedly to the house. Charlotte opened the door and ran onto the porch to greet him.

"Hi, Billy. I wasn't sure you'd be able to make it," she said as she threw her arms around him.

"I wouldn't miss seeing you for anything in the world," said her friend, as they turned and walked into the house. Once inside he put his hands on her shoulders and kissed her. After a few seconds he sat on the couch, pulling her onto his lap.

"It was nice of Mrs. Royce and her husband to go away and let you use their house," said Billy.

"Well, don't get too used to it. They'll be back in a few days."

"I know, and back to reality for us," he answered as he stroked her hair. Then, with a more serious tone, he asked, "Have you thought any more about what we talked about?"

She rubbed his cheek, then moved to the couch next to him.

"You know how I feel about you, Billy, but...I just don't know. I don't think I can just take off like that."

"What do you have to keep you here? Except your father, I mean?"

"Well, that's something. I know he and I ain't that close, but I couldn't just go away and leave him without saying nothing."

"And if you told him you know he'd never let you do it."

"I just don't know, Billy," she said as she wrung her hands.

"It's not about Gerald, is it? You don't love him."

"I know that."

"And he don't love you. He just wants to own you. If you settle down with him, you'll never be happy. He just wants a woman he can show off to his friends like some...like some huntin' trophy."

"I know. And it's not about him. New York is just such a long way off and so different. You sure your friend's gonna get you a job there?"

"I'll be playing trumpet at one of the finest nightclubs in Greenwich Village, and you can get a job as a waitress. We can work together at night, sleep till noon, then go to school in the afternoon. Charlotte, you know that's the only way we can be together. And it's the only way I can ever do anything with my music. There ain't nothing for me here. Neither one of us is suited for this little town."

The cat came into the room and sat at Charlotte's feet. She picked her up, paced around the room, then turned back to Billy.

"I don't know what to do. You know I love you and want to be with you, but it's such a big decision. Why do we have to do this now?"

"I'm twenty-two years old, Charlotte. I know that don't seem old, but this is the only chance I'll have to do what I want with my life, and it's the only chance we have to be together. I don't have anybody here except my aunt, and you know how her and I get along."

She walked around the room, rubbing the cat and looking at Billy.

"Okay, Charlotte, I'll make this easy for you. I already told Mr. O'toole that I'm quitting. If you want to go with me then meet me at the bus station Thursday morning. The bus leaves at ten-fifteen. If you're not there then...well, I'll understand."

"Oh, Billy, this is awful. I do love you and want to be with you, but...I just don't know. I wish I could talk you out of this."

"I love you too, Charlotte, but this may be the only chance I'll have to get out of this town and make something of myself. Whatever you decide, I'll understand."

She put the cat down, and walked to the door and stared outside. After a few seconds she turned back to him.

"You got your trumpet in the truck?"

"Yes, why?"

"Go get it and play me something."

"That trumpet is pretty loud, you know."

"The nearest neighbor is a mile or two away. I want to hear you play," she said as she moved closer. "Maybe if you play real nice it'll help me make up my mind."

"Girl, you get much closer, and...and we might still be here when Mr. and Mrs. Royce get back."

"I got all afternoon, but I want to hear you play the trumpet first."

PART ONE

ONE

SEPTEMBER, 1988

The assignment was simple enough. Write a two to three page essay on yourself and how you became the person you are. At first, Emily Ward found it boring, but as she spent more time thinking about it, it became more interesting. It was the first time in her eighteen years that she'd consciously spent time analyzing who she was, and in doing so she'd learned much about herself. Now, she had to stand in front of her freshmen English Composition class and read her report. Why was it necessary to read a report for a composition class? That should only be for a public speaking class. Still, with some trepidation and a little excitement she began to read.

"A friend once asked me what is the first thing a person notices about someone when they meet them for the first time. I wasn't sure what she was getting at, but I told her it was probably their height or weight. She told me that she didn't agree - that the first thing you always notice is if the person is a male or female. After I thought about it a while, I agreed - with one exception - me. With a white father and a black mother, the first thing a person notices about me is that I'm bi-racial.

"I was five years old when I first realized I was different. You see,

my mother and father were just - well, my mother and father. And my little brother looked just like me, so, as crazy as it sounds, I never thought of myself as being different. That all changed when I started kindergarten. One day another little girl felt it necessary to tell me that I was a half-breed. I didn't know what a half-breed was, although, from the way she said it, I knew it must be something horrible. So when I went home I asked my mother why she'd called me that. She then explained the obvious - at least the obvious to everyone but me. She said that she and my dad were different races, and that there would be some people that didn't like people from different races marrying. When I asked her why, she just said that some people just didn't like anyone different from themselves. And she also told me that I shouldn't worry about it, because she and my dad loved each other very much, and loved my brother and I more than anything in the world, and that that was what was really important.

"Of course, as I grew older, I endured more prejudice, although it was rare that anyone said anything to my face. Usually it was just a glance, or a stare, or a whisper when they thought I wasn't looking. I guess, if I'd been born twenty or thirty years earlier, it would've been a lot worse, but hopefully people are a little more tolerant now than they were in the good ole days.

"So, as an adult, how has being bi-racial affected me? That's a difficult question, and I'm not sure I have the complete answer yet. I think some things are obvious. I do my best to treat everyone the same, and, even though my friends sometimes call me wishy-washy, I try to always look at everyone's point of view in a situation. And while this may shock some people, I sometimes struggle with thoughts which might be considered biased or prejudiced. For example, I know that young black males are at a great disadvantage in society, so am I biased if I only date white men? And I've been told I'm a great athlete like my father, and, even though my mother is not athletic at all, I wonder if my abilities are because of my black heritage.

"Someone once asked me if I felt more black or white. And, while I thought it was an insensitive question, it made me think. You see,

through my veins flows the blood of slaves as well as slave owners. I'm German, English, African, and a little Hispanic. My ancestors have been conquerors as well as the conquered. They have lived in the ghetto and in palaces. They have been princes and paupers. In short, I'm the result of thousands of years of human interaction and life.

"I had a friend who recently began researching her ancestors. As a blond-haired, blue-eyed girl, she was surprised to discover that one of her great-great-grandparents was African. I also read somewhere that if mankind survives another couple of thousand years, with inter-racial marriage becoming more common, there will eventually be only one race. So I guess I just got a little head start on most of you. But I suspect, if that actually does happen, people will still find another reason to discriminate against one another. Because, like my mother said, people still feel uncomfortable with someone even a little different from themselves. And for society to advance, that has to change. "

Emily finished her essay, and to her surprise and enjoyment, received a nice applause from the other students. She thanked the class and returned to her seat.

It was only the second week of class and Emily was still adjusting to college life. While the University of Tennessee campus was only twenty minutes from her parents' house in north Knoxville, it seemed as if it was in another universe. As the oldest child, and with a reputation of being self confident and fearless, she hated to admit that she was homesick. It was only three days, however, until she would join her family for their Friday night dinner, a tradition that began when she was a small child. There was a lot she could tell them about her past week at school.

With many thoughts on her mind she returned to the dorm room she shared with her roommate, Candy, a pleasant but shy girl from Shelbyville, Tennessee. Since it was mid-afternoon, Candy, like most of the other girls in the dorm, was still in class. Taking advantage of the quiet, she opened her English Literature book, sat at her desk, and began to read. She forced herself to read John Keat's, *Ode to a Grecian Urn.* Her class was to discuss the meaning of the poem the next day.

After reading it for the third time, it finally began to make sense. The two lovers, their picture captured while running towards each other on the urn, would never meet. While their joy at their anticipated reunion would be captured forever, their love would never be realized. It was a bittersweet tale - one for all eternity.

Proud that she had finally understood what Keats was saying, she closed the book and walked to the tiny window that overlooked the parking lot.

It's too nice a day to stay in here, she thought to herself. She quickly changed into shorts and a sweatshirt, grabbed her basketball, and left for the gym. Even though the building was open to anyone when there were no gym classes or basketball practices scheduled, there were only a few students present when she arrived. The gym held three basketball courts, the first of which was used for pick-up games. The other two courts were designated for students who just wished to shoot baskets. Emily watched the game between two teams of male students for a minute, then went to an unused net and began practicing foul shots. Although she'd been a starting forward on the Murfreesboro High School girls' team, it had been over six months since she'd handled a basketball. She loved the game - there just had not been time to play with everything going on; her graduation from high school, her parent's moving to Knoxville, and her beginning college.

She had the court to herself for a few minutes, before she was joined by a male student who appeared to be about her age.

"Mind if I shoot some hoops with you, girl?" he asked.

"That's fine," she answered.

The two shot without talking for some time. Then, when Emily made a forty foot shot, the boy turned to her with a smile.

"Say, sister, that's one fine shot you got there."

"Thank you. It just takes a little practice."

"You on a b-ball scholarship?"

"No, I just played a little in high school."

"You ought to try out for the team this fall. They're looking for fine talent like you."

"For Coach Summitt's team? No, I've seen those girls play. Believe me, I'm not in the same league."

"Don't cut yourself short, girl," he said as he moved closer. "You got a lot of talent, and not too bad looking, if I do say so myself."

She ignored his last remark, and took her next shot.

"Whatcha name?" he asked as he held out his hand.

"Emily. And yours?" Emily answered as she shook his hand. He was rather handsome, and muscular too, although a bit arrogant, she surmised.

"I'm Julius. Dr. J some people call me," he answered, referring to the professional basketball player, Julius Irving. "You want to play a game of horse?"

"Oh, I guess so," answered Emily, hesitantly.

They began shooting, each trying to match the other's shot. If one person hit a shot and the other missed, that person received a letter - a H or an O, etc., until one person spelled out H-O-R-S-E. After a few minutes the score was tied with both having H-O-R-S.

"Let's say who ever loses has to buy the other one a soda." said Julius.

"I guess that's fair," answered Emily.

Emily again made her forty-foot shot. Julius took the ball and copied her shot. The ball hit the rim and fell to the floor.

"Looks like I owe you a coke, girl. Want to go to the student lounge?"

"Right now?"

"Sure, girl. No time like the present."

"I don't know. I'm kind of sweaty."

"They don't mind, and it'll only be for a few minutes."

"Okay. I guess we can do that."

As they headed off the court, Julius turned to her.

"You got a fine shot, sister, but you hold the ball too much in the palm of your hand. You need to just let it slip off the end of your fingers."

"Well, why don't you save your suggestions until after you beat me, then you can tell me what I did wrong."

"All right," he answered with a laugh. "That's fair."

The student lounge was almost deserted when they arrived. They picked a table where they placed their basketballs on the chairs, then went to the vending machines. Julius bought Emily a Pepsi and handed it to her.

"You want something else - like a bag of chips or something?"

"No thanks. I'm not hungry."

They took their drinks and returned to the table. Emily soon learned that, like her, he too was a freshman.

"So, how come you came to UT?" asked Julius.

"They have a good law school."

"You going to be a lawyer?"

"That's my goal."

"I'm impressed."

"Thanks. What about you?"

"Just General Ed. I still have some time before I decide. Where are you from?"

"I grew up in Murfreesboro, but my parents just moved to Knoxville this summer."

"So you could go to school here?"

"Oh, no. It was just a coincidence. My dad just took a job as the Regional Editor for the Tennessean."

"The Tennessean? I know I heard of it, but..."

"That's the statewide newspaper. He worked for them in Nashville, and just got promoted this summer. What about you? Where are you from?"

"Jefferson City. You know where that is?"

"We actually played them once in the state tournament, but that was at Cookeville, so I've never been there. It's somewhere east of here, right?"

"Yep. Just about an hour." Julius studied her for a minute.

"What are you thinking?"

"I hope you don't mind me askin'," he said.

"Go ahead," she answered, knowing the question that was on his mind.

"So, are you...?

"White father and black mother."

"Well, you're one of the finest looking sisters ever I laid my eyes on."

"Why do you talk like that?"

"Like what?"

"Why can't you just say that you think I'm attractive?"

"I just did. That's just me. Why?"

"Never mind."

There was an uncomfortable silence for a moment, then Julius spoke.

"So, how did your parents meet?"

Emily thought the question a little strange, but then figured he might be nervous and was just thinking of something to say.

"At college at Middle Tennessee State University."

"That's in Nashville, right?"

"Close - Murfreesboro, which is right outside of Nashville."

"They grew up in Murfreesboro?"

"No, not really. My grandfather moved there when my mother was a teenager, but my father grew up in Greeneville. I think that's probably near Jefferson City."

"You're kidding."

"What?"

"I lived in Greeneville when I was young. We left when I was about four, so I don't remember much about it."

"How come you left?"

Julius looked down at the table for a second, then back at Emily.

"I'm not sure I should tell you."

"Why? Not much you could have done at four that you could be ashamed of."

"That's true," he said with a laugh, then became more serious. "My mother was embarrassed to live in the town any more."

"Why?"

"My father sort of held up a gas station and got caught."

"Oh, I'm sorry."

"Yeah, so was my mom. She moved us to Jefferson City to live with her sister. She didn't want me and my little sister growing up in that environment."

"That was nice of her. She still live there?"

"Yep. She's been working for the county now for about fifteen years."

"And your father? I guess he's long been out of jail?"

"Well, sort of. He only got three years for the gas station, but I guess some people just can't make it on the outside. He sold some cocaine to an undercover cop a few years ago, so he's back in the slammer."

"I'm sorry."

"Me too. Let's change the subject. You want to go to the Vol's game with me Saturday?"

"I heard it was sold out? You got tickets?"

"I'm Dr. J, remember?"

"Oh, okay. That sounds like fun."

The two continued talking for a few minutes. Soon Emily took her last sip of Pepsi and said, "Well, I guess I better go. I've got a lot of studying to do."

"I thought maybe you would like to get together later this evening?"

"You sure move fast, don't you?"

"Why take it slow?"

"Because, that's the way I am. Saturday will be fine, though."

The two picked up their basketballs and walked toward the door.

"What's your last name?" asked Julius.

"Ward - Emily Ward. What's yours? Since my dad grew up in Greeneville, he might have known your dad."

"It's Russell. My dad is Ted Russell, but I doubt if they ran in the same circles."

TWO

Her mother's minivan and her dad's Mustang were already in the parking lot when a fellow student dropped Emily off at the restaurant. Both cars being there told her that her father had worked late again, and didn't have time to come home before going to the restaurant. Emily and her brother, Justin, were very young when the family began the tradition of eating out on Friday night. Each week a different family member got to select the restaurant. This week her mother had chosen a Mexican restaurant on Clinton Highway near their home north of Knoxville. While she still enjoyed the weekly get-togethers, it was not as much fun since they'd moved to Knoxville, and her Grandpa Robertson was still in Murfreesboro. The family had tried to convince him to move, but had yet been unsuccessful. As a professor at Middle Tennessee State University in Murfreesboro, he still had a few years remaining before retirement. They hoped he would join them in Knoxville at that time. At least he made frequent trips to visit them, and they planned on visiting him on Thanksgiving.

At six-foot-four it was easy to spot Emily's brother, Justin, as she entered the restaurant. Still, he waved his hands getting her attention

"Hey, sis, over here."

Her mother and father arose and gave her a kiss as she joined them. Justin put out his hand to give her a high-five, a gesture which she ignored with a shake of her head.

"You're too old to give your big sister a hug now?" she asked as she moved closer and wrapped her arms around him.

"Not too old - just too cool," said their mother, Sally. "Starting quarterbacks don't do emotional things like hug their sister - or mother."

"Or dad," added their father, Ethan.

"Hey, what is this?" asked Justin. "Pick on Justin night?"

The four laughed and sat down. Justin smiled and pulled out the chair for his sister.

"So, how was school this week, sweetie?" asked her dad.

"It was good, Daddy. It's still just a little overwhelming."

"Well, it's only been two weeks, honey," said her mother. "How's your roommate?"

"Candy's fine. She's the perfect roommate - that is unless you want somebody to talk to."

"She's still as quiet?" asked her dad.

"I guess she's getting a little better. I mean, she's nice enough, she just hardly ever says anything unless I ask her a question."

"Sounds like my old college roommate," said her dad.

"That's right," added her mother. "He was really strange. What was his name?"

"Rudolph Reynolds. Rudolph Reynolds, from Louisville."

"That's right," said her mother with a laugh. "That's how he always introduced himself. What a strange character."

"From what I've heard about him," said Emily, "I don't think Candy is that strange - just pretty shy."

"Is she cute?" asked Justin.

"What?" asked Emily quickly.

"Is she cute?" repeated Justin. "Maybe I can come by and help her get rid of her shyness."

Her mother and father laughed as Emily stared at her brother.

"Yeah, little brother, that's what every college girl wants - a sixteen-year-old high school sophomore."

"A sophomore starting quarterback. Not many of those around."

"Whatever. And how come, Mr. Starting Quarterback, you're not playing tonight?"

"We have a bye week. You can come next week and see me play at Oneida."

The waitress interrupted the conversation by taking their drink orders. When she left the family continued catching up on each other's lives. Soon their father turned to them with a serious look.

"Kids, I'm afraid I have some bad news."

"Uh-oh," said Emily. "Is this about Grandpa Ward?"

"Yes. Unfortunately, his cancer has come back. How could you possibly know that?"

Emily's ability to somehow know the unknown had been the subject of many family discussions.

"I don't know, Daddy - I just had a feeling. Besides, you always worried it might come back someday."

"That's true, I said that many years ago, but I didn't think it would happen after this long."

"But from what the doctor said, it could actually be unrelated to the first cancer," said their mother.

"What difference does it make?" asked Justin. "The news is still as bad."

"But there's a lot of new treatments today, Dad," said Emily. "Have the doctors said what they recommend?"

"My Dad didn't want to talk about it, and Mom said he doesn't want any treatment. He said he'd rather die than go through what he did the first time."

"You going to go see him soon, Daddy?" asked Emily.

"Your mother and I'll probably go over Sunday. You guys want to go?"

"I will," said Justin.

"Maybe it's better if we split it up rather than all go at one time. I only have morning classes on Wednesday, so I can go see him then and still be back by dark. That is, if I can use one of your cars."

"I think that's a good idea, Emily," said her mother. "We'll work something out with the car."

Soon the waitress returned with their drinks and took their orders. After she left, Emily's mother turned to her.

"Anything new at school this week?"

"I had to read my essay on how I got to be who I am today."

"Oh, really. What did you say?"

"Well, I talked about what it's like being bi-racial."

"You're bi-racial?" asked Justin.

"Sometimes you're a jerk, little brother," she returned quickly."

"Just ignore him, honey," said her father. "He's just a dumb jock, you know."

Emily laughed at her dad's comment, while Justin gave him a nasty look.

"Go ahead, honey," said her mother. "These two can entertain themselves for a while."

Emily told them about reading her essay and the response she received from the other students. She then turned to Justin, awaiting another comment.

"That's actually very good, sis. I wished I had thought of some of those things."

"Well, you're just a sophomore starting quarterback."

"Anything else exciting happen this week?" asked her father.

"Well, sort of. A nice young man asked me to go to the football game with him tomorrow."

"That's nice," said her father. "You have a class with him?"

"No, not really. We met on the basketball court. We were just shooting hoops and started talking."

"What's his name?" asked her mother.

"Julius. Julius Russell. He likes to be called Dr. J."

"Ha," said Justin, "that's pretty arrogant to name yourself after the best basketball player of our time."

Emily's father gave her mother a quick, concerned look. "His last name is Russell?" he asked. "Do you know where he's from?"

"Actually, Daddy, that's the most unbelievable part. He's from

Jefferson City, but his dad grew up in Greeneville. You might know him. His name is...oh shoot."

"Ted....Ted Russell," said her father in disgust.

Emily gave her mother a confused look.

"So, do you know him, Daddy?"

"Yes, I do, Emily, and I don't want you to have anything to do with that boy."

"I don't understand," she said, looking back and forth between her mother and father, "Julius told me that his father has had a lot of problems, and that he's in prison now, but that has nothing to do with him. Why are you saying I shouldn't see him?"

"Listen to me, Emily," said her father as he leaned forward, "that family is no good. I've known his father and uncle all my life, and they've been nothing but trouble. And, as the saying goes, the fruit doesn't fall far from the tree. I don't want you to see that boy again."

"Daddy, I don't understand," said Emily with a trembling voice, "Why are you acting like this? You've always taught us to judge a person for theirself, and now your acting crazy when you don't even know him."

"I don't have to know him, Emily. I know what he's like. Let me ask you a question. You said you met him shooting baskets. I'll bet you were already on the court when he came up, right?"

"Yes, but..."

"Then do you think it was just a coincidence that you met? He already knew who you were and planned it to meet you."

"That's crazy."

"Emily, out of 20,000 students at UT, what do you think the odds are of meeting someone whose father I went to school with?"

"And out of all the people in Tennessee," Emily answered, "what are the odds of you meeting a man on a dusty country road, then years later meeting and marrying his daughter?"

Emily was referring to the time, twenty-five years earlier, when her grandfather Robertson, along with a friend, went to Greeneville to look at a hunting dog. Getting lost on a dusty country road, they stopped a young boy, thirteen year-old Ethan Ward, and asked for directions. To show their appreciation, they offered him a ride to his friend's house. Only minutes later they were stopped by a deputy sheriff who pulled his gun on them. Her grandfather's friend, however, drew his gun and shot and killed the Deputy. The men escaped, leaving Ethan the only witness who, for years, lived in fear of their return. Then, six years later, while attending Middle Tennessee State, Ethan and Sally met and began dating. A year later, when the Professor was arrested for his part in the crime, Ethan testified that he believed the Deputy would have killed the men had he not been shot. It was his testimony that helped free Professor Robertson. A short time later Ethan and Sally were married.

Emily stared at her dad for a second, then, as she arose from the table, turned to her mother.

"Mom, I really don't want to spend the night at home tonight. Can you take me back to my dorm?"

With that she turned and walked out the door. Her mother stared at her father for a second, then arose and followed after her.

"I'll go and try to get her settled down before she hitchhikes back to the dorm."

After the two women left, Justin turned to his father.

"That went well, huh?"

Sally Ward found her daughter standing beside her minivan, arms folded. She opened her mouth to speak, but before she could do so Emily interrupted her.

"Can you just take me back to campus, please?" she asked.

"I will after we talk for a minute," said Sally calmly, "if that's what you still want."

"Why did Daddy act like that, Mom? I don't understand. I don't think I've ever seen him that unreasonable."

"I know that he was pretty upset, but...I guess he's never told you anything about Ted and Ed Russell before?"

"I don't think so, Mom. I'm sure I would've remembered it."

"Maybe he hasn't. He doesn't like to talk about it. Your father is a very open-minded and reasonable man, Emily, but there's probably nobody in the world that he dislikes more than Ted Russell and his brother Ed."

"Why is that?"

"I don't know everything, and I don't think your dad even knows why, but those two boys started picking on him when they were young, and continued until he moved away from Greeneville. He and Ted actually got in a fight when they were about eighteen."

"An actual physical fight?"

"Oh, yes. He didn't even tell me until some time later."

"Over what?"

"I don't know. Ted just kept picking on your dad until he'd had enough."

"Who won?"

"I guess your dad got the best of him. I think that's why your dad is so concerned. He thinks Ted may be behind this to get even with him."

"That's ridiculous. It's just a coincidence."

"I think you're probably right, but even if it is, can you see how upsetting this is to him?"

"I guess so, Mom, but I still don't think I should make my decision on who to go out with based on something that happened between the two of them years ago."

Sally stared at her daughter for a minute, and then put her arm around her.

"I'll tell you what. Let's go back inside and we won't talk about this until after dinner. Then, when you're both calmer, you can discuss it again. Then, if you still want, I'll take you back to the dorm."

"Mom..."

"I know you're upset, Emily, but you know how much your dad loves you. Just give him a chance to calm down. Okay?"

"I guess that's fair."

The two women walked slowly back into the restaurant and returned to their table. Sally explained that they were not to discuss the subject until later. While there was much tension in the air, the family made it through the meal, helped considerably by Justin's jokes and comments. After the meal, Sally and her daughter got into the minivan and headed home, followed closely by Ethan and Justin.

After returning home, Ethan went to his bedroom and read for a while before again talking to his daughter. Shortly before bedtime he put down his book, said a quick prayer, and walked to Emily's room. She lay on the bed watching TV. He stood in the doorway waiting until she saw him. Soon she looked up at him and pointed the remote at the TV, turning down the volume.

"Can we talk?" asked Ethan.

"Okay," answered Emily flatly.

Ethan walked into the room and sat on the edge of the bed. Emily could tell that her dad was embarrassed and remorseful about their earlier conversation. Even though the two had a good relationship, they had had their share of disagreements over the years. Emily could not remember, however, when she had seen him so upset over something which she felt should not be an issue.

"Emily, I'm sorry I got so upset, but I hope you know it's only because I love you and worry so much about you."

"I know you love me and worry about me, Daddy, but I think there's more to it than that. I also think you were upset for yourself - that Julius's dad might be behind this to get even with you."

"I guess that's a fair statement. And I'll admit, that there's no one's son I would hate more for you to become involved with. But the important thing here is that I have a need and responsibility to protect you. And from what I know about the family, they have always been bad news, and will always be bad news."

"I'm sorry, Daddy, but just because his father and uncle are evil people, doesn't mean that Julius is. You're the one who always said that each person is responsible for their actions. And you also told me that no child can get into heaven because her parents were saved. Everyone has to make their own decision to accept Jesus or not, so therefore each person makes their own decisions on what type of person they are."

"Good point. So, are you saying Julius is a Christian?"

"I don't know. I hardly know him, but my point is that what his father has done has nothing to do with what kind of person he is. And there's another thing. You think that his father might have put him up to this - to meeting me - just to hurt you. Well, I think it might be just the opposite."

"What do you mean?"

"I think, based on what you and Mom told me, that his father would be just as upset as you are if he knew that his son was going out with me. I really doubt if his father knows anything about this."

"Hmm," said Ethan as he rubbed his chin. "I guess I never thought of that. Anyway, where does that leave us?"

"I don't know, Daddy. I love you and respect you, but I'm not going to cancel my date with him tomorrow because you and his father hate each other."

"Okay, sweetie, then all I ask is that you be very cautious with him. And I'll be praying that you made the right decision."

"Thanks, Daddy," she said as she sat up and hugged her father's neck. "Besides, after he spends some time with me he may never want to see me again."

"Then he'd be a bigger fool than either his father or his uncle, and I don't think that will happen. You sleep tight, pumpkin."

He kissed his daughter and walked out of the room. As he walked down the hallway, Justin called to him from his room.

"Hey, Dad."

"Yes, Justin?"

"I just had a question."

"What's that?"

"Well, there's this new girl at school, and she's kind of cute, so I was thinking of asking her out, but I wanted to know what you thought."

"Yes," Ethan said cautiously.

"She said her father is quite well known. I've never heard of the guy, but she says his name is...now what was it...Oh, I remember - Manson

- Charles Manson. Do you know anything about him?"

"Justin."

"Yes, Sir?"

"Go to bed," he said, trying not to smile.

Ethan heard his wife and daughter laugh as he walked toward the bedroom.

THREE

Greeneville, Tennessee
November, 1982

The crowd at the General Morgan Inn was much larger than expected. Of course, it wasn't every day that a small town like Greeneville celebrated the election of a State Senator. And almost everyone in the town had known Tommy Bell his entire life. Born and raised in the town, he became their favorite son when, in 1969, he was wounded in Vietnam while saving his best friend, Ethan Ward. A few years later he was elected the town's first black Mayor. And while his term was not without trouble and conflict, the great majority of people felt he'd done a good job. It was with the people's support and encouragement that he'd run for State Senator. The race was thrown wide open when the incumbent of thirty years, Ed Peterson from Morristown, retired. It was the support of the people from Greeneville that had helped Tommy win the election. And while he was a registered Democrat, he embraced ideals from both parties. He agreed with the Democrats on issues of gun control and government programs to help the sick and poor, but he shared the Republicans' views on abortion and business. He made a promise to himself before being sworn into office earlier in the day - that he would vote with his heart no matter what his party's position on the issue.

The Democratic Party had put pressure on Tommy to have a sit-down dinner and only invite the biggest contributors to his campaign. He had refused, saying all of the town should be included in the celebration. For that reason, and perhaps the free food, the crowd at the hotel overflowed into the lobby. Still everyone enjoyed themselves as they waited for the guest of honor to appear. Soon, Ethan Ward, the MC for the evening, appeared at the podium.

"I'd like to thank you all for coming this evening," he said, trying to be heard above the roar of the crowd. "Boy, it's a good thing we didn't serve alcohol," he yelled.

"Where's Tommy?" someone yelled.

"He'll be here soon," answered Ethan.

"We love you, Ethan," yelled a woman, "but this is Tommy's night."

"I understand that, but if you all can just calm down for a second, I'll introduce him," he shouted. The crowd grew somewhat quieter. "This is a rare occasion. It's not often you have the chance to elect someone from your hometown as State Senator. But then it's not often you have the chance to know someone like Tommy Bell. I believe we all agree that he is a sincerely good individual. I've known Tommy for over twenty-five years now, and I can sincerely say he's one of the finest people I've ever known. You can say many things about a person at a time like this, but I think the thing about Tommy that is most profound is that he makes everyone he meets want to be a better person. Ladies and gentlemen, I would like to introduce my best friend and your new State Senator, Tommy Bell."

With those words, and to the cheer of the crowd, Tommy entered from the side and waved to his supporters. Shaking hands and hugging people, it took him a few minutes to make his way to the podium. As he did so, he looked around at his family and friends who awaited him at the head of the room. His mother was there, as well as a few distant relatives whom he rarely saw. His best friend, Ethan was there, along with his wife, Sally, and their two kids Emily and Justin. Sally's sister, Rita, who Tommy had met on a few occasions, was standing beside her sister. Ethan's mother and father, Buster and Hilda Ward, along with their older son, Horace, and his wife and son, were also in attendance.

Tommy looked around to see another classmate from high school, Rachel Mills, and her husband, Allen Banks. Tommy thought of the strange way God worked. When they were young, he and Rachel did not care for each other. Now, she was among his greatest supporters. She attributed the change in her life to accepting Jesus. While Tommy knew that Jesus could change people's lives, he had been skeptical about Rachel's conversion. Like everyone else, however, he soon saw that her change had been real and complete. And, since being born again, she had also become hugely successful and famous. As a movie star and singer, she owned houses in Nashville and Los Angeles, as well as Greeneville. As many times as he had seen her in the past few years, Tommy realized that this was the first time he had ever met her husband.

Tommy was also glad to see another old friend, Carl Benlow. Being about the same age as his father, Tommy had first met Carl Benlow when he stopped his father for going through a stop sign. At that time a Greene County deputy, Benlow only gave his dad a warning and told him he didn't want anything to happen to his young son. His father thanked him graciously and later told Tommy what a good man he was. It wasn't easy for a black man - minister or otherwise - to get off with only a warning in 1950's Tennessee.

Police Chief Carl Benlow and Tommy Bell had become good friends when Tommy had been elected Mayor of Greeneville a few years earlier. He was one of the people he would miss most when he left for Nashville.

Tommy's only regret for the evening was that his father, the reverend Oscar Bell, could not share in his joy with him. He died in 1977 at the age of fifty-two from a heart attack. The irony of his death was that he had just returned from the hospital to visit a church member recovering from a heart attack when his occurred. His wife found him slumped over his desk in the church office. While Tommy had been brought up to not question any of God's decisions, this was his ultimate test.

He could not understand how he could let someone so wonderful and useful in bringing people to the Lord be struck down at age fifty-two. While he eventually got over his anger, eleven years later he still missed his father. Oscar Bell had not been an emotional man - and Tommy could count on one hand the number of times he had said he loved him - but he knew that he did. He showed it every day in all the things he did for him. Now, at one of the most important times in his life, his father was not there to share it with him. However, Tommy knew he was looking down on him and always acted accordingly.

The cheering continued as he took the podium. He raised his hands in an attempt to quiet the crowd. Finally, after a short time, the cheering died down enough so that he might speak.

"Wow, that's quite a reception. I never knew I had so many friends."

"You're the man," shouted someone down front who Tommy could not recall ever seeing before.

"Thank you, thank you," he said as he again raised his hands. "I can't tell you how much it means to me having all of you here this evening. And you electing me your Senator is more than I could have ever hoped. Now you all have endured my speeches for the past few months, so this will be very short and to the point. When I began running for this seat, I made myself a couple of promises. I said if I was elected, I would always do what God puts in my heart to do. And in times when the answer is not clear, I will make my decision based on what I feel is right for the greater number of people."

"Sounds good to us," yelled a lady near the front.

"Thank you," returned Tommy. "And I know tonight is sort of like a honeymoon..."

"And we're virgins," yelled one man near the back, receiving a lot of laughter.

"I know...it sounds silly, but that's what it feels like," continued Tommy. "Anyway, I just want you to remember, in the near future, when you disagree with me, that I'm trying to do what is right. And I want you to know that my door is always open, so please, don't be shy about letting me know where you stand on the issues. And I promise that I will do the best job I can in representing the people of Greeneville. Now, enough of that kind of talk. We came here to have fun, so everyone have something to eat and drink, and let's celebrate."

The noise became almost deafening as Tommy turned to hug his mother.

"Congratulations, Son. I just wish your father were here to see this."

"Me too, Mom," he answered as he wiped a tear from his eye.

The rest of Tommy's relatives and close friends gathered around to hug and congratulate him. Soon Ethan embraced his best friend.

"Congratulations, brother. You'll make a great Senator."

"I hope so, Ace. Thank you for everything."

"For what? I haven't done anything."

"Then for being such a good friend."

After talking to his family and friends, Tommy made his way into the crowd, hugging and shaking hands with his fellow town members. As he was making his way to the refreshment table, he turned to see an old acquaintance, James Foster. He and Mr. Foster did not know each other very well, but had met through Ethan. He owned a gas station in Harriman, Tennessee, which was half way between Greeneville and Nashville. Tommy had stopped at his station many times when driving to visit Ethan and Sally.

"Mr. Foster," greeted Tommy, "How nice of you to be here."

"I wouldn't a' missed it for tha world," he said as he held out his hand. "Congratulations, Senator."

"Thank you. You came all the way from Harriman just to congratulate me?"

"Yes, sir. It's a great day for black people, and for tha state'a Tennessee. I always knew you was gonna do somethin' great. I'm mighty proud'a you son."

"Thank you, Mr. Foster."

"Thank you, son."

The two continued talking for a short time before Tommy excused himself. As he was walking back to his mother, Tommy ran into Sally's sister, Rita Simpson, as she was making her way to the refreshment table.

"This is quite a bash," she said. "It looks like you have quiet a few friends."

"I hope they're this happy in a year or so," he answered.

"It looks like they are pretty satisfied with their new Senator."

"Yes, but from what I learned as Mayor, public sentiment can change in a second. Anyway, I'll worry about that when it happens. I haven't talked to you for some time. How are you and your son doing?"

"We're doing okay, I think."

He looked at her more seriously. "Are things starting to get back to normal for you, Rita?"

Tommy was referring to the loss of her husband, Robert Simpson, a few years earlier.

"Well, it's taken some time, but yes, I don't cry too much any more. Thanks for asking."

"I guess when I move to Nashville we'll probably be seeing more of each other."

"I think that would be nice," she returned with a slight smile. "I'll be glad to show you around the town if you would like."

"That sounds like a good plan. I would appreciate that."

The two were interrupted by Ethan as he put his hand on Tommy's shoulder.

"I hate to do this, buddy," said Ethan, "but I think we're going to have to leave."

"So soon? Is everything okay?"

"Oh, yeah. Justin is just a little tired, and Sally is just getting over a cold. It's been a long day. Do you mind giving Rita a ride back to the motel?"

Tommy and Rita gave each other a quick glance.

"Sure, that's fine with me, if she doesn't mind."

"That's fine. I would appreciate it."

"How about breakfast in the morning here at the hotel for everybody?" asked Ethan. "Nine o'clock? Is that okay?"

"That sounds good to me," said Rita.

"Me too," answered Tommy.

"Sounds like a plan," said Ethan.

The threesome was soon joined by Sally and the kids. The Ward family said goodbye to Rita and the new Senator, and left the party.

Nashville
March, 1983

Tommy Bell got out of his car and walked hurriedly around to the passenger's side and opened the door. Rita Simpson took his hand as he helped her out of the car. With his arm around her waist, they walked into her house in suburban Nashville.

"Would you like another glass of wine?" Rita asked as she took their coats and hung them in the closet.

"No thanks. Two was enough for me. I'm a public figure now, you know. You never can tell when someone with a long range camera is watching."

"You had a lot of problems with that?"

"No, but you never can be too careful."

"Well, I'm not a public figure, so I think I'll have one more glass," she said as she walked into the kitchen. "How about a Coke?"

"That would be fine, thank you."

She soon returned with the drinks, sat them on the coffee table, and went to the stereo and put on a Johnny Mathis album. She stood listening to the record for a few seconds, then joined Tommy on the couch.

"I had a really good time tonight," said Rita.

"Me too. Of course, I always have a great time with you. That was a great restaurant."

"Too bad they didn't have a band."

"The night was still young. We could've gone somewhere else to dance."

"I know, but I told Dad I'd pick up Bobby early in the morning. But, if you like, we could dance here."

"Well, of course. Mrs. Simpson, would you like to dance?"

"I'd love to."

Tommy took her hand and led her to the floor in front of the stereo. Johnny Mathis sang *The Twelfth of Never* as Rita put her head on his shoulder.

"This is one of my favorite songs," she said.

"It is nice. He has a great voice."

They continued dancing silently for a while before Tommy raised her chin and kissed her. Rita put her arms around his shoulder and returned the kiss. They continued dancing until the song ended, and then returned to the couch. They sipped their drinks and continued listening to Johnny Mathis. Soon Tommy turned to Rita again and kissed her on the neck.

"You know what?" she said.

"What?" he asked.

She sat her glass of wine on the coffee table, then took his drink from his hand and sat it near hers. Then she arose and sat in his lap.

"This should make it easier for you," she said with a smile.

"That's very thoughtful of you," he answered.

The two continued kissing for a few minutes. After a while, Rita stopped, moved back and looked at Tommy.

"What's wrong?"

"What do you mean?"

"I don't know. I just feel like something's wrong - like you don't really want this."

Tommy looked around the room for a second, then back at her. "It's just that..."

"It's okay, Tommy," she said as she arose and sat beside him again. "We don't have to do this."

"Rita...," he began.

"It's all right, Tommy. I thought we wanted the same thing. I didn't mean to throw myself at you."

Tommy looked at her for a moment, then arose and went to the stereo and turned it down. He turned back to Rita with a serious look.

"Rita, there's something I think I should tell you."

"Uh, oh. I'm not sure I want to hear this. I know - you just want to be friends?"

"No, that's not it. And you have to promise me you're not going to laugh."

"Laugh? What - are you going to tell me that you prefer men?"

"What?" Tommy laughed. "Absolutely not! Now are you going to promise me?"

"Okay."

He went back to the couch and sat beside her again. She waited as he took another sip of his drink, and then looked back at her.

"Well?" she asked.

"I'm thinking. You're probably not going to believe this, but.... I'm not sure how to say this. It's just that..."

"Will you please tell me before you drive me crazy?"

"Okay, you see, I've never actually...well, you know I've dated a few women, but I've never..."

"What? Tommy, you're not actually going to tell me that you've a virgin?"

"Well, yes, I guess so."

She looked at him for a second, then burst out laughing.

"You promised me you wouldn't do that."

She looked at him for a second before realizing he was serious.

"Tommy, I, uh...I'm sorry. I really thought you were kidding, but you're serious about this."

"Yes, so you can go ahead and say whatever you want."

"I don't know what to say. I have to tell you though, that I'm really surprised - no, shocked. I mean, you're a handsome, smart thirty-three year old man who could have any woman you want, and...."

She looked at him for a moment, then shook her head and folded her hands.

"Tommy, I'm sorry. I just realized what you told me. I know how much your religious beliefs mean to you. I just never thought...well, a lot of people say what God means to them, but there are very few who live it like you do. I apologize for acting that way."

"Thanks."

"So, has it been difficult?"

"Has it been difficult?" he repeated with a laugh. "Well, of course. Here I am with a beautiful woman, and I've had a couple of glasses of wine, and I'm thinking to myself, *What are you, an idiot? What difference does it make? Everybody sins, and this should be no different.*"

Rita laughed at his comment.

"Well, I'm sorry, but I have to tell you, I'm glad I have that effect on you. And, if you don't mind me asking, how have you been able to do it? I mean, I know you've dated a few women."

"Not that many, actually. I think only three seriously."

"And, you don't have to answer this if I'm getting too nosy, but what did you tell them? Did you tell them...?"

"No, you're the only one I ever told this to. I would just sort of put things off and tell them I wanted it to mean something - you know, those things a woman usually tells a man."

"And Ethan doesn't know about this either?"

"Oh, no. He's my best friend, but there are things one man just doesn't discuss with another."

"I see. So, what does this mean as far as our relationship? Are you telling me this to let me know you don't want a physical relationship?"

Tommy picked up his drink and took a sip. He then put his knee on the couch as he turned to face Rita.

"Rita, the reason I'm telling you this is...well, I think I'm falling in love with you and..."

"Wow. That's nice to hear."

"And... I...it's just very difficult. I find you extremely attractive, but I have my beliefs and..."

"It's okay, Tommy. I understand. However you want to handle it is okay with me."

Tommy waited for a minute, hoping she would continue, but she said nothing else. Finally, he turned to her with a question.

"So what do you think about what I just told you - how I feel about you? Are you happy or disappointed or what?"

She gave him a slight smile and said, "Tommy, I just need a little more time. I know it's been four years since Robby died, but it's still a little difficult. But I feel very close to you, and you're one of the handsomest and kindest men I've ever known, so please be a little patient with me and I think we could have something permanent, if that's what you want."

Tommy looked at her and opened his mouth to say something, but stopped.

"Is there something else you wanted to say?"

"Well, yes. I guess since we're having this discussion I should tell you everything."

"Oh, boy. Don't tell me - you're dying or you're a spy, or something like that?"

"No, nothing that interesting. As you said, my beliefs are very important to me. I think, if this does become a permanent relationship, the fact that I'm a Christian and you aren't would become a problem for us."

"I believe in God."

"But the Bible tells us that even the demons believe in God and shudder."

Rita gave him an angry look. "What a nice thing to say. Thanks for putting me in with such nice company."

"I'm sorry," Tommy quickly answered. "I didn't mean that the way it came out. I just mean that believing in God is not enough. Jesus said that He was the way and the truth and the light, and that no one came to the Father except through Him."

"I know, Tommy - and we've had this conversation before, but I still don't know what I believe. It's hard for me to believe that is the only way to get to heaven. It must be nice to have such a strong belief and to be so certain of something."

"Well, then, who do you think Jesus was?"

"I think He was a wonderful and very moral man - possibly the greatest to ever live - but I still don't know if I believe He was God."

"I'm sorry, but those two things can't go together. He couldn't have been a wonderful and moral man if He wasn't God."

"I'm not following you. What do you mean?"

"There are really only three possibilities as to who Jesus was. He was either insane, a liar, or He was who He said he was. His life has been examined more than anyone's in history, and there is absolutely nothing that shows Him to be insane or even slightly unstable. As far as Him being a liar, again there is no proof of that. Virtually everything He did or said was recorded - usually by more than one person - and there is not one time He strayed from the truth. The final option is that He was who He said He was - God's own son. So a person has to decide what they believe about Him, but they can't say He was a just a good and moral man who went around saying He was God, because that's an impossibility."

"Hmm," answered Rita, "I never thought of it that way. It gives me something to think about."

Tommy took her hands in his. "Look, Rita, I know everyone has to make their own decision about this, and I can't force my beliefs on you. One thing I would suggest, though, is for you to pray about it and ask God to show you the truth."

"Okay, I think that's fair."

Tommy looked at her for a second, and then shook his head. "Boy, I've really dumped a lot of stuff on you tonight, huh? I hope I haven't freaked you out too much."

He looked at her for a moment, but got no response. "Are you okay?"

She picked up her drink and stared into the glass, then ran her finger around the rim. After a second she turned back to Tommy.

"Yes, I'm okay, but, since we're being so open with each other tonight, there's something I need to share with you."

"Okay," he answered slowly.

She took another sip of her drink and then turned to Tommy with a sad look in her eyes.

"What I'm about to tell you I've never told another person."

"Not even Sally?"

"No. No one."

"Okay, I'm listening."

"All right. You were there a few years ago when that mad man entered my life and tore my world apart."

Sally was referring to the time, five years earlier, when an old acquaintance began stalking her and killed her husband, Robert. The nightmare was made even worse when the authorities began investigating her as a suspect in her husband's death. The truth was not revealed for months, when she was cleared of the charges.

"Oh, yes," answered Tommy. "He sure put you through hell."

"And the hell is not over."

"What do you mean?"

"There's one other thing that he did that no one else knows about."

"What's that?"

She took a sip of her drink and stared at the floor for a few seconds before turning back to Tommy with tears in her eyes.

"He raped me."

"What? And you never told anyone? I don't understand how..."

"It was before he killed Robby."

Tommy's mouth fell open as he stared at her. "I'm sorry, Rita. I don't understand. If that was before he killed Robert, why didn't you tell the authorities?"

"Because I didn't know."

"What? I'm sorry, but this is not making any sense. How could he rape you and you not know?"

"He drugged me. He got the key to our house when Robby was out of town with Daddy and drugged my food or drink or something - I don't remember. I was unconscious and didn't even know about it until...until..."

"Until the night he broke into your house and abducted you?"

"Yes. That's when he told me what he did. And - well, the rest of it you know, since you and Ethan were there when he was killed."

"But why didn't you tell anyone then? No one could blame---oh, I see"

"Yes - because of Bobby. That evil bastard told me that he wore a condom when he had sex with me. He said he didn't want me to get pregnant until we could be together permanently. What a twisted mind he had. Anyway, I had no way to know if my child was his or Robby's, so I didn't want to tell anyone."

"But now, there are still tests you can take. I'm sure you can get both of their blood types and..."

"I know, and I thought of that, but now when I look at Bobby, there's no doubt in my mind that he's Robby's son. If you see a picture of Robby when he was that age they look like twins."

"So, you feel comfortable that..."

"Oh, yes. For the first year or so I didn't really know. But then, as Bobby started to get older, I could see more and more of his father in him. I don't have any more doubts, but it's been tough."

Tommy leaned forward and took her in his arms. "I'm sorry, Rita. You've sure been through a lot."

She sobbed for a moment, then composed herself and pulled back.

"Thank you. I just had to tell someone. Promise me you will never tell anyone else."

"I promise. I don't think there's any need to keep it a secret anymore, and you don't have anything to be ashamed of, but that's your decision. I won't ever tell anyone."

"You're a good man, Senator Bell."

"Thank you. I try to be."

They sat silently for a moment before Rita stood and took her glass from the table. She finished her drink, and then took a deep breath and looked at Tommy.

"Well, this has been quite an interesting evening."

"Yes, it has," he answered as he arose and put his arms around her. "Are you okay?"

"Actually, yes, I feel pretty good. Better than I have in a long time. I appreciate you listening."

"It was my pleasure. So, where do we go from here?"

"I guess that depends on you, Senator Bell. But right now I'm exhausted, and I have to get up early in the morning to get Bobby."

"Then how about a good night kiss, and I'll talk to you tomorrow?"

"As Ethan would say, *Sounds like a plan.*"

The two kissed for a few seconds before Tommy left her arms and walked out the door. Rita watched from the window as he got into his car and drove away.

FOUR

Berlin, Germany
July, 1945

It was a day like any other for the past few weeks. For the fifth time this morning, Corporal Clarence Ward made his way around the four blocks he was assigned to patrol. By now most of the residents knew him by name and greeted him as he made his rounds. In broken English they asked him the same questions - when would the water wagon arrive, or would there be food rations this week? It was heart wrenching to see how the people lived, but there was little he could do. Their diet consisted mostly of bread, cabbage, and potatoes, and there was little or no health care for the sick and elderly. And many infants had died from malnutrition since his tour had begun. His instructions were to keep order in his assigned area, but he felt more like a babysitter than an enforcer. The people were simply too tired and too weak to cause trouble.

As a veteran of many battles, he had first hated the German people. Like other soldiers, he'd seen the concentration camps, and had been shocked and horrified at what human beings could do to each other. At first he felt that the entire German race must be sub-human to let such a thing occur, but then he found the truth to be much more complicated. He learned that much of the population was unaware of what was happening in the concentration camps. He also discovered that those who had spoken up against the government quickly disappeared. In fact, many of the German people were themselves victims of Hitler and his reign of terror. And now, even though the war was over, the suffering continued. And each day he saw firsthand the pain and agony of a fallen people.

There was, however, one bright spot in his day. Each morning he watched as an attractive young German woman walked down the street with her head held high, smiling to people as she passed by. And each afternoon she returned at the same time - a quarter past one. She was tall and lean, and had an air of gracefulness about her. Corporal Ward wondered what her secret was - how she could appear so cheerful in such a place. Each day she would smile and nod to him as she passed by. As he saw her approaching from afar, he crossed the street and awaited her arrival. Again she smiled and nodded. For a reason unknown to him, this morning he did more than smile back.

"Good morning, pretty lady," he said. "I shore wish ya spoke English."

"Guten morgen to you, soldier," she answered as she passed by. "And I am sorry that you do not speak German."

Taken aback by her remark, it did not take Corporal Ward long to recover. Quickly he moved to walk along side her.

"Ya speak English?"

"Ja, I speak English."

"Well, what's your name?"

"Hilda. Hilda Gruenberg. And what is your name?"

"Clarence. Clarence Ward, but my friends all call me Buster."

"Buster? Buster is not a name that is known to me. That is a strange name, no?"

"It's a nickname."

"A nickname?"

It's just somethin' ya call somebody - like buddy or bubba. Understand?"

"Ja, I understand. Why? Do you not like to be called Clarence?"

"It's sort of a sissy name, I reckon. I like Buster better."

"You reckon?" she repeated. "I have never heard that saying before."

"It's a word used by people from tha south. It means, 'I guess'. Ya sure know your English. How do ya speak so good?"

"From my uncle. He lived in your country for many years before the war, then returned home. He lived with us for some time, and taught us to speak English. He was a very - how do you say - bright man."

The two walked together for a while as Corporal Ward tried to think of something clever to say. Soon Hilda spoke again.

"What state in the south are you from, Private Ward?"

"It's Corporal Ward, and I'm from Tennessee. Ya heard of Tennessee?"

"Ja, I have read about it, but I do not know much about the state. Are there many famous people from Tennessee?"

"Ya heard of Davy Crockett?"

"Ja, I reckon," she answered with a smile. "He is very famous."

"Yes, and believe it or not, I'm from the same town where he was born. Greeneville - Greeneville, Tennessee."

"Of course I would believe it."

"And Andrew Johnson - President Andrew Johnson - was from Greeneville too. Ya heard a him too, I reckon?"

"No, I am afraid I do not know this name. He was one of your presidents?"

"Yep. That's funny. Ya heard a Davy Crockett but not Andrew Johnson."

"I am sorry, Private Ward, but after all, I am German."

The two walked on a bit further before Corporal Ward turned to her with a question.

"If ya don't mind me askin', Miss Gruenberg, where do you go every morning'?"

"I go to help at the Waisenhaus - the orphanage."

"Oh, I didn't know there was an orphanage around here."

"It is about two kilometers away. It is in a church - one of the few buildings left undamaged."

"Well, that is awful nice that ya work there. Ya got many kids?"

"We have over twenty children."

"And how many people ya got that works at the Wisehouse?"

"Waisenhaus."

"Right."

"There are three nuns and one other volunteer, so that is five of us all together."

"Well, I'm sure the kids appreciate it."

"I hope so."

Soon they came to the edge of his patrol territory. Corporal Ward nervously turned to say goodbye.

"I have to stop here, Miss Gruenberg, but I sure enjoyed talkin' to ya."

"And as have I, Corporal Ward."

"Then maybe I'll talk to ya again when ya come back by."

"That would be nice, Corporal. I shall talk to you then."

With that she turned and walked away. He stared for a moment, then turned and crossed the street to continue his patrol.

At one-fifteen Corporal Ward lit a cigarette and leaned against the only remaining wall of a bombed-out building and waited for Hilda Gruenberg. The wait was not long. Soon, looking as cheerful as always, she came strolling down the street. Again he greeted her and walked alongside of her.

"So, how was your day, Miss Gruenberg?"

"It was very good, Corporal Ward, thank you. And yours?"

"'Bout the same as always, but I can't complain. Better'n most folks around here, I reckon. If ya don't mind me askin', how can ya be so happy? I mean - working with tha kids and all - and I know ya ain't got much ta feed them or no medical care."

"That is true, but I think people are as happy as the make up their minds to be. If I were not here, the children would still have the same problems, so perhaps I am making it a little better, no?"

"You're right. I guess ya got a good outlook on life," he said. "So where do ya live?"

"It is only a few blocks from here. Do you wish to walk me home, Corporal Ward?"

"As far as I'm able. I have a certain area which I have ta patrol."

"Then you can walk with me until then."

They continued to talk as they walked. Corporal Ward soon discovered that she lived with her mother and brother and sister. She told him that her father had died during the war.

"I am sorry to hear that, Miss Gruenberg."

"So am I, Corporal Ward. The war has been horrible on everyone. Perhaps the world has learned something from it, though."

"Well, I hope so. Is your house still standin'?"

"We have been luckier than most. We have two rooms that are still in living condition - our kitchen and dining room, and our bathroom, but, of course, there is no water. My brother works to repair the rest of the house, but I think it will take many years."

"I'm sure, and if I'm not gettin' too nosey, do ya have enough food ta get by?"

"Again, we were luckier than most. My father was a soldier so he was able to get some food for us up until he died. And my mother is a smart woman. She had preserved much food and put it in our cellar. Still it has been difficult. Many times we have only had cabbage soup and a piece of bread. As you know, we now get rations from your army."

"And ya uncle - does he still live around here?"

"No, I am sorry to say that he died some years ago."

"I'm sorry to hear that. He was killed in tha war?"

"No, he died before the war. He was only forty-one years old. At least he did not see what became of his beloved country."

Soon they were again at the edge of his patrol territory. Corporal Ward wondered if she enjoyed his company as much as he did hers. Nervously he rubbed his hands as he turned toward her.

"Miss Gruenberg, I was just wonderin' - we have a little club a few blocks from here where soldiers go and listen ta music and have a beer. Would you like ta join me sometime for a beer and listen ta some music? It's usually just one or two soldiers playing a guitar and singing, but it's something ta do."

"And do they have food in this place?"

"Yep. I can get ya a hamburger or a sandwich."

"Then I think that would be nice, Buster. How about this evening?"

"This evening?" he responded, happy, but surprised at her quick acceptance of his offer. "Well, sure, that'd be fine."

"Then you may come by my house at seven. Is that acceptable?"

"Well, of course. That's very acceptable."

Hilda gave him directions to her house. He shook her hand, then, with a smile on his face, turned and walked away to finish his patrol.

––––––––––––––

At seven o'clock Corporal Ward was standing in front of the Gruenbergs' house - or at least what was left of the Gruenbergs' house. All that remained of the front of the house was the foundation and crumbling brick walls. As he looked closer, however, he could see that someone had started to rebuild the left wall. He stepped over the debris and walked to the patchwork door which he assumed led into the dining room. Nervously, he tapped on the door and waited. Soon a young man came to the door. Behind the man, next to a small dining room table, he could see four mattresses on the floor.

"I'm Corporal Ward - Buster Ward. Is Hilda here?"

The man said nothing to him but turned and called to Hilda. Quickly, she appeared in the doorway, which Corporal Ward knew must lead into the kitchen.

"Good evening, Buster," she said. "I see you have met my brother, Horace."

She turned to her brother and said something in German. He turned to Corporal Ward and nodded. He did the same. Corporal Ward could not tell if her brother was upset that he was there, or if he was just a beaten young man like the hundreds of others he had seen in this country. Corporal Ward smiled at him briefly, then turned back to Hilda.

"So, ya ready ta go?"

"Ja, I am ready," she replied, then turned toward the kitchen and yelled, "Mutter, Ich gehe jetzt."

Her brother again nodded but said nothing as they turned to leave. When they were out of earshot, Buster turned to her with a question.

"Was your brother in tha war?"

"Ja, unfortunately he was. He was injured and was sent home."

"It seemed like he didn't like me coming ta see ya."

"You should pay no attention to him. My brother has many problems from the war. I think he will never be a normal man again. He is always like that. We can hardly get him to speak."

"And where was your sister?"

"She has left this very day to stay with our aunt and uncle in the country. There will be more to eat there, and she will have a room with our cousin. It is good for her."

"How's she gonna get there?"

"We have a friend who has a small farm on the edge of town. He has a horse and carriage. He has agreed to take my sister to my aunt and uncle's house."

Soon the two were at the soldiers club - a large tent between two bombed-out buildings. There were a couple of dozen soldiers sitting around the scattered tables. Hilda was glad to see there were also a handful of other young women there, although no one she recognized. They found a table, and soon a young German woman came to take their orders.

"Would ya like somethin' ta eat?" asked Buster.

"What do they have?"

"They got Spam sandwiches, hamburgers and hot dogs."

"I have heard of Spam. I would like to try that please, with one beer."

"I'll have the same," said Buster with a laugh.

The waitress returned soon with their food and beer. Buster watched with a smile as Hilda hurriedly devoured her sandwich. She soon became aware of his stare.

"I am sorry. I do not get much to eat, so this sandwich is very good."

"That's fine. Ya can have another, ya know."

"Perhaps I will later. Thank you."

The couple enjoyed their meal as they got to know each other. Soon Hilda turned to Buster with a question.

"How long will you be in this country?"

"Well, I don't rightly know. I still got another year before my time in tha army is up, but I don't know if they will send me back home before then or not. What about you? What plans do ya have for tha future?"

"As you can see, the future for people of my country is not bright at the present, but some day I would like to be a teacher."

"Have ya been to college?"

"I had started school when the war began. Then, with both my brother and father leaving to serve in the military, I quit to take care of my mother."

"If ya don't mind me askin, how old are ya?"

"This fall I shall be twenty-four. And you?"

"Well, yur a little older than me. I just turned twenty-three a month ago."

"Well, happy late birthday, Buster Ward," she said as she raised her glass of beer. He tapped her glass and took a drink.

"And if I can ask another question, what do ya think of the war?"

"War is always horrible."

"Well, I guess what I'm askin', is what do ya think of Hitler?"

"I think people are only now beginning to see Adolph Hitler for the monster that he was."

"Really? I'm a mite surprised that ya would say that?"

"Why?"

"From what we heard, all Germans were in love with Hitler."

"That was probably true during most of the war. The people had no way to know what was really happening. I understand, in your country, the radio stations and newspapers can say or print anything they like, yes?"

"I guess, pretty much so."

"Well, unlike in your country, the radio stations and newspapers here were controlled by the government. And those people who did question what the government was doing were not seen again, so people learned not to give their opinions. But near the end the truth became clear. I think many people are just now beginning to see how Hitler lied to the people and destroyed our country."

"And your brother and father volunteered for tha army?"

"My father volunteered. Since he was older, he was made a guard at Dachau. My brother was drafted."

"Your father was a guard at Dachau?"

Hilda saw the look in his eyes, and understood the meaning behind it. She leaned closer.

"Yes, he was there. In the beginning I was proud, but now - well it is not something I wish most people to know. And..."

Buster waited for her to finish. She dropped her head for a moment, and then turned back to him.

"I told you that my father was killed in the war. The truth is, when he knew all was lost, he took his own life. At least that is what was told to us by the SS."

"Wow - I'm sorry. And ya don't believe them?"

"I guess it is true. It happened just before the end of the war. They sent us pictures of his body and a letter saying he was a coward for not fighting until the end. They said that he was a disgrace to the German Army. But then, shortly after his death, those same soldiers abandoned the camp when your army drew near."

Buster watched as she took a handkerchief from her pocket and wiped her eyes.

"I'm sorry, Hilda. Like you said, war is hell. I won't tell anyone what you have just told me."

"Thank you."

They continued their conversation as they ate their meal. Buster studied her face for a moment, wondering if he should ask the next question.

"What is it that you wish to know?" she asked.

"I'm not sure if I should ask."

"Then how can I answer?"

"Okay. Have ya visited Dachau since tha war ended?"

Now she understood his hesitation.

"It is a long way from here. No, I have not visited it, but your soldiers took people from our neighborhood to see Sachsenhausen. It is another camp not far from here."

"Yeah, I know where it is. What did you see?"

"There were many dead bodies. We were told they had either starved to death or died from disease. Men, looking like - how do you say - scarecows?"

"Scarecrows," said Buster with a slight laugh.

"Yes, scarecrows. And women also - but the worst - the worst - was the young children. It was quite horrible. Have you seen such things?"

"Yes - before I was assigned here, I was on burial detail at Dachau."

"Oh, I did not know that. Then what you have seen was probably much worse."

"Yes, it was pretty bad."

The two stared at each other, each unwilling to discuss further the horrors they had seen at the camps. Knowing that the other one had seen the carnage was enough.

"It's horrible what people do ta each other," said Buster.

"Ja. And the Nazis called it ethnic cleansing. And yet it is difficult to tell a Jew from a German."

"Did ya know anybody that was sent ta the camps?"

"When I was younger I had Jewish friends, but as our country began to change my father told me to no longer play with them. I know many have disappeared, but I do not know if they were put in camps. I still wonder what happened to the young girls I used to play with. Perhaps someday I will know."

"I reckon your country has been through a purty rough time."

"Ja, but it is similar to what has happened to your country with the negroes, no?"

"Well, I don't think that's the same. We ain't never had no concentration camps for the Nig...Negroes."

"Ja, but you made slaves of them, which is as bad. And they are still not treated as equals today."

"I reckon there's some truth ta that, but...."

"But what?"

"I don't know if I should say."

"Say what?"

"Well, I reckon there's a mite difference between the Jews and the Negroes."

"Different? How are they different? You mean because of their color?"

"Well, yes....I mean, no. Yeah, they're darker, but they're also...I don't rightly know how ta say it."

"Please try to explain."

"Well, I guess what I'm trying ta say is that they ain't as civilized or as smart as white folks. They're more emotional and easier ta get riled up. And they always seem angry about something."

"Perhaps they are angry at being slaves for a few hundred years, or for being beaten or lynched. Do you think that is a possibility?"

Clarence stared at her for a second, then moved closer. "Ya ain't never actually known any Negroes, have ya?"

"Ja, I have," she answered as she returned his stare. "When we went to war with America, Hitler said that all Negro American are demons. He said that they are cannibals and that if women are captured by them they will be raped and then cooked and eaten. I did not believe these things, but still I worried when your soldiers came closer. Then, after the war was over and I went to the orphanage to help out, one day we have a group of Negro soldiers show up. They offered their help and brought food and water for the children. They have been very kind and continue to help when they have free time."

"I reckon that's purty nice of them, but..."

"Corporal Ward, I did not think you would be a racist."

"I'm not a racist. I'm a realist. I just see things as they are."

"And do you believe in God?"

"Yes, Ma'am."

"Then do you believe that God created man?"

"Yeah, but I reckon he created monkeys too."

She started to take a drink of her beer, but stopped and sat it down and stared at him.

"Corporal Ward, that kind of thinking is exactly why you are here. Have you learned nothing from what has happened in my country?"

"I guess you're right," he answered. "I should be more open-minded. Can we talk about somethin' else?"

"Okay," she answered, "but if we get to know each other better, it is something I wish you to give more thought to."

"Agreed," he answered as he sipped his beer. "So, if we can change the subject, from what ya said I guess you're a Christian?"

"Ja, I am."

"Wow, you're just full of surprises."

"Why do you say that?"

"It's just that - well, I never expected there to be a lot a Christians in this country."

"There are many things you do not know about our country. Yes, there are many Christians here. And what about you, Buster? Do you believe in God?"

"That I ain't sure of yet. If He does exist, he sure ain't done too good a job so far."

"This is a subject we can spend much time on, but first I think I will have another Spam sandwich. Is that acceptable?"

"Yes," answered Buster with a smile. "I think I can arrange that."

October, 1945

The muggy summer air had given way to a crisp clear autumn breeze. While the city was still in shambles, life had gradually returned to the streets. Many of the wrecked vehicles had been removed, and the citizens had been working to repair the damaged buildings. It had taken time for the people to get over the shock of what had happened to their country and begin to build for the future. There was the tragedy of lost husbands, sons, fathers, and brothers they had to deal with. But the main reason life had returned to the city was simply an increase in the food rationing. No longer forced to live on the bare minimum it took to survive, the people simply had more energy.

Buster Ward had seen Hilda Gruenberg almost every day in the past three months. He would meet her on her way home from the orphanage and they would sometimes take a stroll in the park, or just sit by the lake and watch the pigeons. Occasionally, they would dine at one of the few restaurants which had recently opened. But more frequently they would return to the soldiers' club where they had their first "date." Buster had tried to converse with Hilda's mother and brother, but had little success. While her mother understood some English, and was pleasant enough to him, he could tell that she was not happy with him seeing her daughter. And her brother was in a world of his own, hardly ever speaking to anyone, even his family.

He sipped his beer and looked at his watch. Hilda was fifteen minutes late - a rarity for her. Just when he had decided to leave the club and walk toward her house, she walked in. He stood and gave her a kiss, then pulled out her chair to join him.

"I was gettin' worried about ya."

"Sorry, I was talking to my mother."

"Is everything okay?"

"It is okay and not okay."

"I don't understand."

"Then I will explain, but first I must order something to eat, if that is okay?"

"Sure," he answered as he waived for the waitress to come over. She ordered a hamburger and beer. After the waitress left he again turned to her.

"Do ya want ta wait till your food comes?"

"No, I will tell you now. My mother has decided that she and my brother shall join my sister at my aunt's house. She is making plans to leave."

"Wow. When are they gonna do that?"

"It will be soon - as soon as they can arrange for transportation. It will be crowded at my aunt's house, but they will be warm when the winter comes."

"And what about you? I reckon your mother wants you ta go with them?"

"Ja, I reckon," she said with a laugh. "But I have not yet made up my mind what I wish to do. It will be difficult for me to stay here by myself, but I do not wish to live with my aunt and uncle."

"Why?"

"My aunt is very nice, but my uncle - he is not so nice. I do not like him. He can be very cruel at times. And it will be very crowded at their house. My mother will have to live in the basement, and my brother will sleep on the couch. I do not know what to do."

Buster looked at her for a moment, and then smiled.

"What is funny about my news?"

"I'm sorry, it's not funny," he explained. "But I got some news today also."

"Really? And what is your news?"

"Well, I reckon I'll be going home soon."

"Going home?" she repeated wide-eyed. "When did you learn this?"

"Just this mornin'."

"And when will this happen?"

"In a few weeks."

She stared at him for a moment, trying to think of what to say. Finally she said, "Then I guess we shall not see each other again."

"Unless..."

"Unless what?"

"Unless you came back to the States with me."

"But how can I do that? I know no one there but you, and I have no job, and..."

"I guess none of that would matter if you were my wife."

Hilda clutched her hands to her chest as she sat back in her chair. She knew that Buster cared a great deal for her, but she had assumed it was just a wartime romance which would end when he went home. Now his words totally shocked her.

"You are asking me to marry you?" she asked as she leaned forward.

"Yes, ma'am. What do ya think?"

"I do not know. It is such a surprise."

"Why? You know how I feel about you. I ain't exactly made it a secret."

"Yes, I know but this....this is so sudden. It is quite a shock."

"I know, Hilda, and if ya don't feel the same way about me, I'll understand."

"It is not that. You know that I also love you. But this is such a big decision in my life. And America is such a different country, and I would be leaving my family. When must you have a decision?"

"Well, like I said, I'll be leaving in a few weeks, but if ya want ta go back with me we need some time ta make plans. The sooner the better."

"Oh, I do not know, Buster," she said as she wrung her hands. "I will give you my answer this week. Is that okay?"

"That sounds find ta me."

He smiled and took her hand as the waitress returned with her beer.

FIVE

September, 1988

D r. Warren Robertson removed the letters from his mailbox and walked toward his house. There were the usual items - bills, advertisements, and political mailings. He smiled to see a letter from his granddaughter, Emily Ward. One letter in particular caught his eye. It was a simple white envelope like most of the others, but the return address was Vanderbilt University in nearby Nashville. He wondered why they would be writing him.

He took the letters into his house and threw them on the table. He poured himself a glass of lemonade and then seated himself. He again picked up his granddaughter's letter, smiled for a second, and then put it aside. He would save it for after dinner when he could take his time to enjoy it. He picked up the letter from Vanderbilt and opened it. He read:

> *Dear Professor Robertson,*
>
> *As Director of Human Resources at Vanderbilt University, one of my responsibilities is to attract educators to the college. With your skills and experience, we feel that you would make an excellent addition to our staff. If you are interested, I would enjoy the*

opportunity to meet with you to show you what Vanderbilt has to offer. I'm sure we can make an attractive offer. Please call me at the number below to set up a time when we can discuss this matter further.

> *Sincerely,*
> *James O. Nesbit,*
> *HR Director,*
> *Vanderbilt University*

Professor Robertson stared at the letter in confusion. Why were they contacting him about a job at the University? He was fifty-nine years old, would probably only teach for another three to five years, and had no plans of changing jobs. Middle Tennessee State University had been good to him. It was over twenty years ago that they had made him the first black professor at the college. They had always treated him well, and he enjoyed his job as an English Professor. Even when his daughter, Sally, and son-in-law, Ethan had moved to Knoxville and tried to get him to go with them, he had remained behind. Of course, if his other daughter, Rita, and her husband, Senator Tommy Bell, had not been in the area it might have been another story, but still he was comfortable with his life and job. He had no interest in the offer from Vanderbilt, but it still confused him as to why they had sent the letter. Then the answer came to him. Things had changed a lot in the last twenty years. Now there was much pressure on colleges to hire minorities. And a black English Professor had to be in high demand. He was being courted more for his color than his abilities.

He smiled and threw the letter back on the table. No need to respond. He would finish his career at MTSU, and then spend the rest of his life enjoying his family. But the letter did make him think about his life. As he prepared dinner for himself, he thought about the many twists and turns his life had taken. He thought of himself as a young boy growing up in Harriman, Tennessee over a half-century earlier. He remembered the responsibility of being a husband and father when he was not much more than a boy himself. He recalled the difficulties he and his wife faced in raising two young girls while still trying to better themselves in a racially prejudiced world. He recalled the first time he met his son-in-law, Ethan, and how the encounter had led to a deputy's death and him eventually being charged with murder. But, as difficult as being arrested had been, losing his wife had been even more devastating. It had been over twenty years since her car was hit by a drunk driver. Her death was bad enough in itself, but he also had to deal with the possibility that perhaps he could have prevented it. He could have driven her to the meeting that night, but instead he chose to stay home and watch a basketball game. While he knew it was irrational to blame himself for something he could have never foreseen, his heart would not let him forget.

He shook his head to bring himself back to reality, and finished preparing his meal. He said grace, and then began eating as he picked up his granddaughter's letter.

Emily Ward closed her books, and picked out what clothes she would wear to the football game. She glanced at the clock as she headed to the bathroom, which was shared with the adjoining room. It was only half-past eleven, and thirty minutes before Julius was to pick her up for the game. She had plenty of time to get ready. Her roommate Candy had left a few minutes earlier to have lunch with friends. She showered and dried her hair, then wrapped a towel around her and went back into her room. As she left the bathroom, she gasped at what she saw.

"What are you doing here!" she yelled.

"Calm down, sister," answered Julius who was sitting on her bed. "I knocked on the door, but no one answered. It was open so I just let myself in to wait for you."

"You mean it was unlocked, not open. And you're fifteen minutes early," she yelled.

"I hate to be late. Why don't you calm down so the whole building don't hear you."

"I don't care if the whole building hears me. You're not supposed to be in here anyway - especially when I'm half dressed."

"That part don't bother me none," he answered. He stared at her for a second, then arose and headed for the door. "But I don't want to upset you, so I'll just wait outside. Don't be too long."

After he left she stared at the door, furious at him for coming into her room. After a few seconds she calmed down. The question now was what to do. Perhaps she had overreacted. Perhaps the door had been ajar. And how could he know that she would be only wrapped in a towel when she came out of the bathroom? She got dressed and combed her hair. Deciding she would not let the incident ruin her day, she soon left the room and locked the door behind her. Julius was leaning against the building outside the entrance. She stared at him as drew nearer.

"Look, Em...I'm sorry about that. I didn't think it would upset you so. And I didn't know you would be coming out of the bathroom in a towel."

"All right," she answered. "Just don't do anything like that again."

"Sure. That's cool. Anyway, you shore look hot. Let's get to the game while the players are still warming up. Your roommate going to the game?"

"No, she doesn't care for sports. She went to lunch and shopping with some other girls."

The LSU Tigers were already on the field when Emily and Julius arrived. Soon, the roar of the crowd told them that the Volunteers had just made their appearance. While both her father and brother had been to games before, this was her first time inside Neyland Stadium. She noticed that almost everyone except her was dressed in orange and white.

"This is unbelievable," she said as she looked around. "How many people does this stadium hold?"

"Oh it's only about half full now," answered Julius. "They'll be ninety thou here soon."

The two watched the Volunteers as they went through their warm-up drills. After a few minutes, the teams left for the dressing room.

"They're going in for their final pep talk before the game," said Julius.

"Yes, I know. Then, in about fifteen minutes, they'll come back out and make their grand entrance and run through the "T" made by the cheerleaders."

"I thought you didn't know anything about football," said Julius.

"I didn't say that. I just told you I'd never been to a UT game. I watch them all the time on TV with my father and brother."

"Oh. That's cool."

Shortly thereafter, the teams again took the field and the game began. At times Emily found the roar of the crowd to be almost deafening. And when the home team made a big play, the stomping of the feet actually made the stadium shake. Soon a vendor came by selling peanuts and popcorn. Julius waved to the vendor and then turned to Emily.

"Do you want any peanuts?"

"No thanks," she answered. "I'll wait for the hot dog vendor."

"Might be a while. These peanuts are great."

"No thanks."

Julius turned back to the peanut vendor and yelled, "Two bags please."

The vendor tossed the bags to Julius as he passed the money down the line. After receiving them he turned and offered one bag to Emily.

"I told you I didn't want any peanuts," she said irritably.

"So maybe you'll change your mind later," he answered as he put the bag under his seat. He turned back to the field as she continued to stare at him. Soon he turned back to her.

"What's the problem?"

"You really have a need to control everything, don't you?"

"What? Because I got you a bag of peanuts in case you want it later. If you don't want it I'll eat it, okay."

She stared at him for a few more seconds, but said nothing. After a few seconds, she returned to look at the game. Soon a timeout was called, and Julius took the opportunity to explain the intricate details of the game to Emily. He explained that he thought the Vols should easily defeat visiting LSU. She was relieved when play resumed, and his attention was focused on the game. While Emily did not wish her home team to lose, she did enjoy the fact that, with each score by LSU, Julius grew quieter. With a final score of LSU 34 and Tennessee 9, his mood changed significantly. With over 90,000 disappointed fans, they left the stadium.

"I'm sorry your prediction didn't hold true," said Emily.

"Hey, no big deal. Their minds just wasn't in the game. They must'a been thinking about next week's game. They'll bounce back."

"I'm sure."

"So, do you want to go have a beer?"

"I don't drink, thank you."

"Well, you're over eighteen now, girl. You need to get with the program."

"I have my own program, thank you."

"Then we'll just have a coke or something."

"No thanks. I have an awful lot of studying to do before Monday, and tomorrow I'm going over to see my parents."

"This is not about me showing up early, is it? Cause I already apologized for that."

"No, but I still think that was very inconsiderate. I told you, I just have a lot of studying to do."

"Okay," he said irritably.

A few minutes later, as they neared the entrance to her dorm, Julius turned to her with a question.

"So, do you think Candy's back yet?"

"How did you know my roommate's name was Candy?"

"I guess you must'a told me."

"No I didn't," said Emily with fire in her eyes.

"Sure. You told me when we first met."

"No I didn't. I've never told you Candy's name - I just referred to her as my roommate. Now I want to know how you knew."

"What's the big deal, sister? What difference does it make?"

"It makes a big difference to me. Now, are you going to answer my question?"

She stopped and stared at him, awaiting an answer. He looked around uncomfortably for a second, and then turned back to her.

"Okay, so maybe I asked a few questions. So what?"

"A few questions? Of who?"

"Just around - you know, people in your building."

"What? You've been spying on me?"

"No - now calm down. I just wanted to know if you were - you know, available. So I asked around, and the name of your roommate just came up."

She stared at him for a moment, saying nothing, and then turned and walked hurriedly toward the entrance to the building. Julius caught up with her and grabbed her by the arm. Emily jerked away, and turned towards him.

"Don't touch me!" she shouted.

"Just calm down, sister," he said. "I don't know why you are making such a big deal of this."

"I come out of the bathroom and find you sitting in my room. You try to control when and what I eat. And now I find out you've been going behind my back and asking questions of my friends. Our relationship, what little there was of it, is over."

With that she turned and pulled the door open. Julius quickly moved forward and put his foot against the door. Emily turned to him with fire in her eyes.

"Move your foot!"

"Not until we have a talk. You ain't gonna just get rid of me like that."

"I said move your foot," she repeated as she pulled against the door. He moved closer to her and grabbed her arm and squeezed it.

"Oh, you're hurting me. Let go."

"I paid for your ticket to the game, and now, just because I talked to some of your neighbors, you're dumping me? I don't think so."

Emily pulled away from him. Then, as she was trying to decide what to do next, there came a shove from the other side of the door. Julius looked at her for a second, and then removed his foot. The door opened and out came one of her dorm-mates, Linda, and her boyfriend, Rick. It was obvious to the couple that something was wrong.

"Is everything okay here?" asked Rick.

"It will be when he leaves," said Emily.

Julius stared at her for a second, then back at the other man, then turned and walked away. After he had gone a few steps he turned back to Emily.

"This is not over."

Seeing that she was shaken, Linda put her arm around her.

"Are you okay?"

"Yes, he's just a jerk."

"You need us to call the campus police?" asked Rick.

"No, I'm fine. I'm sure there won't be any more problem. Thank you both for helping."

Linda told her to let them know if there was another problem, and the two then turned and walked away. Emily walked to her room, took out her keys and opened the door, then locked it behind her. She sat silently for a few moments, trying to calm her self. She then picked up the phone and dialed her parents' house. Her father picked up the phone on the third ring.

"Hi, Daddy," she said.

"Emily, what's wrong."

"It's that obvious?"

"Well, I'm your father. What's wrong?"

"I'm such a fool, Daddy" she cried.

"What happened, Honey? Are you okay?"

"I....I'm okay. It's just that....oh, Daddy, you were right. Julius is such a jerk."

"What did he do?"

She told him about the afternoon's events. He listened patiently, comforting her as she spoke.

"Do you want us to come over there?"

"No, Daddy. I'm fine. And I'm sure I won't have any more problems with him. He's just not a very nice person."

"Well, I think we should call campus security."

"Daddy, I don't want to do that. It's really okay. He won't do anything more. If I thought there would be any more of a problem I would tell you."

"Okay, Pumpkin. But just be careful."

"I will, Daddy."

"I think you should go over to see Grandpa with us tomorrow."

"Oh, I have a lot of studying to do. What time will you be back?"

"We'll leave early, so we'll probably be back by four or five. What do you think?"

"I guess I can do that. That sounds like a good idea."

"Great. We'll pick you up around eight."

"Thanks, Daddy. And thanks for not saying, 'I told you so'."

"Sure, Honey. I love you, Emily."

"I love you too, Daddy."

SIX

It was a dreary, overcast morning as Ethan Ward left home. The drive from Knoxville to Greeneville was a little over one hour on Interstates 40 and 81. That was not always the case. He remembered as a kid growing up in Greeneville, and before the Interstates were finished, that the trip took almost twice that long. Of course then the only way to get to Knoxville was via route 11 which went through the towns of Morristown and Jefferson City. And not only was the trip much longer back then, US 11 was also very dangerous. He remembered, in 1972 a deadly wreck in Bean Station, not far from his home in Greeneville. A bus and a tractor-trailer had a head-on collision, killing fourteen people. It was said that the crash could be heard for miles. Today the trip was safer and more pleasant, even a little boring. Still, this being his second visit to Greeneville in the past few days, he would be glad to get to his parents' house.

He and his family had driven to Greeneville on Sunday and had been upset and shocked at how frail and weak his father looked. It brought back memories of his first battle with cancer twenty years earlier. The difference was that then his father had been a younger and much stronger man. He was now sixty-six and seemed to have no resolve left to fight the disease. And while his mother rarely, if ever, complained, he could tell the illness was taking its toll on her as well. That was the main reason Ethan had decided to take the day off work and return home so soon - to give his mother a chance to get out of the house and perhaps renew her energy and spirits.

It was a little before ten when he arrived at his parents' house. He knocked on the door, and then turned the knob.

"Anybody home?" he called as he entered the house.

"What did ya expect?" answered his father weakly as he looked up from his makeshift bed on the couch. "Ya think we'd be out partyin'?"

"Hi, Dad," said Ethan as he walked over and kissed his father on the top of his head. "How are you doing?"

"Good as ever, I reckon. How was yur trip?"

"Fine. Not much traffic this morning. Middle of the week is always slow, I guess."

He looked up to see his mother come in from the hallway, carrying a prescription bottle in her hand. She walked to her son and gave him a hug.

"Glad you could come by, Ethan," she said.

"My pleasure."

She turned and went into the kitchen, then returned with a glass of water. She removed a pill from the bottle and handed it to her husband.

"Here, Buster. It's time for your pill."

Her husband took the pill, then a sip of water.

"What's that for?" asked Ethan.

"This one's for nausea," answered his father. "Got so many danged pills I get 'em confused sometimes. Guess that's what I got a wife for."

"Yes, and you only have two of these left. We need to get them refilled. You want to do that, Ethan?"

"Sure, or I can stay here with dad if you want to get out for a while. It might do you good to get out of the house."

"No, I'm fine."

"Oh, ya go on out, Hildy," said Buster. "You need a break, and I reckon Ethan can stay with me for a little bit. I'll be fine."

"You sure, Buster?"

"Oh, yeah. Go on in ta town. And take your time. Maybe do a little shopping."

"Well, okay. I guess Ethan can look after you for a while."

Hilda got her purse, and took the keys off the wall, then walked over and kissed her husband goodbye.

"Better take your umbrella," said Buster. "TV's callin' for rain."

She hugged her son, then removed an umbrella from the closet, and walked to the door.

"I'll be back in a short time," she said as she left.

Ethan pulled a chair near his father and sat down.

"You need something, Dad?"

"No, I'm fine son. It was nice a you takin' off ta come and see me. How's tha family?"

"They're fine. Emily said to tell you she's sorry she couldn't come by today. She was going to take off this afternoon, but she had a report come up she's got to work on."

"She sure is a real sweet girl."

"That she is."

The two spent their time together talking about anything but Buster's cancer. They talked about earlier times when Ethan's dad would take him and his brother Horace hunting and fishing. They talked about their old house, and their old car on which Ethan first learned to drive. They talked about sports, mainly the Tennessee Volunteers and their terrible start to the football season. They talked about anything but his father's illness. After some time, Buster began to tire.

"Son, I think I need ta go sleep for a while, and it's not too comfortable on the couch. Can ya help me back to bed?"

"Sure, Dad."

Ethan helped his father to his feet, and then guided him down the hallway to the bedroom. He gently helped him into bed, and then stood beside him as his father lay back.

"Is there anything else I can do for you, Dad?"

"No, thank ya, son. I just need ta rest a mite."

Ethan started to leave, but turned back to his dad.

"Dad, don't you think you should begin the chemo treatment like Doctor Anderson said?"

Buster turned and looked at his son.

"Ethan, I know this is hard for ya ta accept. It's hard for me ta accept, but that chemo ain't likely ta help me none, and, as bad as I feel now, it'll make it ten times worse. No, I reckon if God says my time is up, ain't nothing I can do. But I shore appreciate your concern."

"Okay, Dad," said Ethan. He stood looking down at his dad, wondering how to ask the next question. His dad sensed his hesitation.

"Somethin' else ya wanted ta say, son?"

"Well, yes, I guess there is."

"Well, don't be shy, Ethan. What's on yur mind?"

"It's just that....well, Dad, you know that God can heal you if He wants."

"Sure. I reckon that's true."

"But then there's a chance He won't heal you also."

"Yeah, I know that too."

"So, if He doesn't heal you, do you know if you'll be going to heaven when...when?"

"When I die. Ya can say it, ya know."

"Yeah, I know. So...do you know?"

"Well, I reckon I ain't been such a bad old Joe. Yeah, I feel pretty certain of where I'll be goin'.."

"But you know, Dad, Jesus said the only way to heaven is through Him."

"Son, I know that's what ya believe, but it's a mite hard for me ta accept. Now, I believe that there's a God - it just makes plain sense. But they's plenty good people all over the world that ain't never heard of Jesus. Ya goin' ta tell me that none a them are going ta heaven?"

"Well, that's what He said."

"Okay, Ethan. I appreciate what yur tellin' me, but I'm too tired to go into it right now. Besides, maybe they'll be a back door into tha place."

"What?" laughed Ethan, surprised at such a comment from his normally stoic father.

"Just havin; some fun with ya, son."

"Okay, Dad. I just hope you'll think about what I said, and maybe pray about it. Will you do that?"

"Sure, son. Now I think I got ta take a nap."

"Okay, Dad. Just let me know if I can do something else."

"You're a good boy," said his father as he turned on his side to sleep.

Ethan went back into the living room and stared out the window into the gray sky. He had never felt so helpless. When he was younger he had felt that it was a real tragedy when someone died young, and that it would be easier to take if the person had lived a long life. Now he wondered how he had ever believed such a thing, since he couldn't imagine feeling any more sadness than he felt now. He walked into the kitchen and poured himself a glass of orange juice, and then picked up the Greeneville Sun, and stared blankly at it, awaiting his mother's return.

It was almost an hour later that his mother walked in the door.

"That was quick," said Ethan. "You should have taken some time and gone shopping like Dad said."

"There is nothing I need. Besides, wherever I go I meet people who want to ask me how your father is doing, and I know they mean well, but I get tired of talking about it."

"Oh, okay."

"How is he? He went back to bed?"

"Yes, just after you left."

His mother went to the closet and returned the umbrella, then went to the kitchen and placed the prescription bag on the counter.

"Do you want something to eat or drink, honey?" she asked her son.

"I had some juice, Mom. That's fine."

His mother went to the refrigerator and removed a package of frozen chicken.

"Can you stay for dinner?" she asked.

"Sure, Mom. I'll leave around six, that way I should miss most of the traffic going home."

She placed the chicken in the sink to thaw, then picked up an envelope lying on the counter.

"Oh, shoot."

"What?" asked Ethan.

"I forgot to mail this letter to the insurance company. They want more information about your dad's illness. It's already late."

"Can't you just give it to the mailman?"

"I want to send it registered so they can't cause any problem by saying they didn't get it. Oh, well, I guess I'll just go back to the post office."

"I can take it if you want, Mom. That is unless you'd rather do it yourself."

"No, that is fine, son. If you don't mind, that would be great. Your father probably won't be awake for a while anyway, so you can visit with him when you get back."

Ethan took the letter from his mother, kissed her goodbye, and left for the post office.

It was beginning to mist as Ethan left his car and ran toward the post office. As he neared the building, he saw an old friend inside walking toward the entrance. He stood near the door waiting for her to look up. After walking through the doors, she looked in his direction and smiled.

"Hi, Ethan," she said as she hugged him.

"Hi, Rachel," he answered. "How are you?"

"I'm fine. I'm so sorry to hear about your father. How's he doing?"

"Not good. But who knows? He may fool us all and make a full recovery."

"I hope so. He's a good man. I'm really sorry for what you're going through."

"Thanks, Rachel. I really appreciate that. So, what are you doing in town?"

She glanced around for a second, then turned back to him.

"That's a long story. Do you have time to talk?"

"Sure. Just let me mail this letter and I'll be back out. Where are you parked?"

"I have the silver BMW parked over there," she answered as she pointed toward the parking lot.

"Nice car. I'll be out in a minute."

As he walked into the post office, Ethan thought of his relationship with Rachel over the past twenty-five years. They had known each other since they were children, and had dated through much of high school. Then, in their senior year, he broke up with her when he decided he could no longer take her arrogance and selfishness. Later, when Ethan had gone away to college and began seeing Sally, Rachel moved nearby and attempted to break them up. When that failed, neither Ethan nor Sally heard from her for a while. Then, sometime later, she came to Sally and begged her forgiveness, saying she was now a Christian and wanted to atone for her past behavior. While Sally had been cautious, she found Rachel true to her word. When Sally's father was arrested for murder, it was Rachel who found defense attorney Ellen Cornblossom-Williams and paid her fees.

Now that Rachel had become a successful singer and movie star, Ethan and Sally hardly ever saw her. Still the couple considered her a true friend. He wondered what it was she wanted to discuss with him. The mist had turned into a downpour as he left the post office. He ran to her car, opened the passenger door, and climbed inside.

"You're soaked," she said. "Don't you have an umbrella?"

"It's not bad. You sound like my mother."

"How is she holding up?"

"Well, you know how she is. Germans always have to be tough. But it's pretty rough on her. That's why I came over - to give her a little break. So, what is it you wanted to talk about?"

She put her hands on the steering wheel, looked ahead at the rain for a few seconds, then turned back to Ethan.

"Allen and I are splitting up," she said bluntly.

"You're kidding."

"No, I'm afraid not."

"Wow. I....I don't know what to say. I'm just shocked."

"Really?" she said sarcastically.

"Sure. Why do you say it like that?"

"Well, let me ask you a question. In the past twenty years how many times have you and I seen each other?"

"I don't know. I guess a couple of times a year, maybe more. Why?"

"And how many times have you seen my husband?"

"Oh. Not that many, I guess....maybe three or four. But I just thought that was because of your careers. You both always had commitments which pulled you apart."

"Oh, yeah. We convinced ourselves that we had a 'modern' marriage. We put our careers and our success ahead of everything else. I guess it should have been no surprise that the marriage failed, but I didn't see it coming until it was too late."

"But, Rachel, is it that bad? I mean, you don't think you can work things out?"

"He had an affair, Ethan," she said bitterly. "An affair with his secretary. Can you believe that? And this will probably sound catty, but I don't think she's even that attractive. But I guess she was there for him when I wasn't."

"Oh. I'm sorry, Rachel. I don't know what else to say."

"There's not much else you can say."

The two sat silently, staring into the rain. After some time she turned to him with a more peaceful look.

"You know what I wonder, Ethan?"

"What?"

"I wonder....no, maybe I shouldn't..."

"Go ahead. Tell me what's on your mind."

"Well, I just wonder what would have happened....you know, with you and me, if I hadn't have been such a nasty person when we were younger."

"Rachel, you weren't such a...."

"Ethan, I'm not in the mood to be patronized. I was a bitch, and we both know it."

"Okay," he laughed, "you were pretty bad."

"I know. Of course, growing up with my parents, I think anyone would have been the same, but I guess that's no excuse."

"I'm not sure if I should say this, but I always thought your parents were pretty nice."

"You're kidding, right?"

"No. At least they were always nice enough to me."

"I guess that's true. They put on a good front, but trust me, there was no love lost between the two of them. A symbiotic relationship."

"A what?"

"A symbiotic relationship. You know....two parasites living off of each other."

"I know what the word means. I'm a newspaper man, remember? I just thought it was an unusual way to describe a marriage."

"They have an unusual marriage. I don't know why they ever got married. I don't think my mother likes my father, and my father doesn't like....well, anybody. Anyway, I guess I shouldn't blame them. We all have things we have to overcome in our lives. I guess I just didn't do a very good job at it. But, ever since I accepted the Lord, I've really tried to live a good life. And now this happens."

"I know, Rachel, but we both know that being a Christian doesn't mean that you're not going to have problems in your life."

"Yeah, I know."

"Anyway, I guess the press will love getting this news."

"Oh, I don't know. In case you haven't noticed, my career hasn't exactly been hot lately."

"Well, you're still doing a lot of shows in Nashville and Vegas, right?"

"Yeah, some. Still, I think my career is on the down slope."

The two became quiet again. Rachel tapped her fingers on the steering wheel, then again turned towards Ethan.

"You know what I remember?" she asked as she stared ahead into the rain.

"What?"

"The short time we were together in Nashville."

"Yes," he said slowly, "we had some good times."

"Before I blew it."

"I wasn't going to mention that."

"It's okay, but there's something I want you to know, Ethan."

"What?"

"I know I always manipulated people back then, but I also really cared about you. That was one of the best times of my life."

"Me too," answered Ethan, but then, afraid of where the conversation might lead, he attempted to change the subject. "So, is this general knowledge yet?"

"No. Allen just told me about the affair a couple of days ago. I came home to tell my parents, but haven't gotten up the nerve yet. You're the only other one who knows."

"Again, Rachel, I'm sorry."

"Thanks," she said. Then, after a deep breath she asked, "So, how's Sally and the kids?"

"They're doing fine. Emily just went away to UT, and Justin is starting quarterback this year."

A look of sadness came over her. She turned away from him toward the window.

"Did I say something wrong?"

He heard her muffled sobs as she leaned her head against the window.

"Rachel, what did I say?"

She turned back to him with tears in her eyes.

"We always put off having kids. It was when I went to him and told him that I wanted to start a family that he told me he wanted a divorce."

THE THIRD GENERATION   77

Ethan removed his handkerchief from his pocket and wiped her eyes. She leaned her head against his shoulder as he rubbed the back of her neck. Soon she raised her head and looked into his eyes. Her lips drew near his. The kiss was soft and tender, and lasted only a few seconds before Ethan drew back. Rachel straightened herself, and then put her head in her hands.

"I'm sorry, Ethan," she whispered.

"No, I'm sorry, Rachel. I should have never let that happen."

"It was my fault. And Sally is a good friend. I....I'm so ashamed."

"It's okay. Let's just forget this ever happened."

"Okay. But I'm glad to know that at least I'm still attractive to somebody."

"You are a beautiful woman, Rachel. And if things were different.... but you know..."

"Yes, I know. Anyway, thanks for listening to me and letting me cry on your shoulder."

"Is there anything else I can do?"

"I guess just keep me in your prayers."

"I can do that."

"And please don't mention this to anyone until I have a chance to at least talk to my parents."

"Of course."

"And please don't start feeling guilty and tell Sally about....you know."

"Yes, I know."

"And thanks for being such a good friend."

"Always."

He leaned forward and kissed her on the cheek. She squeezed his hand, and then he turned and opened the door.

"And I'll keep your father in my prayers."

"Thanks," said Ethan as he closed the door and ran through the rain to his car. He watched through the foggy window as the taillights from Rachel's car faded in the rain.

SEVEN

October, 1988

The footsteps echoed down the empty school hallway. As they drew closer to Sally Ward's room, she looked up from her desk to see an unfamiliar woman standing in her doorway.

"Mrs. Ward?" asked the woman.

"Yes."

"I'm Eleanor Cooke," she continued. "I'm Richard's mother."

"Ricky Cooke, in Miss Malone's third grade class?"

"Yes," answered the woman as she walked toward Sally's desk. "You don't know the names of the kids you teach?"

"I'm the reading specialist for all six grades, Mrs. Cooke, of which there are a couple hundred kids," answered Sally, in a tone that let the woman know she didn't care for her comment. "And he told us he wants to be called Ricky."

"Oh," said her visitor indignantly.

"What can I do for you, Mrs. Cooke?"

"I want to talk to you about your report regarding Richard's reading ability."

"Yes? What about it?"

"Well, in the report you stated that he only reads on a first grade level."

"Yes, that's true."

"I don't understand that, Mrs. Ward, since at his old school last year there was never any mention of a reading problem."

"Well, I can't address what happened at his old school, Mrs. Cooke," said Sally as she arose from her desk. "I can only tell you that, like I said in the report, your son only reads on a first grade level."

"Then what can be done about it?"

"As I also said in the report, I'm working with him two days a week. While it is still early in the school year, I think it's safe to say that you should see a big improvement in his reading by the end of the year."

"Is there something else that can be done to help him improve?"

As Sally looked at the woman, it became obvious that the only part of her report that Mrs. Cooke had read was the part about her son's reading level.

"Again, as I mentioned in my report, it would be very useful for your son if you or your husband read with him every evening."

"Okay. We can do that. I only have one other question."

"What's that?"

"Does your report go into his permanent record?"

"I give the report to Miss Malone. It's up to her what she does with it. Why?"

"Because I don't want it coming back to haunt him years from now."

"Haunt him how?"

"Like when he's ready to go to college or is looking for a job."

Sally stared at the woman for a moment, wondering if she knew how ridiculous her concern was. She knew that she had to be tactful when dealing with parents, but she felt that she had to address her concern.

"Mrs. Cooke, I think the only thing to be concerned with when he is older, is him still having a problem reading - not what was in a report when he was in the third grade."

"That may be so, but just the same, I'd like to make sure your report doesn't go in his permanent record."

"Then I think you need to talk to Miss Malone."

"Is she in now?"

"No, I think most of the other teachers have left."

"What about the Principal?"

"I think Mrs. Jackson, the Assistant Principal, is still in."

"Good. I think I'll stop by and see her."

"That's your right."

With that, Mrs. Cooke turned and left her room. Sally shook her head as she watched the woman walk down the hall. It had been a long and difficult day. She had spilled a cup of coffee on her dress at breakfast and had to change before leaving for work. A wreck tied up traffic on the way to dropping her son off at his high school, which made her late getting to school. An irritated teacher's aide was waiting in her classroom with the student with whom she was to work. She had had a disagreement with another teacher on the techniques used to evaluate a student. And her meeting with Mrs. Cooke ended the day the way it began. She looked at her watch. It was almost five o'clock. She would have just enough time to stop at the supermarket and get something for dinner before picking up her son after football practice. She locked her desk, put her keys in her purse, and walked out of the room. As she walked past the office, the secretary, with one ear to the phone, motioned for her to come in.

"*Oh great,*" she said to herself, "*probably another problem or parent complaint.*"

"It's your husband," said the secretary as Sally neared her desk. "He's on line one."

Sally walked to a nearby vacant desk and picked up the phone.

"Hi, Ethan," she said.

"Hi, Sweetie."

"What's wrong?"

"It's that obvious, huh?"

"Yeah. What's wrong?"

"Horace called a few minutes ago. They took our dad to the hospital?"

"Wow. The cancer has spread that fast, huh?"

"Well, actually, he has a bad cold - possibly pneumonia. I'm sure it's related to the cancer. The doctor said other illnesses are quite common when somebody's immune system is weakened from the cancer."

"I'm sorry, honey. How bad is it?"

"Horace said we should come over a soon as possible - tonight if possible. We should plan on staying at least a day or two. I talked to Emily and she said she wanted to go and she was sure her teachers would have no problem, but if you can't get off work on such short notice, I understand."

"Of course I'll go, honey. It'll take me a few minutes to track down a substitute, so I won't have time to go by the supermarket, so can you stop and pick up something to eat - maybe Chinese - and I'll pick up Justin and meet you at home in a little while. We should be able to leave in a couple of hours."

"Okay, honey. I'll pick up Emily and then Justin and see you at home."

It was half-past seven when the Ward family climbed into their minivan and headed for Greeneville. The drive was quiet and somber, with each family member lost in his or her thoughts about what they would find when they got to the hospital.

Laughlin Memorial Hospital sits just east of downtown Greeneville on a small hill off of highway 11E. The hospital began as a clinic founded in 1939 by Dr. C.B. Laughlin. The facility continued to expand as the community grew. It now contained 177 beds, one of which was being occupied by Clarence, "Buster" Ward.

Ethan Ward and his family were met in the waiting room by his older brother, Horace, and his wife, Emily, or 'Big Emily' as the family called her to distinguish her from 'Little Emily'. They arose from their chairs and embraced Ethan and his family.

"How was the trip?" asked Horace.

"As good as can be expected," answered Ethan. "Is Mom in the room with Dad?"

"Yeah, and Edward is keeping her company," he answered, referring to their teenage son.

"So, how's he doing?" asked Sally.

"Not too good, Sal," answered Horace. "They have him kind of doped up so he's not in much pain, but he's pretty weak."

"Any prognosis?" asked Ethan.

"Well, Dr. Anderson just stopped by a few minutes ago, and....oh, here he comes now," answered Horace as he turned toward a gray-haired man walking down the hall toward them.

Ethan had known Dr. Merle Anderson as long as he could remember. Besides being friends with his father, he had been the family's doctor since he and Horace were children. And while he had a great reputation as a physician, Ethan had never felt comfortable with him. He found him to be cold, arrogant and condescending. Still, of all the doctors he knew, he would rather have him handling his father's illness than anyone else. He turned to greet the Doctor as he drew near.

"Hi, Doctor Anderson," said Ethan as he held out his hand. The Doctor gave a quick handshake.

"Ethan," he responded with a quick nod, and then turned to the other family members.

"Oh, Doctor Anderson, this is my wife, Sally, and our kids, Emily and Justin."

"Hello," he said bluntly, then turned back to Ethan. "You just get here?"

"Yes, sir. Horace was just telling us about our dad, but now we can get it from you directly."

"Not much I can tell you. We got him on an IV to try to get rid of the infection and help with the pain. Probably be a day or two before we'll know if we caught it in time."

"So the infection is from the cancer."

"Probably. We got germs around us all the time, but usually our body fights them off with no problem. Your dad's immune system is just too weak, so, like I said, we'll just have to wait and see."

"And if he recovers from the infection, how do things look?"

"Not too good, I'm afraid. Told him to start the chemo but he refused. He'd had a fair chance it would have worked if he'd started it a few weeks ago."

"Can he still do it?"

"Kind of late now. Cancer is too advanced."

"Oh," said Ethan as he lowered his head. Sally moved to his side and wrapped her arms around him.

"Well, sorry, got to run. I've got a couple other patients to see," said Doctor Anderson as he turned and walked away.

The family stood in silence for a moment, then turned and seated themselves. A short time later they were joined by Ethan and Horace's mother, and Horace and Emily's son, Edward. Ethan and his family arose to greet them.

"Hi, Mom," he said as he hugged her.

"Hi, honey," she answered as she clung to him.

Sally and the kids quickly joined Ethan in embracing his mother, then Edward. Sally took a tissue from her pocket and wiped the tears from Hilda's eyes. The two women had bonded from the moment they first met. Ethan's mother told Sally that she had seen in her native Germany what hatred and racism had done to people, and was determined it would not happen to her family. She had taught her sons to treat everyone the same, regardless of color or nationality. Sally loved her for that, and she loved Sally for being such a good wife and mother.

"How's he feeling, Mom?" asked Ethan.

"Better than when they brought him in. I think the medication is working."

"Can we go see him?"

"Sure, honey. It's a small room though, so maybe just two at a time."

The family stared at each other.

"You and Mom go ahead, Dad," said Emily. "Justin and I can go in afterwards."

"Oh, okay," said Ethan.

Horace gave them the room number, and the two walked down the hall. As they drew nearer his room, Sally remembered the first time she had met Buster Ward and what a difficult time he had in getting used to his son marrying a black woman.

"What's wrong, son?" he had asked, "ain't they got no decent looking white girls over ta tha college?"

While Ethan's father had been polite to her, it was clear she was not the person he had hoped Ethan would marry. Even when Emily was born, it was months before his father would visit them. When he finally did, the baby had melted his heart. He told Ethan that in Emily he could see him twenty years earlier. Sally felt that, more for Emily's sake than anything else, he attempted to get to know her better. She felt that his relationship with her and the children had helped erase those feelings of racism he had been born into.

Buster Ward was lying quietly, with his eyes closed, as they entered the room. He soon opened his eyes and offered a weak smile.

"Hi," he said to them. "How ya'all doin?"

"Fine, Dad," answered Ethan. "But how are you doing?"

"Finer'n frog's hair," he answered.

"Glad to see you still have your sense of humor," said Sally as she bent forward and kissed her father-in-law.

"So, you feeling better than when they brought you in here, huh?" asked Ethan.

"Yeah, some better. Be all right once I get rid a this infection."

Ethan and Sally visited with his father, talking about anything but his illness. They talked about their jobs, the weather, and the Tennessee Vols football team.

"How's Emily likin' college?"

"Okay, I guess. I think she felt a little homesick at first, but she's adjusting," said Ethan, not wishing to go into his daughter's experience at the game, and certainly not wishing for him to know that she had gone out with Ted Russell's son.

"She'll do fine. She's a smart girl. And how's my boy, Justin - the sophomore starting quarterback?"

"He's doing fine, too. Matter of fact, they're both waiting to see you. Is it okay to send them in then we can talk later?"

"That'd be mighty fine, son. But how about them comin' in one at a time?"

"Sure," answered Ethan slowly, curious of his father's request. "We'll go get them, and then we'll stop back by before we leave."

"Sounds good, son."

Ethan and Sally left the room to talk to their children. Soon Emily entered the room and stood nervously at the foot of her grandfather's bed, waiting for him to notice her. Thinking he was asleep, she waited for a few seconds, then, not wanting to wake him, turned and started to leave. As she did so, he opened his eyes and smiled.

"Hi, sweetie," he said.

"Hi, Grandpa," she said as she moved forward and gave him a kiss on the forehead. "I'm sorry you're sick."

"Me too, sweetie. But I'm much better now that you're here. Come'n sit next to me," he said as he slid toward the center of the bed.

"Are you sure it's okay?"

"Sure," he answered, patting the bed next to him.

"Okay," said Emily as she sat next to him and took his hand. "How are you feeling?"

"Not too bad, considerin' tha circumstances."

"I wish there was something I could do, Grandpa."

"You are, Honey. I'm glad you came ta see me, cause there's somethin' I been wantin' ta tell ya."

"Really. What's that, Grandpa?"

"I just wanted ta thank ya, sweetie."

"Thank me for what, Grandpa?"

"For saving me."

"For saving you? I don't understand. Saving you from what?"

"From myself."

"You're not making much sense Grandpa. Are you sure you're feeling okay?"

"Sure, honey," he laughed. "I guess I should explain. I reckon your parents talked ta ya about how I acted when I heard 'bout them gettin' married?"

"No, they never really said much about it."

"Okay," he said as he laid his head back and stared at the ceiling for a moment. He then turned back to her and continued.

"Emily, when I was a young man I was not tha most...uh, open-minded person in the world."

"Yeah?"

"To be honest, honey, I was a narrow-minded bigot."

"Grandpa, I can't believe that about you."

"I'm sorry, but it's true, honey. They say a man is a product of his environment. Well, I reckon I grew up bein' taught that blacks and whites just shouldn't be together. So when your daddy started dating your mother, I wasn't too happy about it...wasn't happy at all."

"I didn't know that," aid Emily quietly.

"I reckon they didn't see a need ta ever tell ya. Can't blame them neither. Anyway, I didn't go ta see them get married, didn't go visit them afterward, and - I hate ta admit this - but I didn't even go visit when you were born."

"Oh."

"Yeah, I was a purty stubborn cuss. And I'd like ta apologize ta ya for that, Emily. I wish I could take it back, but I reckon it's too late."

"It's okay, Grandpa. It's not like I can remember it."

"I know, sweetie. But it was wrong anyway. But then, a few months after you was born, mostly ta satisfy your Grandma, I went over ta visit your mom and dad, and I saw you for tha first time."

"So, how did I look?"

"Honey," he said as he squeezed her hand. "You were perfect....still are. When I saw ya it was like seein' your daddy as a little baby all over again. And when ya smiled at me and....well, I just fell in love with ya. The first thing I thought was what a fool I'd a been all those years for being so narrow-minded. Of course, it took some time ta get over those old feelin's a bigotry, but it all started with you, and I just want ta thank ya for saving me."

"Oh, Grandpa," she said as she put her head on his chest, "I love you."

"I love ya too, honey. And, Emily..."

"Yes?"

"I just wanted ta tell ya that in case ya ever hear anything bad about me after I'm gone."

"Anything bad, Grandpa? Like what?"

"I don't know. Like anything I might a said or done when I was younger and not so open-minded."

"Okay, Grandpa, but you're not going anywhere. You're going to get well and we are going to have a lot more happy times together."

"I hope so, honey. I hope so. Now I'm gettin' a mite tired. Why don't ya go tell Justin ta come in."

"Okay, Grandpa. And you get better quick."

Emily kissed her grandfather and arose from the bed. She waived to him, then left the room to get her brother.

EIGHT

Clarence 'Buster' Ward died at eight-fifty-three AM on Thursday, October 6th, 1988. His wife, Hilda, and his oldest son, Horace were at his side. His last words were, "Hildy, I'm sure glad ya decided to be my wife." The cause of death was listed as a viral infection, with cancer as a contributing factor. He was sixty-six years old. Besides his wife, he left two sons, three grandchildren, and one sister, Ruby, who lived in Ashville, North Carolina.

It was not necessary for Hilda and her son, Horace, to say anything to the rest of the family when they returned home from the hospital that morning. The news could be seen in their eyes. Ethan and Sally were at the table having a cup of coffee when they walked in, while Emily slept on the couch, her brother and cousin on the living room floor. Horace's wife, Emily, was taking a shower. Ethan and Sally arose from the table and walked to his mother and wrapped their arms around her.

"I'm so sorry, Mom," said Ethan.

"Thank you, honey. So am I."

Sally rubbed her head as her mother-in-law sobbed on her shoulder. Emily awoke to see her father and Uncle Horace clinging to each other.

"Daddy?" she said as she sat up and wiped the sleep from her eyes.

Ethan and Emily walked to the couch and sat beside their daughter.

"I'm sorry, honey," he said.

"Grandpa...?" she asked.

"I'm sorry, honey. Yes, he passed away just a little while ago."

"But I thought...I thought he was doing better."

Her grandmother walked to the couch and stood by her son as he talked to Emily.

"His body was just too weakened from the cancer, honey. He just couldn't fight the infection," said Ethan.

Emily stared at them for a moment, then put her hands to her face and began to sob. Soon Justin and Edward awoke, and, although an explanation was not necessary, Horace told them about their grandfather. Hearing the discussion and sobs from the bathroom, Emily soon joined the group. The family spent the morning reminiscing and laughing and crying as they comforted each other. At a little after eleven o'clock Horace announced that he and his wife would go to the funeral home and make arrangements.

"You don't have to do that, honey," said his mother. "I can take care of it."

"No, Mom. You don't need to worry about it. We'll do it."

"Do you need me to go with you?" asked Ethan.

"No. You and Sally should stay here with Mom. We'll be back in a little while."

After Horace and Emily left, Sally told the family that she would make hamburgers for lunch. Hilda arose and went to her bedroom. After a few minutes, Ethan went to check on her and found her sitting on the bed, staring blankly at the wall.

"Are you all right, Mom?" he asked.

"I don't know, Ethan. It's just too hard to believe."

"I know, Mom. I don't know what to say except that I'm sorry."

"Thank you, son."

The two sat silently for a moment, and then Hilda turned to her son with a sad smile.

"There is some good news, though."

"What's that?"

"Your dad gave me a message for you this morning."

"What was that?"

"He said to tell you that he figured out that there was no back door into heaven, but He and Jesus would see you there someday. What did he mean about no back door?"

Tears came to Ethan's eyes as he explained to his mother about his recent conversation with his father.

"Thanks for talking to him, Ethan," she said as she hugged her son. "It's good to know we'll see him again some day."

Ethan kissed his mother on the cheek before returning to the kitchen. Justin was standing at the sink, drinking a glass of orange juice.

"So, how are you doing, son?"

"I guess as good as anyone else. Do you know when they're going to have the service?"

"Your Aunt Emily and Uncle Horace are going to check on that now, but I don't think it'll be until Monday."

"Are we going to stay here until then?"

"Yes, I don't think your grandmother should be alone, although we may get a hotel room. It's kind of crowded in this little house. But if you want to go back for the football game, we can take you."

"I'm not sure what I should do, Dad. What do you think?"

"I think that has to be your decision, Justin. It's what you're comfortable with. But don't feel like it's disrespectful if you want to play."

"Okay," he said as he pondered his decision. "Grandpa loved to watch me play football," he said with a crack in his voice. "So I guess I'll go to the game if you or Mom can take me."

"Sure, son," said Ethan. He hugged his son for a moment, and then walked away.

The funeral was held Monday morning at ten o'clock at the Greeneville Methodist Church. Over 200 people turned out for the service. The air was crisp and clear with the temperature in the 60's. Almost everyone Ethan knew was in attendance. As he and Horace walked his mother down the aisle, he noticed many classmates he had not seen in years. Sally's sister Rita, and her husband, and Ethan's best friend, Senator Tommy Bell, had driven in from Nashville the day before. Rita and Sally's father, Professor Warren Robertson had come with them. A group of Ethan's coworkers had rented a van and rode together from Knoxville. Teachers from Sally's school had carpooled to the service. Retired Police Chief, Carl Benlow, offered his condolences to the family, as did Rachel Mills. Ethan smiled to see another old friend, Ellen Cornblossom-Williams, the defense attorney who had represented his father-in-law at his murder trial. Within the past couple of years she had gotten married, adopted a child, and moved back to her home in North Carolina As they walked down the aisle, Ethan was surprised to see his father's physician, Doctor Anderson. Perhaps he was not as cold-hearted as Ethan believed him to be.

Ethan's mother sat in the front row, with him and his family on one side, and Horace and his family on the other. As they waited for the service to begin, Ethan thought of how few times his father had been in the church. While his mother made sure he and his brother attended church regularly, his father generally went on two occasions - Christmas and Easter. When, as a small child, he had asked his father why he never went to church, he had responded, "Son, me and God got us an agreement. He don't make me go ta church, and I don't tell him how ta run tha world." Still, he had never heard him complain or criticize their mother for making sure they went to church.

The minister's comments were short and to the point, just as his father would have liked it. To sum it up, he said, "So, ladies and gentlemen, today there is good news. While we will all miss Buster, we can all see him again. I was told by his family that he accepted the Lord before he passed away, so he's now in heaven. I hope, however, you don't wait until the last minute to ask Jesus into your life. What if you decide to call on Him at eleven o'clock, and you die at ten?"

The service was over in less than half and hour, and the family stood outside as the casket was loaded into the hearse. Buster Ward was buried in a small cemetery outside of Greeneville. The family said their final good-byes and climbed into their cars and drove away. Tommy Bell's mother, Gloria, had a reception for the mourners at her house. While her house was larger than the Ward's, it was still cramped for the fifty or so mourners. After a while, Ethan made his way to the patio where he was joined by his friend Tommy.

"How you doing, Ace?" asked Tommy.

"It's rough, Tommy. But then you know that. Does the pain ever go away?"

"Not totally. It's been over ten years since my father passed away, and I still miss him. Every time I come home I still expect to see him sitting at his desk, working on his next sermon. But it does get better. I can now think of him without crying, and just remember the good times. How's your mother doing?"

"I guess worse than any of us. It's going to be even tougher on her when everyone leaves."

"I know. My mother and her other friends here will look after her, but you and Horace should come over and see her as often as possible."

"I know."

"How are your kids doing?"

"It's rough on them, too--especially Emily. She and Dad really loved each other, which is pretty ironic, especially with the way he reacted when he found out he was going to have a half-black grandchild."

"Well, God works in mysterious ways. It's good that she and Justin have spent so much time with their grandparents. Which reminds me - as long as we've known each other - what is it, over 25 years now - you've hardly ever talked about your grandparents."

"Yeah, I know. Well, you know that Mom's father was killed in the war. And I only met her mother once when she came to visit when I was about six. She passed away a couple of years after that."

"And what about your dad's parents?"

Ethan took a sip of his soda, then shook his head.

"My grandpa Ward was not a nice man - a real SOB, you might say. He always scared me."

"You never told me that."

"I never really liked to talk about it. He was just a very unpleasant person to be around. He always criticized Horace and me, and always seemed angry about something."

"And your grandma Ward?"

"I felt sorry for her. If I had to guess, I would say he abused her, but back then men could do whatever they wanted to their family. She was always quiet - hardly ever spoke. I didn't have much of a relationship with either one of them."

"And they also died when you were pretty young, right?"

"Yeah. I was about ten when my grandpa Ward died, and my grandma passed away a couple of years later."

"That's sad. At least your kids had a good relationship with their grandparents."

"That's true. Let's change the subject to something more pleasant."

"Okay. How about this? Guess what your old buddy Randy Richmond is doing now?"

Randy Richmond had been the District Attorney at Professor Robertson's murder trial. He later became Mayor of Greeneville, but was defeated in his bid for a second term by Tommy. Then, years later, as an investigator for the Tennessee Bureau of Criminal Investigation, he oversaw the investigation of Rita's husband's death.

"Wow. That's a name I haven't heard in a while. Did you see him?"

"No, but I happened to be talking to a state trooper who worked in the Greeneville area when your father-in-law's murder trial was going on. We just started talking about the old days, and Richmond's name came up."

"What did he think of him?"

"Not much, but then Randy didn't have a lot of fans."

"So what happened to him? Whose life is he trying to ruin now?"

"You won't believe this. He's a real estate agent in Memphis."

"You're kidding? Well, maybe he's found his level of competence."

"Right," laughed Tommy, and then took a sip of his drink.

"So, brother, now that you've been a Senator for a while, I was just wondering if you have your eye on the governor's mansion next?"

"No, I don't think so. Matter of fact, Rita and I were just talking about that the other day. When my term is over I think I'll retire from public life and just be a civilian again."

"Really? That surprises me."

"Why?"

"Because you've always said that you wanted to accomplish as much as you could in life."

"Yeah, I guess I did say that," he said with a laugh. "That was when I was young and naive."

"And now that you're old and seasoned your outlook on life has changed?"

"I guess, somewhat. It's not easy to live under a microscope for so long. And it has been stressful for Rita and Bobby as well."

"But what about all the good you've accomplished?"

"Have I?"

"Sure you have. You don't think so?"

"I've tried, and I'm sure I've made some difference, but...."

He looked into the distance, thinking over has past few years in public office.

"But then I look around and I see the same problems....the same suffering, and the same corruption, the same prejudices. And it'll still be there when I'm gone."

"I see. Did you ever hear the story about the two guys walking down the beach, and seeing hundreds of starfish washed ashore?"

"No, I don't think so."

"So one guy picks up a starfish and throws it back into the water, and the other guy says to him, 'What difference will it make? There are hundreds of them?' And the first guy says, 'It made a difference to that one.'"

"That's a good story," said Tommy. "And I understand what you're saying, but there probably weren't a bunch of people around yelling at the guy and asking him why he didn't throw all the starfish back. So, unless something makes me change my mind, I'm not going to run for another term."

"Okay, buddy," said Ethan, "but the state of Tennessee will be losing a good man. And what will you do with your time?"

"Probably nothing for a while."

"Well, if I'm not being too nosey, can you afford to not work?"

"Oh, we're doing okay. The state of Tennessee has paid me pretty well, and my wife makes good money, so we'll do okay."

The two turned to see Tommy's wife, Rita walking toward them. She came to Ethan and gave him a hug.

"How are you doing?"

"Okay. Your husband's trying to take my mind off things."

"Did it work?"

"Yes. He's a politician, you know."

"Yeah, I know."

"So, how's your job going, Rita?"

Rita was the director of the Nashville Special Olympics. She had begun with the organization in 1978 as a fundraiser, and had just been promoted to director the previous year.

"It's fine. It's tough seeing what the kids go through and how they are sometimes treated by their families, but it makes me feel like I'm accomplishing something worthwhile."

Ethan nodded his understanding.

"Ethan," she continued, "I just had a talk with your mother, and I told her I would like to come over and take her to lunch someday. It might be good for her to talk to someone who has already been through what she's going through now."

"That's really nice of you, Rita. I really appreciate that."

"Well, Tommy comes over to see his mother quite a bit, so this way I'll also be able to come and keep an eye on him."

"Smart move," said Ethan.

The three continued talking for a few more minutes then went inside to join the others. Ellen Cornblossom-Williams soon came and greeted

Ethan and offered her condolences.

"I'm so sorry, Ethan," she said.

"Thanks, Ellen. I really appreciate your coming all the way from Maggie Valley."

"Oh, it's not that far. How is your mother doing?"

"About as well as can be expected. How's your scholarship program going?"

Ellen had begun a college scholarship program for Native American teenagers from the Eastern North Carolina area. She had begun it with her own money, but for the past year had started receiving donations from businesses and individuals throughout the region. She split her time between her law practice and the scholarship program.

"It's doing okay. We just awarded our third scholarship. Hopefully, as more people hear about the program, donations will increase."

"Well, perhaps I can run a story about it in The Tennessean."

"Won't that be a problem, since it's not even in Tennessee?'

"It's close enough, but I'll have to run it by my boss. I'll let you know."

"Thanks, Ethan. Say, whatever happened to your friend, Dan Ro-driquez, the detective?"

Dan Rodriquez had been Ethan's sergeant in the Army, and later a private detective. Ethan had called him to look into Rita's husband's death.

"He's doing fine. We don't talk very much anymore. I guess you just lose contact with people after a while. He's retired from the private eye business and living in Arizona. When I talked to him about a year ago he was working as a security guard at a local college."

"Boy, life moves on, doesn't it?"

"Yes, it does."

Ethan informed her of Randy Richmond's career change.

"I guess he never got over how you destroyed him in the courtroom," joked Ethan.

"Yeah, and it just took another twenty years for it to fully sink in," she answered.

As the two talked, Ethan's mother walked up. Ellen hugged her and offered her sympathy. As the two women talked, Ethan excused himself to get a cup of punch. As he went into the kitchen, Ethan saw Sally talking to Rachel and her mother. It was the first time he had seen Mrs. Mills since he and Rachel had stopped dating in high school. For that reason, and because of his recent meeting with Rachel in her car, he felt the butterflies in his stomach. As he drew near, Mrs. Mills welcomed him with a hug.

"I'm so sorry about your dad, Ethan," she said.

"Thank you, Mrs. Mills. I really appreciate you coming."

"It was the least I could do. And I finally got to meet your wife and kids. They are so sweet," she said as she looked at Sally, who smiled at her.

"Thank you. Yes, I'm pretty lucky."

Mrs. Mills told him how beautiful the service was and asked him how the family was doing. They continued to talk for a couple of moments, neither mentioning his and Rachel's past relationship. Soon Mrs. Mills excused herself to get another cup of punch.

"How are you doing, honey?" asked Sally as she put her arm around him.

"Okay. What were you two talking about before I interrupted?"

"Well," said Sally, "Rachel just told me that she and Allen are splitting up."

"Yeah, I know," said Ethan without thinking.

"You knew?" repeated Sally as she looked back and forth between the two. "How long have you known?"

"I'm sorry," said Rachel, "it's my fault. I ran into Ethan a few weeks ago at the post office. I told him about it but asked him not to say anything to anyone. I didn't mean he shouldn't tell you, but at least I know that he can keep a secret."

"Oh," said Sally as she looked at her husband.

"I'm sorry, honey" said Ethan. "Like Rachel said, I promised her I wouldn't tell anyone."

"It's okay, Ethan. I can respect that."

Ethan looked at his wife, wondering if things were really okay. If not, he would know soon.

Seeing her alone for a moment, Professor Robertson approached Hilda Ward and, like everyone else, offered his condolences.

"Words can't tell how sorry I am, Hilda."

"Thanks, Warren. I'm assuming that with time, the pain will lessen, right?"

"Yes, it will. It will still be there, but over time it will get better. There will come a day when you can think of your lives together and smile. That time may be a log way off, but it will come."

"That's good to know, Warren."

"And, Hilda, if you need someone to talk to, I'm always there. If you want to call me, or if you want I can come over and take you to lunch some day and we can cry on each other's shoulders."

She smiled at him through her tears.

"That is very nice of you, Warren. I think I may take you up on that."

By one o'clock, the mourners began to leave Mrs. Bell's house. Ethan's mother soon left with Horace and Emily. Ethan and his family left soon afterward. As they drove to his mother's house with their children in the back seat, Ethan said softly to his wife, "So, are we okay?"

She didn't answer, but smiled and patted him on the leg. He smiled at her then looked in the mirror at their children. Justin smiled back at him in the mirror, but Emily sat with her head turned toward the window. A lone tear dripped down her cheek.

NINE

The rain pounded against the windows of the Hodges library as Emily Ward read her book. It was the third time she'd read the same paragraph, and still she didn't remember what it said. It had been like that the past couple of weeks since her grandfather had passed away. She didn't seem to be able to concentrate on anything. Her mind kept flashing back to earlier times with her grandfather. She remembered the time when she was five and he and her grandmother had come for a visit and had brought with them a new bicycle. Her mother and father explained that she was too young for a bicycle, but she learned to ride it within a few weeks. She also recalled when she was eight and her grandfather took her fishing at a small pond near his house. She was so excited when she caught her first fish but then was terrified when he told her she had to take it off the hook. Then he just laughed and removed the fish for her and threw it back into the water. She also remembered her last conversation with him and how he had thanked her for saving him from himself.

She looked around the room at the dozens of other students, busy going about their normal routines. She wondered if any of them had lost a loved one recently and were going through the same thing as her. She doubted it or they wouldn't look so happy. With a shake of her head to bring herself back to reality, she returned to the book, determined this time to concentrate. After an hour, when she felt her mind had absorbed all it could in one setting, she closed her book, put on her parka and walked to the exit. Before leaving, she pulled the hood of her parka over her head and then walked into the pouring rain. She had only walked a short distance when she felt someone grab her by her arm. She turned around to see an unwelcome face.

"Julius! What do you want?" she demanded.

"Relax, sister. I just want to talk to you."

"I already told you I don't want to talk to you ever again," she answered as she pulled away from him.

"Hey, relax, Em. I know we got off to a bad start, but I think if you give me a chance you'll see I'm not such a bad guy."

She turned back to him with fire in her eyes.

"I'll make this as clear as possible. I don't want to ever see or talk to you again. Do you understand that?"

She stared at him for a second, then turned and started away.

"Hey," he said as he grabbed her arm again. "Well, maybe I'm not through talking to you. You ain't gonna just go out with me one time and then dump me like that."

Emily said nothing but jerked away from him. As she did so her foot slipped on the wet sidewalk, and she fell to the pavement. Julius reached down for her, but as he did so, he felt a hand on his neck pulling him backward. He quickly spun around, and drew back his fist. He froze as he looked up to see another student, about twice his size, wearing a Vols jacket.

"You're....your Maurice," he stammered. "Defensive tackle for the Vols."

"Yeah, and somebody who don't like men beating up on women."

"I wasn't hitting her. I was trying to pick her up."

Maurice bent down and helped Emily from the sidewalk.

"You okay, Miss?"

"Yes, I am now, thank you."

"And is this boy bothering you?"

"Yes. Yes he is, and I've already told him I don't want to have anything to do with him, but he won't leave me alone."

Maurice, who stood six four and weighed almost 300 pounds, turned to Julius.

"Did you hear that? She don't want you bothering her anymore."

"Look, brother," answered Julius, "I was just trying to talk to her."

By now a crowd had begun to gather nearby, watching to see what would happen.

"First, I ain't your brother," answered Maurice. "And secondly, it don't matter what you want. The lady has made it clear that she don't want to have nothing to do with you, and that's all there is to it."

Julius stared angrily at Emily, but said nothing. Emily turned to see a campus police officer making his way through the gathering crowd. She watched as he walked up to them and stopped.

"What's going on here?" he asked.

Emily explained that Julius had been harassing her, while Julius told the officer that he had just been trying to talk to her. He turned to Maurice, who explained that he had just come along in time to break up the argument.

"Thank you for your help," he said to Maurice, "but I can take it from here." Then, turning back to Emily and Julius, he said, "Why don't the two of you follow me to the station and we'll sort this out."

Emily eagerly went with the officer, walking alongside him while Julius reluctantly followed behind. Soon they were at the campus police headquarters. The officer, who identified himself as Sergeant Matthews, led them to a small desk in the back of the room. He took out an incident report form, and filled in the day's date, then asked them for their names. He then asked Emily's version of what happened. She described everything that had happened back to when they had first met. Julius tried twice to interrupt, but was cautioned by Sergeant Matthews to wait his turn. When Emily had finished talking, he turned to Julius, who then gave his version of what had occurred. While the details agreed closely with Emily's account, he explained that he had never meant her any harm or distress, and only wanted to make her listen. After they were through, the Sergeant turned to Julius.

"Son, I think she has made it clear that she doesn't want to talk to you again. Do you understand that?"

"But I only...."

"I asked if that is clear?"

"I guess so."

He took the paper on which he had been writing and held it up for them to see.

"Then what I'm going to do is file this report, and if nothing else happens...well, it'll just go away. But if you come in contact with her in anyway, then you'll be suspended for two weeks. And if it happens a second time, you'll be expelled. Is that clear?"

"Yes, sir," he answered.

"And there is also the possibility of criminal charges if something else happens. Is that clear?"

'Yes, sir," answered Julius as he stared at Emily.

"Fine. Then you're free to go."

Emily watched as Julius arose from the desk and angrily walked away and out of the building. The Sergeant then turned to her.

"Are you okay now, Miss?"

"Yes, sir. I appreciate you doing that."

"Sure. Generally, in a situation like this, the guy gets the message, so hopefully this is the end of it. But if you have any other problem with him, you let me know. Now, do you want an escort to your room?"

"No, I'll be fine now. Like you said, I don't think he'll bother me any more. Thank you for everything."

Emily left the building and walked to her dorm. While she kept looking around for Julius, he was nowhere to be seen. She went into her room and locked the door, then threw her books on the table. She sat on her bed and put her face in her hands. What else could happen to her? She wondered how she could have been so wrong about Julius. Her father's warning about him came back to her. After sitting for a moment, she picked up the phone and called her father's office.

"Hi, Daddy," she said.

"Hi, cutie," he answered. "You don't sound too good. Are you okay?"

She told him about her incident with Julius.

"You're kidding. You want me to come over there? I think I need to have a meeting with that boy."

"No, Daddy. There won't be any more problem."

"That's what you said before. I think that boy's dangerous."

"No he's not dangerous, Daddy. At least not in that way. He's just self-centered and stubborn. But I know there won't be any more trouble with him. But that's not the reason I'm calling."

"Oh, really? There's more?"

"No....well, it's just that I think I need to get away for a little while. My last class is over by noon tomorrow. I thought if I could borrow your car I would go over and see Grandma for a few hours. Is that okay?"

"Sure, honey. I can pick you up at twelve-thirty, and you can drop me off at the office on the way, and I'll get someone to give me a ride home. Is that okay?"

"Sure, Daddy. Thanks. Can you call Grandma and see if that's all right with her?"

"Sure, honey. She'll be tickled to death to see you."

The next day Emily arrived in Greeneville a little after two. Her grandmother greeted her with a hug and a smile.

"How nice of you to come and see me, Emily. How was your trip?"

"It was fine."

"Did you have lunch?"

"Yes, thanks. I had a sandwich in the cafeteria before I left."

"Well, I bet you still have room for some of my apple pie. How does that sound?"

"That sounds great, Grandma," she answered with a smile.

Her grandmother led her into the kitchen. She seated herself at the table and waited for her grandmother to bring the pie.

"So, how are you doing, Grandma?"

Uh, all right I guess. I've never been through this before, so I don't know what to compare it to, but it's pretty difficult. And how are you doing?"

She returned with the pie and a glass of milk.

"I think the same, Grandma. I know they say when someone dies you get too emotional and only remember the good things about them. I guess your mind makes them out to be a saint, but I sure miss Grandpa."

"Oh, he wasn't perfect, but he was a good man. He had a good heart. At least he raised two fine young men."

"Well, I think you had little to do with that too," said Emily with a laugh.

"I guess."

Emily took a bite of her pie as her grandmother watched with a smile. After taking a sip of milk, she turned back to her grandmother.

"Have a lot of friends and neighbors been by?"

"Yes, quite a few. Mrs. Bell has stopped by a couple of times, and a few other people from our church have been by."

"What else have you been doing to keep busy?"

"Well, today I've been going through Buster's old clothes and packing them up to take to the Salvation Army."

"Oh, God, that's got to be awful, Grandma."

"It is, honey, but it needs to be done. And there are a lot of people around who can use them, so some good will become of it."

"I know. I would offer to help, but I don't think I can handle it yet."

"That's fine, honey. I can do it. And....well, I don't know if you are interested in this, but there's a trunk up in the attic with a lot of old souvenirs he had collected over the years. I was going to go through it next, but you're welcome to look through it to see if there's something you would like to keep."

"I don't know. I think it's too early - too painful....well, maybe I will. I guess it would be nice to have something to remember him by."

The two women looked at each other with tears in their eyes. Her grandmother moved forward and hugged her. After a few seconds she pulled back.

"Okay, enough of that. I have a quick errand to run. Do you want to go with me?"

"I guess. Where do you have to go?"

"To the social security building. I have to sign some papers to get Buster's death benefit."

"Are you doing okay financially, Grandma?"

"Oh, I'm fine. And I will receive the check for his life insurance in a couple of weeks, so I should be pretty well set. So, when you finish your pie we can take off."

Emily finished her pie and milk, rinsed out her dishes and placed them in the dishwasher. She then turned back to her grandmother.

"You know what, Grandma? If you don't mind, maybe I will stay here and go through Grandpa's old trunk. Maybe I'll find something I can take to remind me of him."

"That's fine, sweetie. I'll only be gone about thirty to forty-five minutes anyway."

Before leaving, her grandmother pulled down the steps that went to the attic.

"I don't know if you remember, but there's a string for the light switch at the top of the steps, and the trunk is just down a few feet on the right."

"I seem to remember seeing it, Grandma."

Emily hugged her grandmother and watched her leave. She turned and climbed the steps and pulled the string for the light. After reaching the attic, she looked around, thinking of the dozens of years of memories that the room contained. On the left side hung a row of clothes which had probably not been worn in years. She walked by and held out her hand to touch the suits and dresses which would probably never be worn again. Next to them sat rows of boxes, the contents of which she had no idea, and guessed that neither did her grandmother. Turning to her right she saw the trunk which her grandmother had mentioned. While she had seen it many times over the years, she had never thought about its contents. Now she wondered what she would find inside. She knelt down and raised the lid.

The first thing she noticed was her grandfather's high school yearbook. While it was faded and frayed around the edges, she opened it to find the pictures were still quite clear. She searched until she found her grandfather's picture. A smile spread over her face as she found the old image of him grinning at the camera. Reading about him, she was surprised to discover that he had been a member of the basketball team. As best as she could remember, he had never mentioned being on the basketball team. She figured that he must have not been too successful, or he would have shared his exploits.

She opened a small box to discover items related to his time in the military. Enclosed were his induction and discharge papers. The box also contained a few pictures of him and other soldiers posing with their weapons. While there was no caption, she figured that they must have been taken around the time that he had met her grandmother.

She continued to look through the items in the trunk, removing them and placing them on the floor as she went. Soon the trunk was empty. The only thing she found that she thought she might want to keep was a medal for sharp shooting which held her grandfather's name. She placed it aside and began to return the items, when she noticed something strange at the bottom of the trunk. There appeared to be a thin removable platform. As she looked closer she realized it was a false bottom. She slipped her fingers under the piece and removed it. Underneath she found only one faded brown envelope. She removed the envelope and examined it, but there were no markings to explain what was inside. She opened it and reached inside to remove the contents. As she did so, she gasped at the photographs inside. Her hand went to her mouth as the contents fell to the floor. Then, slowly, she picked up the photographs and examined them. Her heart raced as she looked at the three pictures, all showing slightly different angles of the same scene. There, hanging from a tree by his neck, and bare from the waist up with his hands tied behind him, was a young black man. Standing in front of him, covered in white sheets, were four figures, guns by their sides.

She turned the pictures over. On the back of one was the handwritten date, *'1946'*. With terror, she remembered the significance of the date. It was the year when her grandmother and grandfather got married. It was the year they returned to Greeneville from Germany.

PART TWO

TEN

Emily's hands shook as she stared at the photographs again. Many questions raced through her mind as she tried to comprehend the meaning of what she had uncovered. Who was the young man hanging from the tree, and what had he done to deserve....no, not deserve..... receive such a horrible fate? Where did this happen? Was it near Green-eville? She had never heard of a lynching in the area, but then, if the date on the pictures was correct, it happened over forty years ago. And why did her grandfather have the pictures? And the biggest and most terrifying question was, could he possibly be one of the men in the picture?

She thought of her last conversation with her grandfather. His words took on a frightening new meaning. Was this what he was referring to when he thanked her for saving him from himself? She examined the photographs closer and noticed three pick-up trucks in the background, partially hidden by the grass, a line of trees behind them. The trucks were blurry, and the license plates were mostly hidden, but perhaps someone would be able to make out their year and make. Which brought her to her final question....what should she do with the pictures? Many options came to her. She could put the photographs back and try to forget she ever saw them. She could destroy them. She could show them to her grandmother and let her decide what should be done with them. None of the options seemed right. She remembered the advice her parents had always given her. *When you have a difficult decision, call on God for advice.* After putting the photographs back in the envelope, she folded her hands and sat silently, asking God to give her direction.

After a moment she opened her eyes, took the envelope and placed it aside, and began putting the items back in the trunk. After finishing, she closed the trunk and picked up the envelope and walked toward the stairs. Remembering something, she returned to the trunk and removed her grandfather's medal, turned off the light and climbed down the stairs. She put the medal on the kitchen table, then went to her car and put the envelope under the passenger's floor mat. After locking the car she returned to the house and sat at the table awaiting her grandmother's return.

Her grandmother was gone over an hour. When she returned, Emily was sitting at the table sipping a glass of lemonade.

"Hi, Grandma."

"Hi, sweetie. I'm sorry it took so long. Nothing is as simple as it should be."

"Did everything go all right?"

"Oh, yeah. It just took a little while. How have you been?"

"Okay."

"Did you go through the stuff in the attic?"

"Yes. I just found this old medal of Grandpa's. Is it okay if I keep it?"

"Sure, honey. That's the only thing that you wanted to take?"

"Uh, yes."

Her grandmother stared at her a moment.

"Is everything okay, honey?"

"Yes, why?"

"You just look like something is bothering you."

"Well, it was kind of upsetting going through all of that stuff."

"And you're sure that's all?"

"Well, I did remember that I have a test tomorrow which I forgot about, so I'll be up late tonight studying."

"Oh, I'm sorry. Well, it was nice for you to come and see me, Emily, but if you need to leave to study, that's okay."

"I can stay a little while longer. I'm used to staying up late anyway."

Emily left her grandmother's house a little after four o'clock, arriving back in the Knoxville area just before six. She stopped at a convenience store and walked to the pay phone. Her father answered on the third ring.

"Hi, Daddy. I wasn't sure you'd be home yet."

"Hi, honey. Yeah, I just walked in. Are you back in town?"

"Yes, well, just west of town."

"How was your trip? Was your grandma okay?"

"She seems fine. Daddy, can I come by and talk to you?"

"Sure, honey. If it's better we can wait until tomorrow when you return the car."

"I need to talk to you now if that's okay."

"That's fine. Your mother and brother won't be home until later. She's taking him out to dinner after his football practice. Is everything okay?"

"I'll explain when I get there."

"Oh. Okay. Then I'll see you when you get here."

Emily arrived at home a short time later. Her father was sitting on the couch watching the news while eating a sandwich. He arose to greet his daughter with a hug.

"Good to see you, honey."

"You too, Daddy. I see you eat well when mom's not home."

"Yeah. I didn't feel like fixing anything. So what's so important that you needed to talk to me tonight? I hope it's not about that Russell boy again."

"No, Daddy, it's not," she answered as she sat on the couch beside him. "Can we turn off the TV?"

"Sure, honey," he answered. He looked at her curiously as he shut off the TV. "This sounds awfully serious."

"Well, I'm afraid it is, Daddy," she began.

She explained to her father about her grandmother telling her to go through the trunk. She told him about taking all of the items out of the trunk and finding the false bottom. And she held up the envelope and told him that she found it in the bottom of the trunk. Her father looked at the envelope and then back at his daughter.

"I'm afraid to ask, honey. What's in the envelope?"

"I think you should see for yourself, Daddy. And I'm sorry I have to show you this, but I couldn't think of what else to do."

Her father took the envelope from her hands and slowly opened it and removed the contents. As she had done earlier, he stared at the photographs in disbelief.

"Oh, my God. What....Who?"

"I know, Daddy."

"I mean, do you know...."

"Daddy, I don't know any more than you do."

"Did you show my mother these pictures?"

"No. I didn't know what to do, so I decided I should talk to you first. I'm sorry."

He continued to stare at the pictures.

"One of them has a date on the back," she said.

Ethan turned the pictures over and stared at the handwritten date.

"1946? That's....that's the year our mother and father got married."

"I know. Did you ever hear of any lynchings around Greeneville back then?"

"No....I mean, this was a few years before I was born, but I'm sure if something like that had happened I would have heard of it."

Ethan held the pictures up and examined them closer.

"Can you tell anything by looking at them, Daddy?"

"I was just trying to see the trucks better, but they're mostly covered by the weeds. You can only make out a couple of numbers from the license plates."

"But you can see the front of the trucks. Did Grandpa have a truck back then?"

"Probably, honey, but about everybody in Greene County had a truck back then, and they were all black."

Emily thought of her next question. As much as she hated to ask, she had to know.

"Daddy, do you think Grandpa was one of the men?"

"Honey, I don't think so. Your grandpa was not the most open-minded man when he was younger, but he always had a good heart. I don't think he could ever do something like this."

"But, Daddy, then why would he have the pictures? And the fact that he knew about it all these years and didn't do anything means something. Why would he keep it a secret unless he was involved?"

"Emily, I don't have the answer to your questions, but there's one thing I have learned in life....things are not always what they appear. Just remember how I met your Grandpa Robertson. So try and not think about your grandpa being one of the men in the picture."

"Okay, but what should we do about this, Daddy?"

"Well, I'm sure you've spent a lot of time thinking about it. What do you think we should do?"

"Oh. Well, you and Mom have always taught us that we have to do what's right, no matter how difficult it is. I think we have to let people know. I mean, I know it's been a long time, but the boy must have relatives somewhere who would want to know what happened to him. And if any of those four men are still alive, they should have to pay for what they've done."

"Five men."

"There's only four, Daddy."

"But someone had to take the picture."

"I never thought of that. But what do you think about what I said?"

"I agree with you, honey. For all the reasons you gave, plus the fact that we all need the truth. Although, understand, Emily, that we may never find out what happened."

"I know. So what do we do next?"

"Well, I have to go see your grandmother. Boy, I don't look forward to that, but it needs to be done. Then, if she doesn't have a problem,

We ll have to go to the authorities with the pictures."

"I think you should make a copy of them first, Daddy."

"I already thought of that, sweetie. I'll do it in the morning at work, then call mom and take off early and go see her."

"Do you need me to go?"

"Not unless you want, honey."

"I don't really want to. But will you tell her I'm sorry for not showing her first. I just didn't know what to do."

"I'm sure she'll understand."

"Are you going to tell Mom and Justin?"

"Yes. Boy, I hate doing that too, but they should know. And, Emily, we shouldn't say anything to anyone else until I go to the authorities."

"I know, Daddy."

They both sat silently for a moment, staring blankly at the pictures. Ethan picked up the pictures, studied them one more time, and put them back in the envelope.

"Do you need me to take you back to school now, honey, or do you want to wait until your mother and Justin come home?"

"How long will it be?"

"Well, she picks him up at practice around six, and they were going to dinner after that, so it'll probably be another hour or so."

"Then I should be getting back. I have a lot of stuff to do for class tomorrow."

"Okay, honey."

Ethan turned toward an end table near the couch and opened the door. He removed an old Newsweek magazine and took the envelope and placed it inside, then returned the magazine to the bottom of the pile and closed the door.

"We don't need your mother or Justin seeing these before I get a chance to talk to them."

"I understand."

The two arose from the couch. Ethan hugged her daughter, and the two left to take her back to school.

Ethan's wife and son were as shocked and upset as he had been upon seeing the pictures. After some discussion, they agreed that the authorities should be notified. At work the next day, when no one was around, he made three copies of the pictures. He put them in his briefcase, and left for his mother's house a little after three o'clock. She had been curious when he called to say he wanted to come by and talk to her, but had not questioned him too much.

With butterflies in his stomach, Ethan walked from the car to his mother's house. She greeted him with a hug and asked him if he had eaten.

"I'm not hungry right now, Mom. It's still a little early."

"Oh. Well, if you get hungry let me know. I have some stew I made earlier and I can warm it up."

"That sounds fine," he responded as he walked to the kitchen and sat his briefcase on the table. He then turned back to his mother.

"Mom, there's something I need to talk to you about."

"You sounded pretty mysterious on the phone. What is it son?"

Ethan explained to his mother that Emily had found something in the attic the previous day that he thought she should see. He apologized for his daughter, and said she wasn't sure what to do about it. He told her that Emily hoped she was not upset with her.

"Oh, I could never be upset with her," she answered as she sat at the table with her son. "Now, what is it that is so important for me to see?"

Ethan opened the briefcase and removed the envelope.

"Mom, I'm sorry. This is going to shock you, but I think you have to see this."

He removed the photographs from the envelope and placed them on the table. He watched as his mother's eyes grew wider as she picked up the photographs. She looked at the photographs, then at him, and again at the photographs. Slowly her hands went to her chest. She said nothing, but began to breathe faster. Finally she turned back to her son.

I hese....these were in Buster's trunk?"

"Yes, Mom, I'm afraid so."

"No, no. This is not possible."

She arose and began to walk around the table.

"Put those things away, please," she said to Ethan.

Ethan took the photographs and put them back in the envelope, but left it lying on the table.

"This, this is not possible. Why would your father have those pictures?"

"I don't know, Mom. I know this is horrible for you, but we thought you should see them. I'm really sorry."

She walked past him and went to the couch.

"I have to lie down," she said as she threw herself on the couch and put her hands to her forehead.

"Are you okay, Mom?"

"I just feel a little lightheaded. I just have to lay here a minute."

Ethan went to the refrigerator and removed ice cubes and wrapped them in a towel. He went to his mother and placed the towel on her head.

"This should help. Just lie there a minute."

He stood by the couch and watched his mother for a moment. Soon she removed the towel from her head and looked up at her son.

"I'm feeling a little better now."

She sat up and placed the towel on the table in front of her. Ethan sat on the couch next to her.

"Do you feel like talking, Mom?"

"Ja. But I don't know what to say."

Ethan smiled at her choice of words. When his mother became overstressed, she sometimes returned to her German language.

"Well, I guess my first question is, did you ever hear of a lynching back in the forties....when you and Dad first came to Greeneville?"

"No. I never heard about any such thing. That was in the forties?"

"Yes, there's a date written on the back. It says '1946', so we assume that's when it happened."

"There's handwriting on the back?"

"Yes."

"Then let me see it, but I don't want to see the picture again."

Ethan walked to the table and returned with the picture with the date on the back. He handed it to his mother, face down.

"Does the handwriting look like Dad's?"

She studied it for a moment, and then looked up at him.

"This is just block letters. You can tell nothing from this."

"Yes, I thought the same thing."

She studied the writing for a moment and then gasped as she put her hand to her mouth.

"What is it, Mom?"

"I remember that summer....it was our first year together."

"Yeah?"

"Your father began having horrible nightmares that year...a couple of times a week. They lasted for a couple of months. When I asked him what they were about he said he was dreaming about the war. I always thought that was strange....to start dreaming about the war a year after the fighting was over. I tried to get him to see a doctor but he wouldn't."

"Wow. Did he say anything in his sleep?"

"No, he would just moan, and I would wake him up. Now I see what his nightmares were about."

She put her hand over her mouth and began to sob.

Ethan sat down again and put his arm around his mother.

"Mom, we don't know that Dad had anything to do with this. We both know, from things we have been through, that things are not always what they appear. We just have to keep an open mind until we find out what really happened."

"But how can we do that, son? This was so many years ago."

"I know, and that's what I need to ask you. What do you want to do about this?"

"Well, what can we do? I do not know what to do."

"Well, the only two options are to keep it to ourselves, or turn the pictures over to the authorities. Of course, you know what that will put the family through, but mostly it will be rough on you."

She rubbed her hands together as she tried to think of what to do.

"Did Dad have a pickup like any of those in the pictures?"

She looked at him for a second, then took a deep breath and turned the picture over. She stared at it for a second, then turned it back over and laid it on the coffee table.

"He had a black pick-up but I can not tell if it was like the ones in the picture. Everyone had a black pick-up truck back then. And I can't tell one from another. Besides, the picture is not clear."

"Okay. So what do you want to do about this, Mom?"

"I don't know. I just don't know. What do you think we should do?"

"Well, I talked to Sally and the kids and we all agree that we have to turn the pictures over to the authorities. I know it will be horrible to go through, Mom, and you can come and stay with us until this blows over if you want, but I think it's the right thing to do."

"But it has been so long ago. I don't know if any good will become of it."

"I know, Mom. But I think somewhere out there somebody still has to know what really happened. And while the victim...the young man in the pictures...was probably not from around here or we would have heard about him missing....I think that somewhere he still has relatives or people that care about him."

"That is true, son. I didn't think of that. Of course you are right. We have to tell the authorities. Who should we contact?"

"I'll take care if it, Mom. I think the logical place to start is with Chief Benlow."

"But he is retired now."

"That's true, but he still knows everybody in the police department and the sheriff's office. And I trust him more than anybody I know."

"Yes, he is a good man, Ethan. That is the best thing to do. And he was a deputy back then. Perhaps he knows something about this - something that will show that my Buster had nothing to do with it."

"Maybe so. So if it's all right I'll call him and see if I can go by and see him."

"Yes, son, you should do that. You're going to call him now?"

"Sure. He's retired, and since his wife died he probably has a lot of free time on his hands."

She took a deep breath and arose from the couch.

"Okay, son, you should call him."

Ethan nodded, and turned and walked toward the phone. He then stopped and looked back to his mother.

"Mom, we haven't told Horace yet. Should I do that first?"

"No. I will do that. You go ahead and call Chief Benlow, and I will call Horace afterwards."

"All right. And, Mom, there's two other things."

"What is that?"

"First, do you want to come and stay with us until this blows over?"

"No, Ethan. This is my home. And what else?"

"I don't think you should tell Chief Benlow or any body else about Dad's nightmares."

"Oh, okay, that makes sense."

Ethan smiled at his mother and then picked up the phone to call his old friend, Carl Benlow.

ELEVEN

As Ethan drove to Carl Benlow's house he thought of the day he had seen Deputy Pratt killed. Sheriff Benlow had been incensed at his Deputy being shot, but had also been sensitive to what Ethan had been through. He remembered his words.

"Son, I know you've had an awful experience, but I'm afraid I have to ask you some questions, and I don't have any time to waste. Can you help me out?"

The following day the Sheriff had come by his parents' house to check on him. Five years later, when the shooting had still not been solved, he allowed Ethan to examine the case records to see if they would jar his memory and uncover some new information. And he remembered the day that he had met with Sheriff Benlow and the county's District Attorney, Randy Richmond. When Richmond tried to intimidate Ethan, the Sheriff had jumped in and warned him to stop. Ethan had been very glad he was there to protect him.

Sheriff Benlow and his wife had never had children. His wife often kidded him that his career was his family. And, since his wife had died just after his retirement two years earlier, Ethan wondered how he was doing. He parked his car behind Benlow's Ford Crown Victoria, removed the envelope from his briefcase, and walked to the door.

"Ethan, son," said Benlow. "It's good to see you. Come on in."

"Good to see you too, Sheriff, uh...Chief."

"Or how about just Carl."

"Oh, okay. That'll be kind of hard to get used to, but I'll try."

"How's your mom doing, son?"

"Son?" Ethan repeated with a laugh. "You know I'm thirty-eight now."

"Well, you'll always be *son* to me."

"Okay. No, my mother's not doing too well. That's really the reason I wanted to see you."

"All right. I'll be glad to help. But first, there's something I want to show you. Follow me."

Benlow turned and walked through the living room and out a door. Ethan realized, as long as he had known him, he had never been in his house. He followed him through the door which went into his garage. Benlow stopped and turned to Ethan and waved his arm toward a shelf along the wall.

"Well, what do you think of them?"

Ethan looked at a dozen or so wooden ducks, all in various stages of completion.

"You carved these?" he asked as he walked over and picked one up to examine it.

"Yep. Pretty good, don't you think?"

"They sure are nice decoys, Ch..., uh, Carl. How long have you been doing this?"

"Since Betty died. It gives me something to keep me occupied."

"I see. And how are you doing?"

"It's like an empty spot inside that never goes away. But, I guess it's better now than a couple of years ago."

Ethan saw a distant look in his eyes as he spoke. While he hardly knew Carl's wife, he understood what he was saying.

"Anyway," said Carl with a shake of his head to bring himself back to reality, "I can get you a good price on one of those if you'd like."

"Don't think I'd have much use for one in Knoxville. I haven't gone hunting since I was a teenager."

"I see. Well, why don't we go back into the living room, and you can tell me what's going on and how I can help."

The two men walked back into the house. Carl offered Ethan something to drink, which he declined. Carl sat on the couch with Ethan in the chair to his right. He turned to Ethan with a more serious look.

"So, why don't you tell me what's in the envelope that's got you and your mother so upset?"

"You're a perceptive man. Okay," he said as he began to open the envelope. "I guess in your career you've seen just about everything, right?"

"Just about."

"Then I guess some pictures like this won't be any shock to you."

He removed the pictures and handed them to Carl. He studied them for a second, then turned back to Ethan."

"Your dad had these?"

"How did you know that?"

"It's the only thing that makes sense. You came here because your mother is so upset. Your father just passed away, so she's been going through his things, and she finds these. Is that right?"

"Well, yes, except she didn't find them. My daughter Emily found them. I just showed them to Mom a few minutes ago."

"How's she taking it?"

"Not good. If you look on the back, one of them has a date."

He turned the pictures over and saw the date.

"Humm, 1946. That was a long time ago. Anything else you can tell me about these?"

"No, other than Emily found them in the bottom of Dad's trunk. It had a false bottom, and when she raised it up, there they were. So, I guess you don't know of anything like this going on back then?"

"No. You asked if I'd seen everything. I guess I have to change my answer. I don't know of any lynchings in the area, or even any rumors of lynchings."

"What about any young black men that disappeared around then?"

"Nope. Of course we don't know that this even took place around here."

"No, but that's the most logical thing. I don't know why my dad had these, but he never traveled far from home. You were a deputy back then, right?"

"Yep. I had just started in 1945."

"After you got back from the war?"

"No," laughed Carl. "I'm not quite as old as that. I was fourteen when the war broke out. When I turned eighteen I wanted to join, but it was almost over by then, and my daddy talked me out of it. I also have flat feet, so I doubt if they would've taken me. So I went and joined the sheriff's department. They didn't care about my flat feet. But, back to your problem, I guess there's nothing else you can tell me about these pictures?'

"That's it Carl. Right now you know as much as I do."

He studied the pictures closer.

"Anything you noticed that we might have missed?" asked Ethan

"Well, this one guy has on cowboy boots with an unusual emblem on the front."

Ethan took the picture from him and looked closer.

"Yeah, it looks like a star. I never noticed that before."

"Could be he was from Texas...you know, the Lone Star State."

"Yeah, that might be helpful. How about the trucks? Anything helpful about them?"

"They look like a couple of Fords and a Chevy. You can make out a couple of numbers on one of the license plates, but I don't think that'll do much good."

"Why?"

"Two reasons. Even if we had the whole license number, that's been over forty years ago, and there would be no records left. No computers back then, remember, so Motor Vehicles won't be able to help. And there wasn't any such thing as vanity numbers then, so no one, even if they're still alive, is going to remember somebody's license plate number from 1946."

"I see. What about fingerprints? Any chance of getting those off the pictures?"

"Well, let me ask you. How many people handled these since you found them? Probably five or six, huh?"

"Uh, well, me and my wife and son and daughter, and then my mother. I guess five. That makes it pretty bad, huh?"

"Yeah, and I think it's safe to say your dad's prints will be on them also. And I don't even know if fingerprints will last over forty years on a photograph. I never had a situation like this before."

"So, is it worthwhile to even have them checked for fingerprints?"

"Yes, we still need to do it. But that means we'll have to get you and your family printed to eliminate them from any other prints. And even after we do that, and even if we find another print on the pictures, there's probably little chance we can match them up to somebody else. Again, there were no computers to store prints on forty years ago, so I doubt if any of these men will be on file."

"It sounds like you're telling me, Carl, that we'll never know what happened to this man, or if my father was involved."

"No, I wouldn't say that. I think there's a good chance we'll uncover what happened."

"Really?"

"Yes. And for one reason."

"What's that?"

"People love to talk. I have to believe that, out of all of these men, at least one of them talked to somebody about it. What we have to do is find that person and convince them to talk to us. The question will be if any of them are still alive."

Ethan looked at the pictures for a moment, then turned back to Carl.

"I figured there were five men, since somebody had to take the picture."

"That makes sense. Of course, they could have used a camera with a timer."

"A timer? They had them back then?"

"Oh, sure. Not much to it. It's just like a little watch inside. You wind it up and when it goes off it takes the picture."

"Oh. I never thought of that."

"It's a possibility. So we really don't know if there were four men or five."

"I see. Another thing I thought of is where would they have gotten them developed?"

"That's stretching my memory quite a bit, but I think there were only a couple of places in town back then to develop pictures."

"That should give us something to go on."

"I don't think so. One of the places went out of business about thirty years ago and the owner moved away. And Mr. Wilson, the owner of Wilson Studios, died around 1970. But there's a good chance that whoever took these pictures developed them themselves."

"Oh, another thing I never thought of. Isn't that pretty complicated?"

"No, not really. You just buy some equipment, picture paper, and some chemicals. I've never done it, but I've seen it done before. I really doubt if whoever took these took them to somebody to have them developed."

The two men studied the photographs for a moment longer before Ethan nervously turned to Carl with a question.

"I hate to ask you this, but do you think my father could have been one of these men?"

Carl saw the fear in Ethan's eyes. He folded his hands and spoke slowly to his friend.

"Ethan, there's just no way I can answer that. Although he was a few years older than me, I've known your dad most of my life. And while I never saw anything in him that would lead me to believe he could do something like this, you can never tell what's in a person's heart. And, unfortunately, when a bunch of men get together, they sometimes do things that none of them would ever do alone. But I guess, from everything you've said so far, that you and your family have decided you have to try and uncover what happened?"

"Yes. We have to know."

"And you know, when this is made public, it could be pretty rough on your mother?"

"Yes, she knows that, but she also knows that it's the right thing to do. And she has to know the truth."

"Okay."

"So, what do we do next?"

He looked down at the pictures again.

"It's obvious that this took place somewhere out in the country, so we need to talk to the Sheriff. And I think we should also have the District Attorney there."

"I don't know much about Sheriff Watson. What's he like?"

"He's okay. A little bit lazy for my liking, but I guess he's okay."

"Really?"

"I guess I shouldn't say that. As police chief I worked with him for a couple of years before I retired. I think he just thinks the Sheriff has an office job, and I was more of a hands on type person. I don't know.... maybe he's right."

"Okay. What about the District Attorney? That's Carol Duncan, right?"

"Yeah. I like her. As you know, she's our first female District Attorney, and I think she's done a fine job. She's a hard worker, and she's tough."

"Randy Richmond was a hard worker and tough."

"That's true," said Carl with a laugh. "Then let's say she's tough and fair."

"So, should I call them?"

"No, why don't you let me do that. If it's okay, I'll call them tomorrow and set up a meeting. How's that?"

"That sounds fine, Carl. I appreciate your doing that."

"No problem. Should I take the pictures?"

"Yes, I made copies."

"Smart boy."

The two men arose and walked toward the door. Carl put his hand on Ethan's back.

"Sorry you and your family are going through this, but try to not jump to any conclusions yet. Things are often not what they appear."

"Yeah, I guess we learned that a long time ago."

"Right. You certainly have had an interesting life, haven't you?"

"That's what my brother keeps telling me."

Carl smiled and patted Ethan on the shoulder before he got in his car and drove away. Carl watched as he drove out of sight, and then returned to the living room to look at the pictures again.

TWELVE

Ethan arrived at his office a little after seven the next morning, but had a difficult time concentrating on his job. As East Tennessee editor for the Tennessean, he was responsible for the news for over thirty counties. Working for him were four reporters, two editors, and a support staff of seven. Getting to work so early, he hoped to get caught up on some things before others began arriving. Unfortunately, his mind kept drifting back to the photographs in his father's trunk, and the implications they held.

One of the first things he had to do was call his brother, Horace. He had gotten in too late the night before to return his phone call. Knowing that Horace did not leave for work until eight o'clock, he called him a few minutes before then. Being a few years older than Ethan, he hoped Horace would have additional information or insight into the photographs.

"I'm sorry, buddy, but I don't know any more than you do," Horace answered.

"Do you remember what kind of truck Daddy had back then?"

"The earliest I can remember is around 1950 when I was about three, so I don't think I can be much help. Mom couldn't tell anything from the pictures?"

"No, she said they had a black truck, but they all looked the same to her. You don't really think Dad could have had anything to do with this, do you?"

"I don't know, Ethan. I wouldn't call him a racist, but he was pretty narrow-minded back then. He became much more liberal as he got older, mostly because of you."

"I'd say more because of Sally and the kids. Horace, I hope you're not upset because I went to see Chief Benlow without talking to you. Mom said...."

"It's okay, Ethan. She's the one that's going to be affected the most from this, so I think it should be her call. And you have the relationship with Benlow anyway, so you should be the one to talk to him."

"I know, but it's going to affect all of us."

"This too shall pass."

Ethan loved how nothing seemed to bother his brother. He wished he could be so carefree. They talked for a short while longer with Ethan telling him about his meeting with Carl Benlow. He told him that Carl was to call him when he had set up the meeting with the Sheriff and District Attorney. Ethan hung up the phone and looked at the clock. It was almost eight. He had one more call to make....a call he dreaded. He and Tommy had been friends for over twenty-five years, and, while he knew how open-minded and forgiving he was, he had never had to share news like this. How would he react to the fact that his best friend's father might have been involved in the lynching of a young black man? While Ethan hated to make the call, he knew he had to tell him about it before the newspaper or radio released the information. He knew that Tommy always started work early. He dialed his office number and nervously waited for the phone to be answered.

"Hello," came the answer.

"You're answering your own phone?"

"Martha has a doctor's appointment so won't be in until later."

"And you don't answer the phone saying, 'Senator Bell'"?

"Why should I? If someone is calling this number they probably know who they are calling. And if it's a wrong number, they won't care who I am."

"You can't escape logic like that. So, how are you doing?"

"Fine. Are you at work already?" asked Tommy. "You usually don't start until eight-thirty."

"Yeah, I came in early today."

"Must be something big going on," he joked.

"Actually, there is, I'm afraid to say."

"What's that?"

Ethan slowly told him about Emily's discovery in her grandfather's trunk. Tommy listened quietly, with only an occasional, *'Hum'*. When Ethan had finished he waited for his friend to say something, but there was silence at the other end.

"Well," said Ethan, "you don't have anything to say?"

"Oh, sorry, I was just trying to recall if my parents' ever said anything about a young black man disappearing."

"And?"

"No, I'm afraid not. I guess he must have been someone just passing through."

"But you don't seem too surprised by this?"

"Of course I am. I'm not shocked, but I'm surprised. What do you think about it?"

"I don't know, Tommy. We're all just stunned. I just hope we can uncover the truth."

"I'm sure. How's your mother doing?"

"Not well. First Dad dies, then this. We tried to get her to move in with us for a while, but she doesn't want to."

"She's a tough lady."

"Yeah."

There was a short silence which made Ethan wonder what Tommy was thinking.

"Tommy," said Ethan, "I hope this doesn't affect our relationship?'

"Why would it?"

"Well, it's not every day you have to tell your best friend that your father might have been involved in the lynching of a young black man."

"I know, Ethan. But that has nothing to do with you."

"I know, but..."

"Ethan, don't worry about it. We're all only responsible for our own actions, so you don't have to worry about it affecting our relationship."

"Okay. Thanks."

"So, what are you going to do about it?"

Ethan told him about his meeting with Carl Benlow, and that he was awaiting a phone call from him.

"What does Carl think?"

"He thinks there's a good chance of uncovering what happened."

"That's good. He's a good man. Too bad he's retired, though."

"Yeah, I know. Well, anyway, I've got to run. I sure appreciate your understanding."

"No problem. And, Ethan..."

"Yeah?"

"We'll be praying for you and your family."

"Thanks. I think we're going to need it."

Having made his phone calls, there was nothing further Ethan could do at present. He tried to put the situation out of his mind and concentrate on his work. It was a little after eleven o'clock when Carl Benlow called.

"I set up a meeting with the Sheriff and D.A. for this afternoon at three. Can you make it then?"

"Sure, I'll be there. Where is it?"

"At Sheriff Watson's office."

"Did you tell them what it's about?"

"Nope. I figured it's best to do it in person."

"That sounds good, Carl. I appreciate you doing this. I'll see you at three."

For the second day in a row Ethan informed his secretary that he would be leaving early. While she gave him an inquisitive look, she said nothing. A little before three o'clock he pulled his car in next to Carl's and walked briskly into the building. The receptionist directed him to Sheriff Watson's office. The Sheriff and Carl were there, talking about old times. While Ethan knew the Sheriff well enough to say hello, this was the first time he had ever talked to him in his official capacity. Sheriff Watson arose to greet his visitor.

"Hello, Ethan."

"Hello, Sheriff."

The Sheriff offered his condolences on the death of Ethan's father. The three men made small talk until District Attorney Duncan arrived. The wait was not long. Soon they heard her hurried footsteps drawing near. Ethan turned to see a petite but attractive woman in her mid-thirties. She had short black hair and glasses. She was not at all how Ethan had expected her to look. She walked directly towards the men and shook their hands. After the greetings were finished, the Sheriff directed the foursome to a nearby table.

"So, Ethan," began Sheriff Watson, "I understand from Carl that you needed to meet with us. How can we help you?"

Ethan turned to Carl and looked at the envelope he was holding.

"I guess the best thing to do is to just show you the photographs," said Ethan.

Carl opened the envelope and removed the photographs, each of which he had placed in a plastic bag. He placed them on the table and waited for the other's reactions. The Sheriff and the District Attorney looked at the photographs, then at each other, then to Ethan and Carl for an explanation.

"Where did you get these?" asked Sheriff Watson.

As he had done with Carl the day before, Ethan explained how Emily had found them in his father's trunk. He also showed them the date on the back of the photographs.

"This must be devastating for your family, Ethan," said Carol Duncan.

"Yes, it is."

"And I just want you to know I appreciate you bringing this infor mation to us. A lot of people would have just put this away and tried to forget about it."

"Thank you. We've always tried to teach our children to do the right thing, but this was really difficult. And to tell you the truth I hope we uncover something that shows my dad had nothing to do with this. But either way, our family has to know what happened."

For the next few minutes the foursome went over many of the questions and issues Ethan and Carl had the night before. Carol questioned Carl about any known Klan activity in Greeneville at the time, but he could provide little information.

"There were a few people we suspected might be involved in the Klan, but we never really had any incidents. Back then, even more than today, there were few blacks in the county, and they pretty much kept a low profile, so there wasn't much opportunity for Klan activity."

Sheriff Watson, who had been fairly quiet during the discussion, picked up the photographs and turned to Ethan.

"Ethan, I'm assuming from what you've said so far, that you want a formal investigation into this situation?"

Ethan gave a curious look to the others, then turned back to the Sheriff.

"Well, yes. I thought it was clear that that's why we are here."

"Okay, but I have to tell you that, after over forty years, I think there is very little chance we'll ever uncover who any of these men are. Why, the chances of any of them even being alive still are very slim. And even if they are, if they've kept a secret this long, I doubt if anybody is going to start talking now."

"I'm not sure what you're saying, Sheriff," said Carol. "Are you saying that you don't want to investigate this matter?"

"No, I'm not saying that. We'll look into it. I'm just saying that I don't want Mr. Ward and his family to get their hopes up. Why, I've got murder cases from a few years back that haven't been solved, so I need to give top priority to those first. But I'll put my investigator on it and see what we can come up with."

Carol looked at the Sheriff for a second, and then turned to Carl.

"Well I understand what you are saying, Sheriff, so I'll make it easy on you. Instead of calling on your limited resources, I think I'll just appoint a special prosecutor for this case. And I have just the right person in mind. Someone who was in law enforcement when this incident occurred, and someone who has the experience and knowledge to handle a case such as this."

She turned to Carl with a smile.

"What do you think, Carl? Would you like to investigate this lynching?"

"You can't do that," interrupted the Sheriff.

"Show me a law or regulation that prevents it. I have the right to appoint a special investigator whenever I deem it necessary. Well, I deem it necessary in this case. So, Carl?"

"Well, you caught me a little off guard with that one, Carol. But, yes, I'll be glad to do it."

"And the county will pay you three hundred a week, plus expenses. How is that?"

"Sounds fine."

"And you can coordinate with the Sheriff's office if you need assistance or additional resources."

She turned back to Sheriff Watson who was obviously unhappy with the arrangement, but said nothing more.

"What will be your first step?" Carol asked.

"Well, as I explained to Ethan, if we're going to solve this case it'll be because somebody in the county knows something and they've never come forward. The best way to begin is to let everyone know what happened so they'll start talking about it. So I'll have a story printed in the Greeneville Sun. Then I'll go out and talk to all those men who were rumored to have been in the Klan back then, although only a few are still alive."

"That sounds fine to me. Any suggestions, Sheriff?"

"Yes," he answered as he looked at Carl, "I would like to be kept appraised of anything you uncover during your investigation."

"Certainly," answered Carl.

The meeting was over soon. Carl and Ethan left the building while the Sheriff and Carol remained behind to discuss other cases.

"Well," said Carl as they walked toward their cars, "that was a surprise."

"Yes, but a smart move on her part."

"I guess we'll see if it was or not."

As they reached their cars, Ethan turned to Carl.

"Carl, I just have one request."

"What's that, son?"

"When you find out something about my father, can you please let us know about it first?"

"Sure."

The two men shook hands and got into their cars and went their separate ways. Ethan stopped at his mother's house, and then left for Knoxville. If there were no accidents on the road, he would be home in time to see his son's football game.

Lewis Scarborough, reporter for the Greeneville Sun, was surprised to get a call from the receptionist announcing Carl Benlow was there to see him. He was even more surprised when he saw the photographs he placed before him.

"Wow," he stated. "Is this for real?"

"I'm afraid so."

Like Ethan had done earlier, he explained how Ethan Ward's daughter had found them in her grandfather's belongings.

"Then these were Buster Ward's?"

"I'm afraid so."

"Then he could...."

"That's all we know right now, Lewis. I'm just beginning my investigation."

"Your investigation?"

Carl told him about the meeting at the Sheriff's office.

"I need everyone in the community to know about this as soon as possible. How soon can you run the story?"

Lewis looked at his watch.

"I can get it in tomorrow. I might have to get them to pull another story, but this is huge news."

"Hmm," said Carl as he thought about the story. "Your Sunday paper is double the circulation, right?"

"About that."

"Then why don't we wait until then. I want everyone to be talking about this."

"I think everyone will be talking about it anyway."

"That's probably true, but it's only one more day. Let's wait until Sunday, and that way I'll make sure everyone in the family knows about it beforehand."

"You're the boss."

Carl went with him while he copied one of the photographs and answered any other questions he had about the case. He then left for home to plan his upcoming investigation.

Carl Benlow arose early Sunday morning and looked out the living room window. The Greeneville Sun newspaper was lying in his driveway. He put on his robe, retrieved the paper and lay it on the dining room table while he made a cup of coffee. He sipped his coffee, opened the paper and read:

GRANDDAUGHTER'S SHOCKING DISCOVERY
By Lewis Scarborough, Staff Writer
It has only been two weeks since Greeneville resident Clarence 'Buster' Ward passed away, and no one in the family was more devastated than his granddaughter, UT Freshman Emily Ward. It was her desire to find a souvenir with which to remember her grandfather that led to a shocking

discovery, the photographs of the lynching of a young black man. According to Miss Ward, the photographs (see insert) were in an envelope at the bottom of her grandfather's trunk, which was in storage in the attic. The photographs were a complete and horrible shock to a family still coping with Mr. Ward's death. One of the photographs had the year 1946 handwritten on the back, which, from the image of the trucks in the background, appears to be when the incident took place. When asked about the photographs, Clarence Ward's son, Ethan, said, "Right now anyone who sees the pictures will know as much about the situation as we do. It's just a total shock to the family". When asked what he thought people might infer from his father having the photographs in his possession, Mr. Ward replied, "I hope they will not infer anything. For all we know they somehow came into his possession and he didn't know what to do with them, so decided to hold onto them."

Hopefully the community will not have to wait long until the details of this horrible crime are uncovered. District Attorney, Carol Duncan, has assigned a special prosecutor, retired Police Chief, Carl Benlow, to look into the case. Said Duncan, "Carl Benlow is the most suitable person to handle this investigation. Not only does he have the experience and skills to handle such a case, he was also a deputy sheriff when this incident supposedly occurred in 1946".

When asked about the case, Benlow stated, "Right now my investigation is just beginning, but I feel confident the perpetrators of this horrible crime will be uncovered and brought to justice." Benlow asks that anyone with any information regarding this incident call him directly at 423-555-4358.

Carl Benlow read the article and nodded his approval. He put down the paper and removed the notebook he had been keeping since being appointed to the case. He again examined the list of names of people he would question. Tomorrow he would start his investigation. Like so many times before, he felt the excitement he got at the beginning of a case. He only hoped the trail of evidence led him away from Clarence Ward.

THIRTEEN

Saturday, October 29ᵗʰ

Upon being elected Mayor of Greeneville, Tommy Bell began a monthly radio address on station WGRV to keep the citizens informed of what was going on in their community. When he was elected Senator he kept the same format in place, but moved the time of the program from Thursday evening to Saturday morning. That way, once a month he would drive to Greeneville and do the program and spend the rest of the day with his mother. As an only child, and with no other relatives nearby, he felt an extra responsibility to look after his mother. He offered to have her move in with he and his family, but she always declined saying she was a small town girl and would not be comfortable in a big city like Nashville. She hoped, by remaining in Greeneville, that when her son's term expired, he would decide to move his family back home.

He arrived at the station a few minutes before nine o'clock, and walked to the waiting area outside the broadcast room. The host of the program, George Walker waved through the glass. During a commercial break, George came out and greeted his visitor. Having gone through the procedure many times, the two men only talked briefly about today's show. Tommy followed him into the booth and took a seat behind the visitor's microphone. After doing the news, George announced his guest to his listeners.

"As we do every fourth Saturday, this morning we have with us Greeneville's own, Senator Tommy Bell. Good morning, Senator."

"Good morning, George. It's nice to be back here."

"And it's always great to have you, Senator. So, tell us what's going on in Nashville."

For the next few minutes, Tommy brought his listeners up to date on pending legislature and laws which might affect their lives. When finished, he looked up toward George for direction.

"Well, Senator, thanks for sharing that information with us. However, as I'm sure you know, the talk around the area for the past week has not been about government affairs, but about the photographs uncovered in Clarence Ward's belongings showing a lynching. Is there any information you can share with us regarding that situation?"

"Well, first, George, Mr. Ward preferred to be called Buster."

"Right. Thank you, Senator. And for those of you who may not know, Senator Bell is Ethan Ward's - that's Buster Ward's son - Ethan's brother-in-law, as well as his best friend. Right?"

"That's correct."

"So, anything you can share?"

"No, not really. You, as well as the public, probably know about as much as the Ward family does right now. It's just a horrible time for them. First Mr. Ward passed away, and now this. They knew nothing about the photographs beforehand, and as far as we know, Mr. Ward - that's Buster - never shared any information about them with anyone."

"And if you don't mind me asking, how has this situation affected your relationship with your brother-in-law?"

"It hasn't. A person is only responsible for what he does in his life. No one can be held accountable for what someone else, even a family member does."

"But you've discussed it with him, correct?"

"Yes, we've talked about it, but there really isn't much to say. Ethan told me how sorry he was, and I told him the same thing I just told you. And besides, we don't know if his father had anything to do with this. He could have stumbled over the pictures and not known what to do with them, so just held onto them."

"But, if he had nothing to do with the lynching, why would he have not gone to the authorities?"

"Again, George, I don't know. All I am saying is that we don't have enough information now, so I just ask people to not jump to any conclusions about this. As everyone knows, Carl Benlow has been assigned as a special investigator to look into this situation, and there's no one better qualified. So, let's just give him some time to do his job."

"And, if I may ask, what was your reaction when you heard about this? Were you as shocked as everyone else?"

"Shocked that a black man was lynched in the area forty years ago? No. Shocked that the photographs were found in Mr. Ward's belongings? Yes."

"So, you say you weren't shocked that a black man was lynched in Greeneville?"

"First, it obviously was not in Greeneville. The pictures show a very remote area, so it was not in town. And we don't even know if it was in the county, although we're assuming that it was. But shocked? No. I guess I was a little surprised, but then there have been more black men than we can count that were lynched in the south in the past couple of hundred years. It's just a sad reflection of our society."

"That's true. But I believe you have been quoted before as saying that racial problems in this country were really not a black-white issue, but just an example of man's inhumanity to man."

"Actually, what I said was that race relations in this country were an example of the evil in men's hearts, and not just a black-white issue. You can look at any time throughout history and find examples of people subjugating and enslaving other races. The Egyptians did it. The Romans did it. And probably the worst example of one race's inhumanity to another was what the Germans did to the Jews. But still, what has happened to blacks in this country is horrible. For centuries black families have been split up, children sold off, and men hanged. Slavery and everything that goes along with it, is an abomination to God. So no, I was not shocked that such a thing could have happened here."

"So what do you say to those people who say that this investigation should be dropped? That too much time has gone by and that the case will never be solved, so it's just not worth the time and effort to investigate it?"

"I wasn't aware that people were saying that. Is that the feedback you have been getting?"

"Well, we've received a lot of calls regarding this, and while most of them believe the case must be solved, there are some who believe, after all this time, that it's not worth the time and money it will cost. They also believe that whoever the men were that did this are all dead and gone so it's not worth it to investigate."

"First of all, I don't agree that all of the men are dead and gone. If this really took place in 1946 as the picture shows, then that was forty-two years ago. That means that the men, if they are still alive, could be anywhere between sixty and eighty years old, so the chances of at least one of them being alive is quite good. And to those people who say that it isn't worth the time, I wonder what they would say if it was a young white man hanging from the tree, and four black men that did the lynching."

"Good point, Senator. Okay, let's open the lines up and take some calls to see what's on people's mind."

Tommy smiled at the sound of the first caller's voice.

"Hello, Tommy."

"Hello, Mrs. Byrd."

"It's Beulah, Tommy. You're not sixteen any more, so you don't have to call me Mrs."

The caller was Tommy's favorite high school teacher, Beulah Byrd. Each time he was on the radio she called in, and each time the conversation had the same beginning.

"It's hard to break such a habit. So, how are you today?"

"I'm fine, Tommy. And I just want to say I agree with everything you said. And I am so sorry that a young black man was lynched here, I don't care how long ago it was. I hope Chief Benlow finds out who it was."

Tommy started to tell her that Carl Benlow was no longer police chief, but then realized that she already knew that and didn't care.

"Thank you, Mrs.....Beulah."

Soon she hung up and another called came on the line. The voice was that of an adult male with a strong southern twang.

"Mr. Bell?"

"That's Senator Bell," said George.

"Whatever. Senator Bell," said the man. "You'se talking about slavery and how horrible it is and all. I don't reckon you know that the Bible approves of slavery?"

George motioned to Tommy that he would hang up on him if he wanted. Tommy shook his head.

"What's your name?"

"You can call me Lloyd."

"Well, Lloyd, no, I wasn't aware of the Bible condoning slavery. Can you tell me exactly where in the Bible it says that?"

"Well, I ain't too good on the verses and all, but it's there. I've seen it afore."

"Well, perhaps you're talking about the twenty-first chapter of Exodus. That's the one most theologians reference when they're talking about slavery."

"Oh. Yeah, maybe that's it."

"Yes, that chapter does discuss slavery, but it doesn't condone it."

"Doesn't what?"

"Doesn't approve it. God was smart enough to know that people were going to do evil things, so he put that chapter in the Bible to make sure if people had slaves they were treated fairly. And do you know how people became slaves back then?"

"Cause other people bought 'em."

"I guess that's true, but under Hebrew law people only became slaves because they had committed a crime or were too poor to take care of themselves. And even then they were only sold into slavery until they could pay their debts. I guess you were aware of that, huh?"

"I only know the Bible says it's all right to have slaves."

"Well, Lloyd, as I just explained, it doesn't say it's all right. But let's assume for a minute that it did. Since everything in the Bible takes place in northern Africa, does that mean it's okay for black people to have slaves? I guess that's what you mean - that blacks can own whites as slaves?"

"You're talkin' like a crazy person now."

"Yeah, I guess I am. What was the purpose of your call, Lloyd? Was it to let people know that blacks should still be in chains?"

His question was answered by the sound of the man hanging up.

"Well, I guess he didn't have a response to your question, Senator," said George.

"No, I guess not," answered Tommy.

"Why don't we take a commercial break and we'll return with a couple more calls for the Senator."

The two continued to take calls until the show ended at nine-thirty. Tommy thanked George and left the studio for his mother's house.

Rita Bell enjoyed a cup of coffee with her mother-in-law, Gloria, as they listened to Tommy's radio interview. Rita's son, Bobby, sat at the table having a bowl of cereal as he also listened to his father's interview. During a commercial break between calls, Gloria arose from the table and walked out of the kitchen.

"Maybe I'll have time for a bathroom break before they come back on," she said to Rita.

As her mother-in-law walked towards the bathroom, Rita watched in horror as a rock came bursting through the window and hit her in the head. Gloria fell backwards against the wall and slid slowly to the floor. Rita and her son came running to her aid. As she attended to her mother-in-law, Rita could hear the sound of screeching tires from the street in front of the house. She ran to the window to see an old green sedan moving out of sight. She ran back to the kitchen and grabbed a towel and ran back to her mother-in-law. As she held the towel to Gloria's head, she turned to her son.

"Bobby, pick up the phone and call 911."

Tommy Bell's heart began to pound as he turned the corner and his mother's house came into view. In her driveway were an ambulance and a police car, both with lights flashing. He parked his car on the street and ran into the house. Sitting on the couch, a bandage on her head, was his mother being comforted by Rita. On the floor was broken glass. He turned toward the front of the house to see a hole through the picture window. He didn't need to be told what had happened. His son, Bobby, ran to him. He put his arm around his son and joined his wife on the couch.

"Mom, are you all right?"

"Sure, son. It's just a little scratch."

Tommy looked up at the EMT technician standing nearby.

"How bad is it?"

"It doesn't look too bad, but she needs to go to the hospital to have an x-ray and have the cut sewn up."

"I'm fine. I'm not going to any hospital," said Mrs. Bell.

"Mom, you need to have this sewn up. Now you can go voluntarily or....," began Tommy.

"Okay, fine. Let's get it over with. But I'm not going to be carried out on any stretcher."

Tommy got up and helped his mother to the ambulance. She finally agreed to lie down on the stretcher for the ride to the hospital. Rita followed them to the ambulance and climbed in after her mother-in-law.

"I'll go with her. You talk to the police and then you and Bobby join us as soon as you can. I've already given them a report."

"Did you see who did it?"

"A green sedan - that's all I saw. The police have the report."

Tommy kissed his wife and mother good-bye, and walked back into the house. Ralph Llewellyn, a policeman who he had known since childhood, came over to talk to him.

"Well, it's pretty obvious what happened here," said Tommy. "Did anybody see who did this?"

"Your wife just caught a glimpse of the car as it drove away. She said it was an old, green sedan."

"I know, but she was in a hurry to get to the hospital. I don't guess she got the license number?"

"No, it was too far away. But we've put out an APB for any old green sedan, so there's a good chance we'll catch them."

"So, since you have a statement from my wife, I guess there's not much more I can tell you."

"Unless you know who might have done this."

"You can check anybody that might have been listening to my radio interview this morning."

"That might be kind of difficult."

"Then I guess there's not much else we can do here, huh?"

"No, Tommy, except say that I'm really sorry and that we'll do everything we can to catch whoever did this."

"Thanks, Ralph."

Ralph put his arm on Tommy's shoulder, then turned and walked toward the door. Tommy and Bobby left soon afterward for the hospital. When they got to the emergency room they found his mother lying on a bed in the hallway, Rita sitting in a chair next to her. After a couple of minutes a nurse came and informed them they were taking Mrs. Bell back to have an x-ray and stitches. The three went to the waiting room and seated themselves on a couch. Rita soon turned to Tommy.

"I can't wait to get out of this place. I hate little red-neck towns."

"You grew up in a town smaller than this."

"Yeah, and I left it as soon as I could. They're all the same - filled with narrow-minded, bigoted people."

"There's narrow-minded, bigoted people in the city too."

Rita gave him a look that told him that they should not continue the conversation. The three sat silently waiting for Tommy's mother to return. Fifteen minutes went by before they looked up to see officer Llewellyn walking toward them. Tommy stood to greet him.

"Any news, Ralph?'

"Actually, yes. We caught the guys."

"That was fast. So there was more than one? I guess that figures."

"Yes. Actually it was two teenagers. A neighbor around the corner saw them racing away and wrote down their license numbers. She didn't know what had happened, but figured the boys were up to no good."

"That's good. Did they say anything about why they did it?"

"Well, yeah. I guess they didn't like how you made a fool of the guy on the radio."

"Hum, that's a surprise," he said sarcastically.

"Right, but for whatever it's worth, the idiot deserved to be made a fool of. There are still a few racists around here, Tommy, but most of the people in town are outraged at the lynching."

"Thanks, Ralph. I appreciate that."

Ralph left the room and Tommy returned to his seat with his wife and son. A few minutes later his mother returned to the waiting room with a bandage on her head. The foursome left the hospital to go home.

FOURTEEN

Tuesday, Nov. 1ˢᵀ

C arl Benlow finished sanding the duck decoy and placed it on the shelves with the others. He would paint it when he returned home later that day. He was glad to hear that the two teenagers who had thrown a rock through Gloria Bell's window had pled guilty. It would keep her from having to testify, although, as strong a woman as she was, he thought perhaps she would like to face the boys in court. He hoped the judge gave them more than a slap on the wrist.

It had been less than two weeks since he had been assigned special prosecutor to look into the lynching case, and, as much as he hated to admit it, he was no closer to identifying the robe-covered men or their victim than when he began. He had talked to numerous individuals that lived in the area in 1946 that he felt might have been capable of such an atrocity, but had gotten little information. Of course, he knew investigating a case like this took time and perseverance. He had to find one person who heard something that somebody had said or done that was suspicious, and build on that. It was sort of like a slow leak in a dam. At first the information would come as a trickle, then, hopefully it would turn into a flood. He just had to be patient and continue his job.

While he was not totally surprised that he had not yet uncovered who the men in the robes were, he was a little disappointed that no one came forward with information on the victim. Surely someone knew the young black man that had disappeared in 1946. And the case had now received statewide attention, so even if he were not from the Greeneville or Greene County area, someone somewhere should know who he was. But as of yet, no one had come forward. In 1946 he would have understood, out of fear, no one coming forward, but not in 1988. He had to assume, therefore, that the young man just happened to be passing through the area from somewhere far away. He just happened to be in the wrong place at the wrong time.

Carl strapped his gun on his hip, put on his jacket, and got into his car. He had a couple of errands to run, then had two people he had already interviewed for who he had additional questions. Perhaps, after they had time to think about it, something would come back to them that might be helpful.

His first stop was at the drug store to get his prescription refilled. Getting old was not fun. Although he was only sixty-one, for the past few years he could feel the changes in his body. He didn't have the strength or endurance he once had, and he had to keep a constant watch on his blood pressure. But the thing that bothered him the most was having to get up to go to the bathroom two times every night. For that reason, Dr. Anderson had put him on medication for his prostrate. A quick stop at the pharmacy to get the prescription refilled and a stop at a fast food place for breakfast and he would be ready for the day.

As he was leaving the pharmacy, he looked up to see his doctor walking toward him.

"Dr. Anderson," he said. "That's a coincidence. I was just getting my prescription refilled."

"That's good," said the Doctor as he put his hand on his arm. "Look, Carl, I may have some information about this lynching case I need to talk to you about."

"Oh, really?" said Carl as the two men walked away from the door and alongside the building. "Let's hear it."

"Well, I was looking at the picture in the paper and I noticed one of the men's boots and it looked familiar."

"You mean the boots with the stars on them?"

"Yes. I know it's kind of blurry, but it looks like one from one of my patients back then."

"Really. And it took you this long to remember?"

"No, it took me this long to notice it. I read the article when it first came out, but never examined the picture that close. My wife and I put the newspapers in the garage until we have enough to recycle. This morning I started to throw the papers out, but decided to read the article again. That's when I noticed the boots."

"I see. And do you remember who this patient was?"

"Oh, sure. It was Harold Pratt."

Carl's eyes widened at the sound of the name 'Pratt'. It was his Deputy, Andrew Pratt, and Harold Pratt's son that young Ethan Ward had seen killed in the summer of 1963. Eventually a judge had ruled that Professor Robertson and his friend were acting in self-defense when they shot the Deputy. The trial had uncovered what a cold and mean person Andrew Pratt was. Now, if what Dr. Anderson was saying was true, it would help explain how he got to be so evil.

"Harold Pratt," repeated Carl. "And he had stars on his boots like the ones in the pictures?"

"Yeah. I remember one time when he came in to see me and he was wearing the boots. I asked him if he was a cowboy. He just laughed and said he just liked the boots."

"Wow. Unfortunately even if it was him it'll be hard to prove since he and almost everyone in his family is dead and gone."

"Yeah, I think the only relative he has left is a nephew over in Kingsport."

"Right. His wife's brother's son."

"Of course, Carl, if it was him then his brother and his son, Andrew were probably the other men involved. They always hung together. And Buster Ward would have made the fourth."

"I don't remember Buster hanging around with the Pratt boys back then."

"Me neither, but if they were involved in something like this that would give them good reason not to hang around together afterward."

"Hmm. I guess that's a possibility."

Carl stood thinking of what Dr. Anderson had just told him.

"So, it looks like I may have solved your case for you," said Dr. Anderson.

"Perhaps, but I still have to continue with the investigation. And I would appreciate it if, in the meantime, you didn't say anything to anybody."

"Sure, Carl. And likewise, please don't tell anyone where you got the information."

"No problem."

The two men shook hands. Dr. Anderson continued into the pharmacy while Carl returned to his car and sat staring blankly ahead. While Harold Pratt was considerably older than him, he had known him, or at least known about him, most of his life. He had always been a sullen and quiet man. In all of the conversations Carl had had with him, he probably said no more than a couple dozen words. They didn't know each other well and had little in common, but from what Carl had heard he was like that with everyone. He was one of those people that no one seemed to know very well. And his wife was even quieter, rarely speaking except to say hello. He remembered thinking how different their son, Andrew, was from his parents. He was a loud and sometimes boastful person. He had never had any serious problems with him as a Deputy, which had always been a surprise to Carl since he knew Andrew liked to throw his weight around.

He tried to remember if Harold had ever made any racial comments to him or if his name had ever come up in association with the KKK. He could not recall any such incident. And as far as he knew, Harold had not been a violent man. At least he had never had any complaint about him while he was sheriff. Carl had never known Harold Pratt's older brother, Herman. Herman Pratt lived in a nearby county and had died in an accident at least thirty years ago. But that would have been many years after the lynching incident.

Removing the photographs from the envelope, he tried to picture the three Pratt men and Buster Ward under the robes. Were the men even the right size? Andrew would have been a young teenager, about thirteen or fourteen, when the incident happened, but he was a large man so he could have appeared as an adult under the robe. Harold and Herman were average-sized men. As he grew older Harold lost weight and actually seemed to shrink in size, possibly because of the stress brought on by the loss of his brother and son, but he still could have been one of the men.

The thing that bothered Carl most about Dr. Anderson's theory, however, was Buster Ward's association with the Pratt family. As far as Carl knew, Buster and Harold and Herman Pratt never hung around together, even before the lynching. He just couldn't see Buster doing something like this, and certainly not with the Pratt boys. But then, he had seen crazier things in his life as a law enforcement officer.

He put the pictures back in the envelope, started his car and drove out of the parking lot. After a quick stop at a fast food restaurant for breakfast, he headed for Kingsport. Other than the fact that he lived in Kingsport, which was less than an hour from Greeneville, he knew two things about Harold Pratt's nephew. He knew that his last name was Morgan, and that he owned a small home improvement business. He could have stopped at the sheriff's office and asked questions which could have helped find him, but he didn't want to share what he knew just yet. He would take a chance and hope he could locate him on his own.

His first stop was at the Chamber of Commerce office. He told the receptionist that he had heard that a contractor by the name of Morgan did good work, but he didn't know anything more about him. Luck was with him. She told Carl that he probably meant Lee Morgan, and that he was a Chamber member. She gave him the name of his company as well as his address and phone number. Carl thanked her and left for Morgan's office.

The trip was quick - only ten minutes. Now, if luck continued to smile on him, Lee Morgan would be in his office. He found the office

In an industrial area of Kingsport, and pulled his car near the door. No one was in the small reception area as he entered. He waited a minute before calling out to anyone who could hear.

"Hello. Is anybody here?"

Soon a stocky man in his fifties came out from an office in the back.

"Can I help you?"

"Yes. I'm looking for Lee Morgan."

"Well, you found him."

Carl put out his hand to the man who returned the gesture.

"I'm Carl Benlow. I'm from Greeneville. Do you have a couple of minutes to answer a few questions?"

"Sure. What's this about?"

"I'm investigating something that took place a long time ago in Greeneville, and I thought maybe you could give me some information."

Morgan stared at him for a moment.

"You look familiar. You used to be Sheriff, right?"

"You got it."

"So, is this about the lynching?"

"You heard about it, huh?"

"Probably everyone in East Tennessee has heard about it. Come on into my office."

He followed Morgan down the short hallway to his office. Morgan pointed him to a seat in front of his desk.

"So, how can I help you?" asked Morgan.

"Well, I received a tip that leads me to believe your uncle and cousin might have had some knowledge of the lynching."

"Might have been involved, you mean?"

"I don't know that."

"I wouldn't be surprised if they were."

"Really? You have some information regarding the incident?"

"No. I'm sorry, Mr. Benlow - there's absolutely nothing I can tell you about that incident, but I know what evil men Uncle Harold and

Cousin Andy were, so there's nothing that would surprise me. I mean, you should know better than anyone what Andy was capable of."

"I guess that's true. Did you ever hear them make any racial comments?

"I don't remember. You have to understand, Sheriff...Mr. Benlow, that I had little to do with them. My father didn't like Uncle Harold, and wished his sister had never married him. We usually only saw them at Christmas or at a wedding or funeral. But to answer your question, I'm sure one or both of them at one time or another made racial comments, but then most white people did back then at one time or another."

"So you have no knowledge of the lynching?"

"Absolutely not. I'm sorry, but there's nothing I can tell you that will help. If I knew something I would tell you. I think it's a shame what happened to that young man. Have you uncovered who he was?"

"No, not yet, but I'm still working on it."

Carl removed the photographs from his pocket and handed them to Morgan. He hoped that he could tell him that he too recognized the boots, but didn't want to lead him. He just handed him the photographs and waited for a response.

"Did the Kingsport paper run these?" asked Carl.

"No. They did a story on the incident, but didn't show the pictures. Wow. It's pretty graphic, huh?"

"Yes. So, nothing in the pictures that triggers anything for you?"

He studied the photographs closer.

"No, I'm sorry. I wish I could help, but nothing stands out."

Carl talked to Morgan a few minutes longer. He soon realized he would get no more information from the man and left his office. As he drove back to Greeneville he again went over in his mind his next course of action. Other than his comment that nothing they had done would surprise him, he had learned little from Morgan. Even though the Pratt family had no other living relatives that he knew of, there had to be someone they were close to. He would have to find that person and talk to them. Of course he knew that he still could not limit his investigation to the Pratts. There were others he had yet to talk to that were around in 1946 and might remember something.

As he neared Greeneville he decided he would make one stop before continuing his investigation. It had been a few weeks since he had visited his wife's grave. For the first few months after her death, he went by almost every day. Then gradually it became once a week, and now once every few weeks. That didn't mean that he loved her any less, only that he had to get on with his life. He pulled the car into the Hazel Valley cemetery just east of Greeneville. The cemetery was not in a valley, but was on a hill overlooking a dale where many cedar trees grew. He parked his car and walked to his wife's grave. He bent down and straightened the flowers that someone, probably his sister-in-law, had put on the grave. He dusted the top of the headstone, and then stepped back and wiped a tear from his eye.

"I sure miss you Betty," he said aloud. "But someday we'll be together again."

He knelt for a moment, telling her everything that was going on in his life. Soon he arose and said good-bye, and walked back to his car. While he was there he decided that he would also visit Buster Ward's gravesite. While he had been to the service, he had not gone to the burial. He felt that was a private thing that should only be attended by the family. He drove around the large cemetery looking for a fresh grave. He stopped at a couple of sites, but they were someone other than Buster's. Then, at the third site, he stopped his car and walked toward the grave. As he got closer, his eyes widened and his pace quickened. On the grave, white paint had been spread in the shape of a cross. The headstone had been pulled from its setting and tossed on the ground. He looked closer to see what he already knew. It was Buster Ward's.

FIFTEEN

Carl scanned the cemetery quickly and saw only an elderly woman some distance from him. After glancing down at Buster Ward's gravesite, he turned and walked toward the woman. The woman informed him that she had only been in the cemetery a few minutes, and had noticed nothing. He walked back to the defaced gravesite and stared at it for a moment. He knew better than to touch anything. He walked in a large circle around the grave, looking for anything the perpetrator might have left, but found nothing. He got in his car and slowly drove away. It was times like this that made him wish he had his police car with its two-way radio.

Acquaintances of Carl and his late wife, Ruth and Tory Ledbetter, lived just outside the cemetery entrance. He knocked on the door and waited. Ruth soon came to the door. "Hi, Carl. It's nice to see you," she said.

"It's nice to see you too," said Carl, "but unfortunately this is not a social call."

He informed her that there had been some vandalism at the cemetery and needed to use her phone. She watched and listened as he called the Sheriff's office and explained that one of the graves had been vandalized. After thanking her, he got back in his car and returned to the cemetery. It was only a few minutes before two county sheriff's cars arrived. He watched for a few minutes as they took pictures and examined the site, then turned and got in his car and left. There was nothing he could do there, and he needed to make sure Hilda Ward didn't hear the news on the radio.

Hilda was just getting out of her car when Carl Benlow pulled in behind her. He came up to her and took the bags of groceries from her arms.

"It was nice of you to show up just to help me with my groceries, Carl," she said.

"Right," he answered.

She looked in his eyes.

"You really didn't come to help me with the groceries, did you?"

"Why don't we take these inside."

She opened the door for him as he went inside and put the bags on the kitchen table.

"So, what is the problem, Carl?" she asked.

"I'm sorry, Hilda, but someone has defaced Buster's gravesite."

"They did what?"

"They removed the headstone and threw it on the ground, then poured white paint on the grave."

"White paint?"

"Yes, in the shape of a cross. I'm sorry."

She looked at him for a second, and then put her hands over her face.

"First, poor Mrs. Bell was attacked, and now this. What's going to happen next, Carl?"

"I don't know, Hilda, but hopefully I can figure out who the men were in the capes, and that will put and end to things."

She shook her head, then walked to the couch and sat down. Carl followed her and stood near the couch. After a second, she looked up at him.

"Was the headstone damaged?"

"No, it looked fine. And they can hose down the grave, so most of the paint should be gone."

"That's good. Thank you. Then I will not go see it until that is done. Are you closer to uncovering the truth behind the pictures?"

He thought a minute about telling her what Dr. Anderson had said, but decided against it. He had no proof of what he had told him, and for the moment, decided to keep it to himself.

"I have a few leads, Hilda, but nothing firm. I'll let you know as soon as I know something for certain."

"That is fine. Thank you."

Carl again told her how sorry he was for everything that had happened. She arose, gave him a hug, and then returned to the kitchen to put away her groceries. Carl got in his car and drove away, trying to decide his next course of action.

While the weather was chilly, the stands were packed for Greeneville High School's last football game of the season. Jeannette Waller cheered wildly as she watched her son, William, a starting safety, intercept a pass and return it twenty yards. Unfortunately, the first half expired before the Greene Devils could score. She sat for a moment to catch her breath, and then joined dozens of others in line at the concession stand.

While standing in line she could not help but overhear the conversation between the two white women in front of her. Most of their talk was about the football game. But then, after a few minutes, the subject changed.

"Can you believe what happened to Buster Ward's gravesite?" said one of the women.

"Yeah, isn't that a disgrace?" said the other woman. "But that's what happens when people take matters into their own hands."

"Well, look who you're talking about. We're not talking about the cream of society here."

Jeannette realized that the people the woman was referring to who were not 'the cream of society' were really black. She knew that she should keep her comments to herself, but, after the last remark, it was more than she could handle.

"Excuse me," she said to the women, "but I guess you forgot about the two men that threw a rock through Mrs. Bell's window. Were they the cream of society you're talking about?"

The two women looked at each other, then towards Jeannette.

"I'm sorry, but no one was talking to you," said the first woman.

"Then you should keep your comments behind closed doors where they belong," Jeanette said.

"Excuse me," said the second woman, "but we have a right to say whatever we want. And if you want to eavesdrop, that's your problem."

The women stared at Jeannette for a second, and then turned back around. As they did so, one of the women's elbows hit Jeanette's arm, knocking her purse to the ground.

"Pick it up!" demanded Jeanette.

"I'm not picking it up. You dropped it," said the first woman.

Jeanette put her hand on the woman's arm.

"You did that on purpose, and you're going to pick it up."

"Get your hand off of me," she answered as she pushed Jeanette away.

"You shouldn't have done that," said Jeanette as she grabbed the woman and threw her to the ground.

The second woman grabbed Jeannette. Soon, all three women were rolling on the ground. A black man standing nearby came to Jeanette's aid, and tried to pull the women off her. Upon seeing that, two white men ran to pull him away. Soon others gathered in, and what began with a few words turned into a free-for-all. Officer Ralph Llewellyn, who was working security for the football game, noticed the commotion and ran to the concession stand. He called for assistance, and within a couple of minutes a dozen other officers were on the scene. Eventually the brawl was brought to a halt, with only a few people receiving minor injuries. The police talked to the participants, whose view of the incident greatly varied. After discussing the situation, they decided to let the three women go with only a warning. Officer Llewellyn walked

Jeanette back to the stands, and offered his condolences for what had happened. He then turned and walked away, wondering what would happen next.

———————

Tommy Bell had just returned to his office when his secretary buzzed him on the intercom and told him that Carl Benlow was on the line. He quickly picked up the phone to talk to his old friend.

"Hey, Carl. How's it going?"

"Fine, Tommy. How are you?"

"Just trying to spend my taxpayers' dollars wisely."

"I appreciate that. So, have you heard about the social unrest that's going on back here?"

"Yeah, my mother keeps me pretty informed. It's a shame about Ethan's dad's gravesite."

"Yeah, and I guess you heard about the incident at the football game?"

"Yeah, and the two guys getting into a fight at the gas station yesterday. Anything else happen I don't know about?"

"No, nothing like that. But I just got some news which I thought you should know about."

"What's that?"

"The NAACP applied for a marching permit for next week to protest the fact that no one has been arrested for the lynching. You haven't heard anything about that?"

"No, I haven't, and I'm surprised. I would have thought, me being black and a Senator from Greeneville, that someone would have notified me."

"Well, the Police Chief just got the request, and called me to let me know."

"Okay. What do you think of that?"

"Well, Tommy, it doesn't bother me that the NAACP wants to hold a march. They have a good reputation, and they are non-violent. The problem is what may happen in response."

"What do you mean?"

"Well, I would have to guess that as soon as this is made public, then the KKK will call for a rally at the same time, and we both know what that can lead to."

"Yeah, I see your point. I've met the East Tennessee Regional Director for the NAACP, Alex Hampden before. Do you think I should call him and try to talk them out of it?"

"Actually, I have an alternative I wanted to talk to you about."

"I'm all ears."

Alex Hampden, regional director for the NAACP, had just left a meeting and was returning to his office when his secretary informed him that Senator Tommy Bell had been trying to get in contact with him. He was not surprised. In fact, he had planned on calling the Senator later in the morning. He went to his office and dialed the number. The secretary put him through immediately to Senator Bell.

"Good morning, Mr. Hampden," said Tommy.

"Good morning, Senator. I was just planning on calling you."

"Then I guess I was reading your mind. Look, Alex, I just heard about the rally you are planning in Greeneville for next week, and to be frank, it worries me a bit."

"I was planning on letting you know about the meeting as soon as the permit was approved. But what is your concern--counter protests?"

"Exactly."

"Well, I understand your concern, Senator, but to be quite blunt, that's something we deal with every time we have a rally."

"I'm sure, but this time I think it could be even more volatile, and it's also in my home town."

"I see, but what are you asking? Are you calling to ask us to cancel it?"

"No, but I do have an alternative I hope you will consider."

"What's that?"

"Well, instead of a rally in the streets, why don't you plan a town meeting at the General Morgan Inn?"

"Hum, I never thought of that. But what difference would that make?"

"Well, since it's private property, the owner of the hotel can control who goes in and out. That should cut down on the hostility from the KKK if they show up."

"Well, I understand what you're saying, Senator, but I'm not sure I agree. The KKK can still rally in the streets outside the hotel."

"That's true, and whether they do or not, we don't know or have any control over, but still, I think it's a much better arrangement than trying to rally in the streets with them nearby. And we can also have a real question and answer session, which will be difficult in the streets."

"Okay, I guess that will work. Can we get the hotel?"

"I've already talked to the owner, and he said we can have the lobby or the main conference room for this Sunday night. How will that work?'

"And will you be there?"

"Of course."

"Well, that's kind of short notice, and we'll have to move the rally up a couple of days, but that should be no problem. I guess we can do that."

"And, Alex."

"Yes."

"One other thing. I would like for Ethan Ward to be able to address the group. Is that okay?"

"I guess. From what I've read and heard about him, he's a pretty stand-up guy. Right?"

"Yes. I can personally vouch for him. And he's also one of the least biased persons you will ever meet. His wife is black, you know?"

"Yes, I'm aware of that. Too bad he and his family are caught in the middle of this mess."

"Yes it is. And one final thing. I would like Carl Benlow to be there also. He's the retired Police Chief that is investigating the case."

"I'm not sure that's such a good idea, Senator. From what I understand, he's not made much progress in solving this case. I don't know how people will respond to him."

"Well, the fact that he's not made much progress is not for lack of trying. Remember, this is a forty-year-old case where the people involved are probably all dead. I'll also tell you that he's a very straight and liberal person who most of the people in town know and trust. I think most people will want to hear from him."

"Okay, I'll go with your suggestion. You're a very convincing man."

"Thanks, Alex. I appreciate it. I'll have my secretary fax information to you on the General Morgan Inn. And we can coordinate about getting information about the meeting to the press."

"Sounds like a plan, Senator. I appreciate your help."

"And I appreciate your flexibility. See you Sunday in Greeneville."

SIXTEEN

Thursday, Nov. 10TH

Carl Benlow took a sip of coffee and walked to the window to see if the paper had come. Awaking so early in the morning, he was usually up before the paperboy made his rounds. This morning, though, the Greeneville Sun was already in his driveway. He put his cup on the end table and walked outside to retrieve it. While the sun had not yet risen, the sky was light enough to tell that it would be a beautiful East Tennessee day. The temperature was already in the lower forties, and would reach seventy by afternoon, and there were no clouds in the sky. It would be winter before he knew it, and he hoped to make a trip to the Smoky Mountains before the park closed for the season. Since being assigned a special prosecutor, however, his time had not been his own.

He brought the paper inside and sat on the couch. He took another sip of coffee, and opened the paper. The story he was looking for was on the front page. He read:

NAACP and Senator Bell Plan Rally to
Address '46 Lynching
  Greeneville's own, Senator Tommy Bell, has announced a town
meeting with members of the NAACP in attendance, to address

the 1946 lynching of a young black man. As almost everyone in Greeneville is aware, photographs of the lynching were found in the personal belongings of Greeneville native, Clarence Ward, after his recent death. A special prosecutor, retired Police Chief Carl Benlow, has been assigned by District Attorney Carol Duncan, to look into the incident. When asked about the investigation, Benlow replied, "I have made some progress, but nothing I can share with the public at this time. I still feel, however, that the case will be solved."

The case cannot be solved too soon for most citizens of Greeneville. Since the pictures of the lynching have been made public there have been many incidents of social unrest. After Senator Bell discussed the situation on WGRV radio, a rock was thrown through his mother's window, causing her minor injuries. Two teenage boys were arrested in that incident and pleaded guilty. A few days later, Clarence Ward's gravesite was vandalized. No charges have been filed in that case. And in the past few days two other incidents related to the lynching have been reported. A disagreement regarding the lynching led to a fight at Friday's Greeneville High football game. No arrests were made in that case. And the following day a fight occurred between two men at a gas station. One man was charged in that incident.

Unfortunately, most of the incidents reported have been between blacks and whites. And that is the situation which concerns Senator Bell the most. He said, "the purpose of this meeting is to let the citizens of Greeneville come together in a friendly, open atmosphere to discuss the situation. Carl Benlow, as well as Ethan Ward, and myself will be there to answer any questions presented to us. I just ask the citizens of Greeneville to be patient, understanding, and tolerant until this situation is resolved." Alexander Hampden, regional director for the NAACP out of Chattanooga, will also be in attendance at the meeting, which will be held in the main ballroom of the General Morgan Inn this Sunday evening at seven o'clock.

Carl read the story twice, then tossed it on the table and took another sip of coffee.

"This should be an interesting meeting," he said aloud.

After putting his coffee cup in the sink, he went into the bathroom to take a shower. There were a lot more people he needed to interview, and he wanted to get an early start. Perhaps, with a lot of hard work and a little luck, he would have something he could tell the people by Sunday night.

Sunday, Nov. 13th

As expected, upon hearing about the rally, members of the KKK announced they too would have a demonstration. The city, in an attempt to prevent any violence, limited their permit to Main Street, which ran in front of the hotel, while attendees to the NAACP meeting were told to use the building's rear entrance. By six-thirty, about a dozen robed men and women were congregating on the sidewalk near the hotel.

Ethan Ward's wife and kids had offered to accompany him to the meeting, but he told them that it was unnecessary for them to do so. In reality, he was concerned for their safety in case trouble did break out. Ethan's friend, Tommy, was already at the hotel when he arrived. Tommy introduced Ethan to Alex Hampden, who thanked him for agreeing to speak to the group.

"I know this has been rough on you and your family," said Alex, "and I really appreciate you doing this."

"Thanks. Let's just hope we can calm things down a bit."

Alex excused himself to use the bathroom before the meeting started. After he had left, Ethan turned to Tommy with a question.

"So, you really think this meeting is going to have an impact on people?"

"I'm not sure, but since Alex was going to have a rally anyway, this is better than being in the street with the KKK trying to antagonize every one. Why? You don't think it's a good idea?"

"I guess. I think the thing that people will want to know is how the investigation is going, and from when I last talked to Carl a few days ago, he's not much closer to uncovering who our hooded friends are than he was a couple of weeks ago."

Ethan looked at Tommy who had a sly smile.

"What? You know something I don't?"

"No, not really. Carl hasn't shared anything with me either, but I think he knows more than he's saying."

"Why do you think that?"

"Because I told him bluntly yesterday that if he had any new information, then this would be the place to share it. He told me that, like any good newspaper man, a detective didn't share information until he had it verified by at least two independent sources."

"Hmm. Then maybe he does know something," said Ethan. "We'll have to talk to him before the meeting."

By six-forty-five, Ethan estimated there were about a hundred people in the room. He had feared that the meeting would only be attended by black members of the community, thereby polarizing the town even more. But he was happy to see that about one third of those in attendance were white. At ten minutes until seven, Carl Benlow had not arrived and both he and Tommy were becoming concerned. Ethan walked out of the conference room and to the Main Street entrance and looked out the door. About twenty members of the KKK were now marching in the street with their banners and signs. One said, *'Stop the Witch Hunt'*, while another read, *'What's Past is Prologue.'* Ethan wondered what that meant. It didn't even make sense, but then, the KKK had never been known for their intelligence. A dozen or more policemen stood nearby watching the marchers. He shook his head and walked back toward the conference room. As he walked down the steps from the main lobby, he looked up to see Rachel Mills entering the building from the rear parking lot. He smiled and gave her a hug.

"I didn't know you were going to be here."

"I just felt it was my civic duty. And I thought you guys might need some support."

"Thanks. I appreciate that. You didn't see Carl Benlow out there, did you?"

"No, he's not here yet?"

"Nope."

The two walked back to the conference room. Rachel took a seat in the audience while Ethan walked to the head of the room and seated himself next to Tommy. As he did so, he noticed that Carol Duncan had joined them, but Carl was still not in attendance. By seven o'clock there appeared to be a couple of hundred people in the room. Tommy waited until a couple of minutes after seven, then whispered to Ethan that they had to begin. Ethan nodded his understanding, and Tommy arose to begin the meeting. To both of their relief, as Tommy arose, Carl Benlow entered the room and came and sat next to Ethan.

"Good evening, ladies and gentlemen," began Tommy. "We really appreciate you coming this evening. As everyone knows, the past few weeks have not been easy ones for the citizens of Greeneville, and, in particular, for my friend Ethan Ward and his family. Since the pictures of the lynching were made public, there has been a lot of social unrest in town, and we hope tonight's meeting will begin to defuse that situation. We hope to accomplish a couple of things here this evening. Ethan Ward would like to make a few comments, then, in a few minutes Special Prosecutor, Carl Benlow, will bring you up to date on the investigation. We encourage everyone to ask questions and give your opinions on the situation, but please do so in a calm and rational manner. And I ask everyone, as we try to get through this, please remain calm and try to not make judgments before we have all the facts. Now, to start us off, I'd like you to introduce the East Tennessee Regional Director of the NAACP, Mr. Alexander Hampden."

The crowd gave a muffled applause for Alex. Ethan knew, as did the other speakers, that they really came to listen to Carl and to hear what his investigation had uncovered so far. Alex gave a few cursory comments, repeating much of what Tommy had already said, and then sat down. Next, Tommy introduced his friend Ethan.

"I know this is difficult for him to do, so I hope you all will please be kind and understanding to Ethan."

With that he nodded to his friend, who took the podium.

"Thank you, Tommy. Yes, he's correct, ladies and gentlemen, this is not easy for me. And while Tommy keeps reminding me that a person is never responsible for what another one does - even his own family - I still somehow feel responsible for everything that has happened. I think it was the right thing to do to make the pictures public, but I'm sorry for the problems it has caused so far. I've heard rumors that some people believe that me or my family knows more than we are telling about the photographs. To me that is insane. What else could we possibly know, and what else could be worse than what we've already shared? But I'd like to go on record and say that right now I have no other knowledge of this incident than anyone of you sitting here. I have been asked if I believe my father was one of the men in the robes. I can only say that I hope not, but I just don't know. And I would just like to repeat what Tommy asked. Please try to keep an open mind and remain calm while Carl Benlow finishes his investigation. Now, I would be glad to take a few questions."

A hand immediately went up in the second row. Ethan's pulse quickened as he recognized the questioner. It was Ed Russell, brother to Ted Russell, and one of the people Ethan disliked most in the world. Ethan looked to Tommy, who knew of his relationship with the Russell brothers. He only shrugged his shoulders. He thought for a second, but then realized he could not ignore him.

"Yes?" said Ethan.

"I'm just curious. Has anyone been arrested for disturbing your father's grave?"

The smirk on Ed's face was probably not evident to anyone but Ethan. The reason for his question was obvious. He wanted Ethan to know that he had been the one that had defaced his father's grave. But Ethan had no proof, and there was nothing he could do about the situation now.

"The police are working on it," he answered bluntly. "Any other questions?"

There were a couple of other questions, mostly about how his family was doing and what he thought of the situation. Soon he turned the podium over to Carl Benlow.

"Now I guess we know what happened to my father's grave," Ethan whispered to Tommy as he sat down. Tommy nodded his understanding.

Carl Benlow stood and removed notes from his pocket and placed them on the podium. As many times as he had done so, he still hated talking in front of a large group. After staring at his notes for a few seconds, he cleared his throat and turned to the audience. And while the meeting had been his idea, it had really been to avoid a confrontation between the NAACP and the Klan. He hadn't expected Tommy to request that he speak to the group.

"Good evening. Thanks for coming. Uh, since I've talked to many of you about this case, everyone should know how much time I have spent on it. And while I've made some progress, there isn't a lot I can share. So I think the best thing is to let you all ask questions and I will answer them best I can."

With that he turned to the audience.

"That was short and sweet," Carol whispered to Ethan.

After a short pause, a white lady in the back of the room raised her hand.

"Well, Chief, uh, Carl, exactly what can you tell us? Have you identified any possible suspects yet?"

"There are a few people I'm looking at but I can't tell you if they are actual suspects, ma'am. Right now I really can't share more than that."

"Are any of them still alive?" asked the woman.

"I'm sorry, but I really can't comment on that. Next question."

A black man and former town council member, George Oliver, raised his hand.

"Yes, George," said Carl.

"Carl, I appreciate that there are certain details of the investigation that you don't want to reveal, but it's been a couple of weeks now, and I think the public deserves to know if you've made any progress, or if we're at the same place we were when you began. Do you have actual suspects that you're looking at or not?"

"George, I would like to answer that question - I really would, but I'm afraid it would compromise the investigation."

"I don't understand, Carl. How can telling us who you are looking at compromise the investigation? This was over forty years ago."

Others in the audience nodded their heads in approval of George's comment.Carl wanted to tell them that the reason he didn't want to reveal who his suspects were, was because it might influence others' memories. He wanted to say that, after forty-six years, people's memories were hazy anyway, and by naming the Pratt family as being involved, it might trigger false memories in others. He had seen it happen before. One witness hears what another has said, and it plants a seed in his own mind. And he's soon remembering things that may or may not have happened. That was why, whenever possible in an investigation, he tried to get two or more independent descriptions of what occurred. He wanted to tell them all those things, but, with the looks on the people's faces, he knew that was not what they wanted to hear. He turned to Carol who understood. She nodded her approval.

"Okay," said Carl. "I will tell you what information I have so far. I have reason to believe that three of the men in the pictures were Harold and Herman and Andrew Pratt."

A buzz quickly filled the room. A black woman in the center of the room raised her hand.

"How did you identify them as suspects? Who or what led you to believe that they were the ones?"

"I'm sorry, but that I cannot and will not reveal."

"And what about the fourth man?" asked George. "Was that Buster Ward?"

"I have no information regarding that. And again, I have not even concluded that it actually was the Pratt family that was involved. That's why I didn't want to provide this information. Remember, right now all I have is one lead that points me in their direction. My investigation is still continuing."

Carl continued to receive questions regarding the Pratt family and their involvement, which he tried to answer, or not answer, as best he could. Soon a young black man raised his hand.

"Yes, sir?" said Carl.

"I would like to know what efforts are being made to identify the victim in this case. It's hard for me to understand, after all this time, that he has not been identified."

"I agree with you," answered Carl. "That has been the biggest surprise for me. I'm almost certain he was not from around here."

"That's probably true. Then what steps have you taken to try and identify him?"

"We've provided copies of the pictures to the police in all surrounding towns. I personally have contacted the police in Knoxville, Ashville, Roanoke, and Lexington. The state police and TBI also have copies of the pictures. We have also provided information to any newspaper that's willing to run a story. I think about thirty have done so to date."

"What about the pictures themselves? Any fingerprints from them?" the man asked.

"You should be a detective. Fingerprints were removed from the pictures, and the Ward family was fingerprinted so that we could eliminate those prints."

"Was Buster Ward's prints on the pictures?"

"Yes, they were, which we knew would be the case since the pictures were found in his belongings. There were also prints of unknown subjects."

"Could any of them be one of the Pratts?"

"Since we have Andy's prints on file we compared it to his and it was not a match. Since the other two members of the Pratt family passed away many years ago, and they had no prints on file, there is no way of knowing if the other prints are theirs."

Carl was very upset that the questioning had become this precise, but with Carol Duncan in the room, and the mood of the audience, he felt he had no other choice. The young man who had been asking the questions, however, soon became satisfied. After a few more scattered questions, the room quieted.

"Thank you for your questions," said Carl. "I'll keep you informed of any progress in the case."

He took his seat and Tommy arose to conclude the meeting.

"Again, I would like to thank you all for coming tonight. And, as Carl said, when we have new information we will pass it along as soon as possible. Now, I would just ask that everyone try to be patient and tolerant until this crime is solved. This has always been a calm and open-minded town, and I would like to keep it that way."

"It's not the people in this room that are the problem," said a lady from the back of the room. "It's the people out in the streets right now."

"That's true," answered Tommy. "And all I can suggest is try and ignore them. Most of them are not even from Greeneville, and only came here to cause trouble. Let's not let them succeed."

The meeting ended, and the speakers waited around to talk to the audience members who lingered behind. Ethan looked around for Ted Russell, but he was nowhere to be found. He had accomplished what he wanted. When possible, Ethan took Carl aside and explained who Ted was and asked him to look into his possible involvement in the defacing of his father's gravesite.

"I'll see what I can find out," he answered.

Tommy joined the two men.

"I was a little worried about you showing up," said Tommy to Carl.

"I'm sorry. I was following up on the Pratt boys."

"Anything more you can tell us?" asked Tommy.

"I really don't want to say anything more until I can verify the information I received."

Both Tommy and Ethan nodded their understanding. The three joined Carol Duncan and Alex Hampden and walked out together. As they left the building, they heard a commotion nearby. They looked over to see a number of the demonstrators had left the street in front of the hotel and had come to the rear of the building near the parking lot. About half-dozen robed figures waved signs and shouted at them as they walked toward their cars. Quickly a group of policemen appeared and ordered the protestors back to the street. Shouting as they went, they left the area and returned to Main Street.

"Well," said Tommy to the others, "this actually went better than I expected."

"I agree," said Alex. "I think the way you all handled this avoided what could have been a real nasty situation."

"You can thank Carl," said Tommy as he put his hand on Carl's shoulder. "He's a smart man."

"Or just an old and experienced one," said Carl.

The group laughed and said goodbye, then got into their cars and drove away.

SEVENTEEN

The past few weeks had been the worst in Emily Ward's life. Her grandfather had passed away, then a short time later, she had the incident with Julius Russell. And the following day, she found the photographs of the lynching. Then, to make matters worse, the newspapers got hold of the story, and most people in the state soon learned of her discovery. While everyone she knew had been sympathetic and understanding, she could see the stares and accusations in strangers' eyes. To have people think that her grandfather could have been involved in the lynching of a young black man was almost more than she could bear.

To get through the past few weeks, she had tried to concentrate on her studies and keep to herself as much as possible. To her surprise, her roommate, Candy, had become her biggest supporter and confidante. While Candy had seemed shy and withdrawn in the beginning - hardly speaking to her at all - Emily soon discovered that she was just homesick and missing her boyfriend. After a while, when she had gotten accustomed to campus life, she became much more outgoing and talkative. Soon the two became very close. When Emily had told her about finding the photographs, she had simply hugged her and told her how sorry she was for what she was going through. The two had hardly talked about the incident since then, but it gave Emily comfort to know that she could discuss the situation with her any time she needed.

This evening, as most evenings in the past few weeks, Emily was lying on her bed reading when Candy returned from the recreation center.

"How's it going?" asked Candy.

"Fine."

"As much time as you've spent with that book, you'll be the most prepared person in the class tomorrow for English Lit."

"I guess," said Emily absentmindedly.

"You still worried about what's going on at the meeting over in Greeneville?"

"A little, I guess."

"Your dad said he'd call you tomorrow and let you know what happened, right?"

"Yep," she answered, looking at her watch. It was eight o'clock, and the meeting in Greeneville had probably just finished.

"So, to take your mind off things, why don't you come down to the T Room with me and some of my friends for a while? There's usually a hot guy or two there."

"Oh, I don't know, Candy. That's nice of you, but I think I'll just stay here."

Candy came over to her and reached down and closed her book.

"Look, Emily, you need to get out. I know this has been rough on you, but you can't continue to sit around and feel guilty for something you had nothing to do with. And you need something to take your mind off things."

Emily stared blankly ahead for a second then turned to Candy.

"Maybe you're right. I guess I should get out, huh?"

"Yes."

"Okay. That sounds good. When are you going?"

"Soon as you can get ready."

"I took a shower earlier, so give me ten minutes to get changed," she said as she took the book and placed it on the desk.

Emily arose from her bed, removed a blouse and pants from her dresser, and went into the bathroom to get ready. Upon returning, the two girls put on their jackets and left for the T Room, a popular restaurant and bar located just on the edge of campus. The air was brisk, with temperatures in the upper fifties, a typical fall evening in Tennessee. The place was crowded and noisy when they arrived. Candy looked around to find her friends. They walked to a large table with a half-dozen students, all talking and laughing at the same time. They waved as the girls drew closer. Emily recognized a couple of the students there, but the others were unfamiliar to her.

"Hi, everybody," said Candy. "In case you haven't met, this is Emily, my roommate."

The others either said hello, or just waved. Emily and Candy seated themselves in the two remaining chairs. As she seated herself next to a male student, he put out his hand and introduced himself.

"Hi, Emily, I'm Marty - Marty Navarro. I have economics with Candy. It's nice to meet you finally."

"Hi, Marty. It's nice to meet you," said Emily, wondering what Candy had told him about her. Thinking he was a cute young boy, Emily wondered if Candy had planned it so she would have to sit next to him. No matter. She would just enjoy his company and see where it led.

The waitress soon came and took Candy and Emily's orders. At Candy's encouragement, Emily ordered a beer with her meal. She sipped the beer as she talked to Marty.

"So, are you a freshman?" he asked.

"Yes, and you?"

"A junior. How do you like it here?"

"It's fine. It took me a few weeks to get used to it, but I like it now. Of course, with my family only a few minutes away, I don't get homesick too often."

"Oh, you're from Knoxville?"

Emily told him about growing up in Murfreesboro, and her family only recently moving to Knoxville.

"Where are you from?" she asked.

"I'm from Atlanta?"

"Oh, that's unusual. You didn't like Georgia or Georgia Tech?'

"My father is from here - a UT graduate. All I've heard about all my life is the Tennessee Vols. If I had gone somewhere else I think he would have disowned me."

"I understand," she said. "My father is the same way."

"He's a UT graduate too?"

"No, he actually went to Middle Tennessee State, but he grew up near here and is a big Vols fan."

The two continued to talk. Emily found Marty to be pleasant and polite. Soon Candy nudged her and whispered in her ear.

"He's pretty nice, huh?"

Emily only turned to her and nodded.

Emily and Marty continued to talk about campus life and their studies. She discovered that he was a pre-law student, and that he planned to go into corporate law.

"Do you plan on returning to Atlanta when you graduate?"

"I don't know. That's still a long way off. What about you? What are your plans?"

"I always wanted to be a lawyer, or maybe just a teacher like my mom and granddad."

"Well either one of those is a noble profession."

They continued to chat through their meal. After his second beer, Marty turned to her with a question.

"I hope you don't mind me asking, but are you Hispanic?"

"No," she answered. "Well, actually, I do have a little Hispanic blood in me, but mostly I'm black and white. I probably have a little Native American in me too, so I'm sort of a Heinz 57."

"Well," he said, "I hope I'm not being out of line, but you certainly got the best traits of all of those."

"Thanks," she said with a smile.

During their conversation Marty noticed that Emily kept looking at her watch. Finally, he decided he had to answer his curiosity.

"Do you have somewhere you have to be?"

"What? Oh, no. I'm sorry, it's just that my father has an important meeting this evening, and I have been kind of worried about him."

"An important meeting on Sunday evening? That's unusual."

Emily wondered if she should tell him the story. She decided there was no reason to keep the truth from him. Most people knew about the situation anyway. She told him about her grandfather and the photographs, and everything that had happened since then.

"So, you're that Emily?"

"Yes, I'm afraid so. I guess you know the story, huh?"

"Yes, and I would just like to say I'm sorry for what you're going through. This must be a terrible time for you."

"Yes, it is, thank you. But, as they say, this too will pass"

"Or, as a friend of mine says, *'a hundred years, all new people'*"

"I never have heard that before. That's funny," she laughed.

They continued talking and laughing through their meal. After a while Emily looked at her watch. It was after nine o'clock. She turned to Marty and informed him she had to go.

"So early?"

"Yes, I want to call home and see if my dad is back yet, and how the meeting went."

"Okay. Do you want me to walk you to your room?"

She thought of how nice he seemed, and how it would be nice to have the company, but then she remembered the situation with Julius. This time she would be more cautious.

"Thanks, Marty, but I'll be fine. It's only a few minutes from here."

"But I'll be glad to walk you."

"Look, I do appreciate it, but I have to take it slow. If you want, though, you can call me."

"That would be great. I really enjoyed talking to you."

"Me, too."

She took a napkin and wrote down her room number and phone number. She then informed Candy that she was going back to the room, and said goodbye to the others. The temperature had dropped in the short time she had been inside, but it was still a pleasant early November evening. She had many things on her mind as she made the short walk back to the dorm. She thought of Marty, and wondered if he was as attracted to her as she had been to him. And, more importantly, she wondered if he was really as nice as he seemed. She actually would have liked him walking her to her room, but then she thought of the experience she had had with Julius, and didn't want to go through that again. If he was interested, he would call her. She would take it nice and slow and see what happened.

The meeting in Greeneville was also weighing heavy on her mind. While her father had cautioned her to not get her hopes up, she still thought something could come out of the meeting that would show her grandfather had nothing to do with the lynching. She knew it was a long shot, but she could still hope. And, knowing he would probably stop at her grandmother's house before heading home, there was a good chance she could catch him there.

There was hardly anyone on the streets as she walked back to her room. She turned off Cumberland Avenue and headed down the side street that led to her dormitory. She had only walked a short distance when she noticed a man standing behind a white van. As she drew closer, she could see that he was staring at what appeared to be a map. The lighting was poor, and she wondered how he could even see what he was doing. She wondered why he had not parked under a street lamp, then figured that was the only parking place he could find. As she walked by, he looked up at her and spoke.

"Excuse me, Miss, but could you tell me how to get back to Interstate 40?"

"Sure," said Emily as she walked a little closer, "you just go back here to Cumberland..."

"I'm sorry. Which is Cumberland?" he asked as he looked down at the map.

"We're right next to Cumberland," she answered.

He said nothing but gave her a blank look.

"Cumberland is the main street right here," she answered as she pointed behind her.

"Oh. Then what?"

"You turn right on Cumberland..."

"I'm sorry, can you show me on the map?"

"Okay," answered Emily as she walked to the man. "I don't see how you can even see anything on the map as dark as it is."

Suddenly the man's arm was around her neck, and a cloth was over her mouth. She tried to pull loose, but he was too strong. She kicked at his legs, but to no avail. Her fingers cut into his arms, but he held her tight. The cloth over her mouth had a strange, but not unpleasant odor. Soon everything began to grow dim. When he felt her body relax, he opened the rear door to the van and pulled her inside.

PART THREE

EIGHTEEN

It was the fourth of July and everyone in Emily's family had gathered at her grandfather Robertson's house. After lunch, the family chose teams for a game of football. Emily, her dad, her aunt Rita, and her cousins, Edward and Bobby, were playing against her mom, her brother, her uncle Tommy, her uncle Horace, and her aunt Emily. Emily caught a pass from her dad, and was heading for the end zone when Tommy grabbed her from behind and pulled her down. He fell on top of her, and was soon joined by everyone else in the family. Soon they were all lying on top of her laughing. Emily tried to tell them that her arms and legs were trapped, and that they were hurting her, but no one would listen. She tried to free herself, but to no avail. She tried to yell, but found someone's hand over her mouth.

It took a few seconds after she came to, to remember what had happened to her. When she did, her dream took on a horrible new meaning. She found her arms and legs bound, and tape over her mouth. Her arms ached from being bound behind her. Her heart felt as if it would explode. She began to moan loudly through her taped mouth. When she got no response to her moans, she began to kick the side of the van. After some time, she heard her abductor's voice.

"Girl, that's not going to do you any good. You might as well just try to calm yourself for a little while longer."

Remaining calm was the last thing on her mind. She continued to kick the side of the van and scream as best she could through the tape. After a while she could feel the van slowing down. Once the vehicle came to a stop, the man climbed between the seats and came to her. She looked up at him, pleading through her taped mouth.

"Okay, I guess it won't hurt to take the tape off now. There ain't no one out here that can hear you anyway."

He reached down and pulled the tape from her face. Once it was removed, Emily breathed deeply for a few seconds, and then looked up at him.

"Why are you doing this?" she pleaded. "What - what do you want?"

"You'll find that out in time, girl. Now you're not going to be able to get free, so you might as well just try and relax and save your energy."

As she listened to the cars going by from a distance, Emily tried to figure out where they might be. It sounded like they were near a highway. She tried to make out the man's face, but it was too dark.

"What are you going to do with me?" she asked.

"Like I said, you'll find out soon enough."

"Please let me put my arms in front. This tape is cutting off the circulation. Please, mister."

The man looked at her for a moment, then bent down and rolled her on to her side and looked at her arms. Emily listened as he removed a knife from his pocket and cut through the tape. He then rolled her onto her back, picked up the roll of tape, and taped her arms in front.

"Thank you," she said.

"Now, I can see you from the mirror, so I wouldn't try to remove that tape if I were you. We'll be where we're going soon, so just relax."

"What do you want from me?" she asked again in a calmer voice.

"I don't want nothing from you," he answered. "Of course, I reckon your family will pay a nice sum to get you back."

"A ransom? That's what this is about? My parents aren't rich. How much money are you going to ask for?"

"A half-million should be enough."

"A half-million dollars! My parents don't have that kind of money."

"I think with your grandparents and your rich uncle Tommy they'll be able to come up with it. Now you just keep quiet and we'll be where we're going soon."

The man got back in the driver's seat and pulled the van back on the road. Emily lay silently, trying to listen to any sounds that might tell her where they were. From the sound of the vehicle and the surrounding traffic, she soon deduced that they must be on an interstate highway. She figured that they must be either on Interstate 40 or 75, the two main highways that went through Knoxville, but which way they were headed, she could not tell. She looked at her watch, but it was too dark to see. She turned herself so that she could see out the windshield, but, from her angle there was mostly darkness and an occasional streetlight.

She thought about her captor. While there had not been enough light to see his face clearly, there seemed to be something familiar about him. Had she seen him somewhere before? She couldn't remember. And there must be some decency left in him since he had taped her arms in front of her as she had begged. And she realized that she was lying on some sort of mattress or perhaps foam pad. He had at least been thoughtful enough to think of that. After a while she stopped trying to understand him or why he was doing this, and closed her eyes and prayed.

A short time later she could feel the van slowing down. From the feel and sound of the vehicle, she believed that they had turned off the interstate. How long had they driven? She could only estimate that she had been unconscious for a half-hour to and hour, which meant that they had now probably been driving between and hour and an hour and a half. Therefore they probably had driven between fifty and eighty miles. Not much help, but at least it was something.

It still sounded as if they were on a highway, but now their speed had decreased. She believed it was a secondary road. She tried to estimate the time but it was difficult to do so. After a while - what she estimated to be between fifteen and thirty minutes - they again came to a stop and turned. Now they were on a winding, twisting road. The vehicle sounded as if it was only going about twenty to thirty miles an hour. This continued for a short time, and the van stopped again and made a turn. Their speed again decreased, and it now sounded as if they were on a bumpy gravel road. Finally, after only a few minutes, it sounded as if they had turned onto a dirt road. This only lasted a couple of minutes before the van came to a halt. She heard the man cut off the engine and open his door. In a few seconds, the rear door to the van was opened. The man shined a flashlight toward her.

"Okay, girl. We're here."

"Where?"

"Now I don't think you really expect me to answer that, do you?"

He climbed into the van and took his knife from his pocket and cut the tape to her legs.

"I'm cutting this tape so you can walk, but don't even think about running. It's pitch black out here so you won't get far."

He pulled her to her feet and led her around in front of the van. He shined the flashlight directly in front of her feet, but there was enough moonlight out for her to tell they were at a small house surrounded by woods. She noticed a motorcycle sitting near the entrance. He opened the door and led her inside. The room had a damp, musky smell. Once inside he let go of her arm and closed the door behind them. He then turned and took a lantern off the wall and lit it. His actions told her that he had been to the place before, probably in preparation for her arrival. The lantern provided enough light for Emily to make out the layout of the room. The room was large, and appeared to take up most of the building. Straight ahead, against the wall were a sink, a stove, and a refrigerator. Immediately in front of them were a small dining table and chairs. To the left of them was a couch and chair. On both sides of the room, in the far corners, were twin beds. To the right of them were two doors, one of which she assumed led to the bathroom, the other probably to a closet. The man took her arm again and led her to the middle of the room where he put the lantern on the table. He then led her to the bed on the right side of the room. As they drew nearer, Emily saw a large bolt sticking up from the floor with a chain attached. On the end of the chain was a handcuff. Her heart began to pound as they came nearer the bed.

"No, mister, please. Don't chain me to the bed."

"I'm sorry, girl. I don't have any choice."

"You don't have any choice?" she repeated. "Why do you say that? Then why are you doing this if you don't want to? Please don't chain me up."

He didn't answer, but led her to the bed and put the handcuff around her wrist and fastened it. When finished he looked up at her.

"This is long enough for you to reach the bathroom. It's right next to your bed. We don't have any electricity, but the water still works."

As she looked up at him, for the first time she got a chance to study his face. He was White, and probably in his early to mid sixties. She estimated he was about six feet tall, and weighed about a hundred and eighty pounds. As she studied his face, a horrible thought came to her. She began to sob, hiding her face in her hands.

"No need for that, girl," he said.

She only sobbed louder and began to shake.

"What's wrong?"

"You're - you're going to kill me."

"No, I'm not."

"Yes you are. I saw your face, so I know you're going to kill me, no matter what my parents do."

"Look at me, girl," he said as he put his hand on her shoulder. "I can't explain why I'm doing this, but I promise you, you won't get hurt, no matter what happens. Do you understand that?"

"Really?"

"Yes, really."

"But I can identify you."

"In a few days, it won't matter. Everyone will know, anyway."

There was a sadness to his last statement, Even though he had abducted her, she almost felt sorry for him.

"It's cold in here," said Emily.

"Well, I can fix that," he answered.

He went to the second door against the wall and returned with a kerosene heater. He put it on the floor and pointed it toward her bed and lit it. Within a few seconds she could feel the heat.

"Thank you," Emily said.

"No problem."

"But what will you use?" she asked.

"Oh, this will warm up the room enough. I'll be fine. I have some food in the cupboards if you want something."

"No thanks. I'm not hungry."

He handed her the flashlight.

"You can use this if you want. I'm going to have me a bite to eat, then put out the lantern and go to bed. You sure you don't want something?"

She just shook her head.

He left her and went into the bathroom. Soon she heard the toilet flush, and he came out and went into the kitchen area. She watched as he removed something from the refrigerator and began to unwrap it. She wondered how it could be cold if the electricity was not working, then realized how cold the room had been. It was probably only in the thirties outside. It looked like a sandwich. He took a few bites, then rewrapped it and put it back in the refrigerator. He removed a paper cup from a bag on the table, then took a carton of milk from the refrigerator and poured himself a cup. After finishing, he threw the cup in a nearby trashcan and turned to Emily.

"You sure you don't want something?" he asked for the third time.

"No thanks."

He nodded, then went to the table and shut off the lantern. The room was in almost total darkness. Emily turned on the flashlight and walked into the bathroom. He had been right - the chain was just long enough for her to reach the toilet. The flashlight showed a filthy room.

She forced herself to sit on the toilet, then flushed it and returned to her bed and pulled the covers up to her chin.

She laid in bed trying to understand why the man was doing this. Did he really think that her parents had a half-million dollars? He seemed to know a lot about them, but there was no way that they could raise a half-million dollars, even with her other relatives' help. And even if they did, would he really release her? His actions seemed confusing. He had abducted her, but then he seemed like he regretted doing it. So far he had been very kind to her. He had removed the tape from her mouth and had re-taped her arms in front of her when she had asked. He had been thoughtful enough to put a pad in the van for her to lie on. He had made sure she could reach the toilet. And he had given her the only heater and asked if she wanted something to eat. And, most importantly, he had not tried to assault her and had promised her that she would not be harmed. He was very confusing. Then she realized that perhaps that was what he wanted her to think. Maybe he really was a monster, and was just being nice to gain her confidence. But then why would he do that when he had total control over her? And why had he said that he had no choice in kidnapping her? And, just as importantly, why had he said that, in a few days, everyone will know? Did he mean that everyone would know who he was? Didn't kidnappers always keep their identity secret?

She closed her eyes and tried to sleep, but could not. She thought of the last few hours. How ironic it was that she had turned down Marty's offer to walk her to her room. She had done so because of the problems with Julius, and now she found herself in an even worse situation. If she had accepted Marty's offer, this wouldn't have happened. Of course, from how much the man knew about her and her family, it appeared as if he had been stalking her. So if he hadn't abducted her tonight, he probably would have later. From everything she had seen in the room, he had certainly planned this for some time.

After what seemed like hours, she turned on the flashlight and looked at her watch. It was a little after one. She turned off the flashlight, and turned on her side. A short time later, she finally fell asleep.

NINETEEN

Monday, November 14ᵀᴴ

Emily awoke to the sound of a dog barking somewhere in the distance. She thought that perhaps that meant they were not in as remote an area as she had first believed. Or perhaps it was just a wild dog roaming through the woods. Dogs sometimes wandered miles from their home. As she wiped the sleep from her eyes she recalled the past ten to twelve hours. Could it really be possible that she was being held captive by a mad man? Perhaps it was all a bad dream. Then she felt the shackle around her wrist.

When it was light enough, she looked over at the man's bed, but he was gone. She arose and went into the bathroom and returned to her bed. Soon she heard the sound of the door opening and looked up to see the man walking in. He closed the door behind him and walked to her bed.

"Did you sleep okay?" he asked.

"I guess as well as can be expected with this chain on my wrist."

"Sorry, but I have no choice."

"You keep saying that, but you do have a choice. Why are you doing this?'

"I already told you - half a million dollars."

"Mister, I don't know who you are or why you picked me, but my family doesn't have anywhere near that kind of money."

"We'll see. You want something to eat?"

"I'm not hungry."

"Suit yourself."

He walked to the cupboard and removed a box of donuts, then opened the refrigerator and took out the carton of milk and poured himself a cup.

"Is that milk still good?" asked Emily.

"I just put it in here a couple of days ago, and as you know, it's been pretty cold in the cabin."

Emily's assumption had been correct. He had obviously planned her abduction for some time - had even been to the cabin to get things ready for her arrival. He raised the cup to his nose and smelled it.

"Smells fine to me. You sure you don't want a donut and some milk? I'm sorry, but that's the best I can do without electricity."

"Okay," she answered reluctantly.

He removed another paper cup from the bag and poured her a cup of milk, then took a donut and placed it on a paper plate and took it to her. He sat them on a small table next to her bed.

"I also have some apples if you want them."

"Maybe later, thank you."

She ate her donut as she studied him. Had she seem him somewhere before? He looked familiar, but she still could not place him. She wanted to ask him if they had met somewhere, but decided it best to let it go. Despite what he had said about not harming her, she decided the less she knew about him the better. Besides, it was probably just her mind playing tricks on her. Perhaps she had just noticed him in the past few days that he'd been stalking her. She finished her donut and looked up at him.

"So, how long am I going to be here?"

"Only a few days - long enough for your family to come up with the money."

She thought of telling him again that her family did not have that kind of money, but decided it was useless.

"When are you going to call them?"

"In a little while. That reminds me, there is something we have to do."

She watched as he walked to his bed and removed a bag from underneath it. He removed something from the bag and walked toward her. As he came closer she could see that it was a tape recorder.

"We just have to make a tape recording for your parents so that they know that you're okay."

"I'm not going to do that."

"If you know what's good for you, you will."

"You promised me that you wouldn't hurt me, and now you're already threatening me?"

"I didn't say I was going to hurt you, but you're not leaving here until you make a recording. Besides, don't you think they'll want to know that you're okay?"

She thought about what he said. She hated to admit it, but he was right on both counts.

"Fine," she said reluctantly.

He brought the tape recorder to her and sat on the bed. She pulled her legs up away from him. He handed the recorder to her.

"You just have to push the red button and tell them that you're okay and to please do what I tell them."

She looked angrily at him, and turned on the recorder and began.

"Mom, Dad, I'm okay. Please do what he asks and he said he would let me go. We're out in the woods somewhere in a cabin, I think about an hour or two from Knoxville."

He took the recorder from her and hit the rewind button.

"You didn't really think I would let you say that, did you?"

"It was worth a try."

He handed her back the machine. She gave him an angry look, and then recorded what he had instructed her to say. He said nothing, but took the machine and placed it on the table. He looked at his watch, then turned back to Emily.

"I'll wait a little while, then go call your parents."

"They're going to want to talk to me in person, you know."

"We don't always get what we want, do we?"

With that he opened the door, turned and walked outside.

For the third time that morning, Ethan Ward picked up the phone and called his daughter's dorm room. The response was the same - no answer. He found that strange, since he knew Emily didn't have class on Mondays until ten o'clock, and it was now a little after nine. And he knew that she wanted to hear about the meeting the night before. He finally decided that she had probably just gone to breakfast with friends and planned on calling him later. And he didn't know her roommate Candy's schedule, but figured that she was in class. He put down the phone and returned to work. It was almost eleven-thirty when he started to pick up the phone to try her again. Before he could do so, however, his phone rang.

"Ethan Ward," he answered.

"Mr. Ward," came the female voice.

"Yes?"

"This is Candy - Candy Wells, Emily's roommate."

"Hi, Candy."

"I'm sorry to bother you at work, but..."

"That's fine, Candy. What's the problem? Is something wrong with Emily?"

"Well, I don't know. Actually, I haven't seen her since last night, and I don't know if I should be alarmed or not."

"Since last night? You mean she didn't come back to the room?"

"No, she didn't."

"Look, Candy, I have to ask - is this something she has done before - I mean, has she ever stayed..."

"No, sir, she hasn't. And, to tell you the truth, it kind of scares me."

"I understand. When was the last time you saw her?"

Candy told him about them going to the restaurant with friends and Emily leaving alone.

"Have you talked to her other friends?"

"Yes, sir, that's why I wanted to call - I wanted to talk to them first - but no one has seen her since she left the restaurant last night."

"Candy, I'm coming over there. Will you be in the room?"

"Yes, sir. My next class is not until one o'clock."

Ethan hung up the phone, grabbed his coat, and started out the door. He then stopped and returned to his desk, picked up the phone, and dialed his home number. He put in the code for the answering machine, hoping that Emily had left them a message at home. There was no message, but he could hear the click of someone hanging up. He shook his head and hurriedly walked out the door. He told his secretary that he had a problem that he had to attend to and would be back later in the afternoon. Twenty minutes later he was at Emily's dorm room talking to Candy. When she could provide him with no additional information, he told her that they needed to go to the campus police. She agreed, and the two hurriedly left the room headed for the police building. They explained the situation to the desk officer on duty, Sergeant Linton.

"Look, Mr. Ward," said the officer, "I know how concerned you are, but this happens quite a bit here."

"What do you mean?"

"A young girl is away at college and meets a young man and goes and spends the night with him. I'm sorry, but that is more than likely what happened."

"I thought there was a rule about girls being in men's dorm rooms?'

"There are ways around it, sir. Trust me."

"Well, I don't care. Emily wouldn't do that."

"Sir, I'm sorry to say this, but that's what I hear every time. Now, someone has to be gone for twenty-four hours before we can file a missing person's report."

"Look officer, this is not acceptable. Even if my daughter didn't want to tell her parents what she was doing, she certainly would have told her roommate."

Candy nodded her agreement. Just as the officer was beginning to respond, another policeman came from around the corner.

"Mr. Ward," he introduced himself, "I'm Sergeant Matthews. I was the one who handled the situation with your daughter and Mr. Russell."

"Pleased to meet you," said Ethan as he held out his hand to shake.

"I'll handle this," he said to the other officer, who nodded and turned and walked away. "Let's go into my office."

Once in the office the three sat down.

"Look, Sergeant Matthews, if you met my daughter, then you know how responsible she is. She wouldn't just take off without letting somebody know where she was going."

"I understand what you're saying, Mr. Ward, but Sergeant Linton was correct in the department requiring a twenty-four hour delay before beginning an investigation. However, unofficially, I'll start asking around to see what I can uncover."

"I appreciate that, Sergeant Matthews. The place I think you should start is with Julius Russell."

"Yes, I'll talk to him."

"And I'd like to go with you."

"I'm sorry, but I don't think that's a good idea. First, as I said, this is not an official investigation. And people are not as likely to talk if you are there - especially young Mr. Russell."

"I see," said Ethan. "But I feel like I have to do something to help find her."

"I understand, sir, but I really believe that it's what Sergeant Linton said - she met someone and spent the night there, and she'll show up soon. I know it's hard for a parent to accept, but young girls grow up."

"I don't think that's the case, Sergeant, but I hope you're right."

"I'm sure it'll be fine. Now please go home and try not to worry. I'll talk to Miss Wells here and get information on your daughter's friends. After I've talked to them I'll call and let you know what I found out."

"Okay," said Ethan with reluctance. He thanked the Sergeant and Candy and slowly arose from his chair. Sergeant Matthews handed him his card. Ethan nodded and walked out of the room.

As he walked to the car he tried to think of what he should do next. He wondered if he should call the Knoxville Police. They would probably also tell him that they had to wait twenty-four hours. He thought of how strange a person reacted when it was his family in crisis. From his years as a reporter, he was aware of the regulation that most police forces had about waiting twenty-four hours before they begin a missing person investigation. But now he forgot all about it - or, more accurately, didn't care. He wanted Emily located, and he wanted it now.

He also wondered if he should call Sally. She would want to know what was going on, but if Emily appeared in the next hour or so it would just be worrying his wife needlessly. As he opened the door to his car, he decided he would give Sergeant Mathews until one-thirty, and then he would call Sally and the Knoxville Police. Instead of going back to the office, however, he decided to go home. He knew he would not be able to concentrate on work, and there might be something he could do to help find his daughter.

It was half-past twelve when Ethan returned home. He immediately went to the answering machine and checked for messages. He hit the play button and listened to the sound of two calls hanging up. He threw his coat on the back of a kitchen chair, then went to the refrigerator and removed a soda to drink. As he sipped it, he thought of one thing he could do that might help. He would call Carl Benlow. He had probably handled a lot of cases like this one and would know what to do. Just as he started to pick up the phone, it rang. He quickly answered.

"Hello...hello."

"Hi."

"Oh, Emily, where have you been? Honey, I've been..."

"I'm fine, but, please do what the man says and he says I'll be all right."

"Honey, what..."

"Mr. Ward," came the strange man's voice. "I have your daughter, and if you want her back you'll have to come up with half a million dollars."

"What! Who is this! I can't...! Let me talk to my daughter again!"

"You're not going to talk to her again now," said the man. "Your daughter is fine. Now, like I said, if you want to get her back you need to come up with half a million dollars."

"A half-million dollars! I don't have that kind of money."

"Then you'll just have to talk to the rest of your family - your father-in-law, your brother-in-law, your brother. And your mother should have received the life insurance on your father by now. Remember - a half million in twenty dollar bills - unmarked and non-consecutive serial numbers."

Who is this man, thought Ethan. And how did he know so much about his family? His voice was soft and raspy, almost a whisper. He was obviously trying to disguise his voice.

"I can't raise that kind of money," repeated Ethan.

"I'll call you again tomorrow evening. You'll get more instructions then. Just get the money and everything will be okay. Don't call the police or FBI, and, if you know what's good for your daughter, don't contact the TV or radio stations."

"No...you can't..."

The man hung up, leaving Ethan talking to himself. He held the phone for a few seconds and then slowly hung it up. He braced himself against the wall and brought his hand to his forehead. After a few seconds he stumbled to the kitchen table and sat down. How could this be happening? Had his daughter really been kidnapped? And what should he do about it? There was no way they could raise that kind of money, even with other family members' help. And what about his demand to keep the police and FBI out of it? He had handled kidnapping cases as a reporter, but now couldn't remember if the ones where the victim had been returned unharmed had immediately called the authorities or not. His mind was a jumble of thoughts and emotions.

He started to pick up the phone to call his wife's school, but then decided against it. There was nothing she could do about the situation, and it would only be a few hours before she would be home. Better to use the time to try and figure out what to do. Ethan arose from the chair and paced around the room for a few minutes, then walked to the phone. There was only one thing to do. Call the person who had a lot of experience in such situations, and someone he knew and trusted. He dialed the number of Carl Benlow.

TWENTY

Ethan dialed Carl Benlow's number and waited nervously. The phone rang a dozen times but there was no answer. He hung up the phone and paced around the room. Perhaps he should call the Greeneville district attorney's office and see if they knew where Benlow was. Or perhaps his mother or Tommy's mother knew? But then the caller said to not let the authorities know. No, he would wait a little while longer and call again. He wondered if he should call Sergeant Matthews again. He wouldn't have to tell him his daughter had been kidnapped - just ask him if he had uncovered anything yet. That wouldn't be a problem. In fact, that would be the thing a father would be expected to do, even if he hadn't received the call from the evil man. He removed Sergeant Matthew's card from his pocket and dialed the number. His answering machine came on. He left him a message asking if he had uncovered anything about his daughter yet.

He waited another fifteen minutes and called Carl Benlow again. He listened to the hollow sound of the phone ringing. He was just about to hang up when the phone was answered.

"Benlow here," came the out-of-breath response.

"Carl," said Ethan.

"Oh, hi, Ethan. I just ran in from outside."

"Carl, Emily's been kidnapped."

"What!

"She's been kidnapped."

"Kidnapped? Are you sure, Ethan?"

"I just got a call from him - the kidnapper."

"Oh, God. I'm sorry. What did he say?"

"He said if we want to get her back we have to come up with half a million dollars. A half-million dollars! We don't have that kind of money, Carl. I don't know what to do."

"Ethan, listen to me. You need to get the FBI involved immediately."

"He said to not let the authorities know."

"I know, Ethan, but you need to call them."

"And what if he finds out and does something to her?"

"Ethan, listen to me. I'm sorry to have to say this, but he's already decided if he's going to let her go or not. It won't make any difference if you call in the authorities or not, so your best chance of getting her back is to get the FBI involved."

"What about the TBI?"

"No, the FBI. They're more equipped to handle things like this. But you'll have to call the police first. On kidnapping cases they have to request the FBI's help."

"Yeah, I know. But again, I want to keep it quiet. You know anyone at the Knoxville Police Department I should talk to?"

"Yes. Call Lieutenant Bob Elliott. I've worked with him on a few occasions, and he's a good guy. Let me look up his number."

Ethan waited while Carl found the number.

"Here it is. It's 615-555-2324."

Ethan found a piece of paper and wrote down the man's name and phone number.

"Okay, Carl. You know what's best."

"Well, let's hope. Ethan, do you have any idea who would do this?"

"Yes, the Russell boys."

"Really? You really think...?"

"Yes, I do. I don't think it was a coincident that Ted's son happened to meet Emily and go out with her. And what about my dad's gravesite? They hate me and have always wanted to do something to hurt me, and now I guess they got their chance."

"I didn't know about his son and Emily. You should tell the police and FBI about that. And I'm sorry, but I haven't been able to prove anything about the gravesite."

"It doesn't matter now. Can you come over, Carl?"

"I'll be there in a couple of hours. In the meantime, you call Lieutenant Elliott."

"Okay."

Ethan hung up the phone and stared at the piece of paper with Elliott's name and number. He wiped the moisture from his forehead as he dialed the number.

"Elliott," came the quick answer.

Ethan told Elliott who he was and why he was calling.

"I'm sorry, Mr. Ward. I'll be at your house in a few minutes."

"And Carl Benlow says we should get the FBI involved."

"Absolutely. They have resources for cases like this that we don't. I'll call SAC Kidwell."

"That's Special Agent in Charge, right?"

"Right. I'll get him to have a couple of his agents accompany me. See you in a little while."

"And, Lieutenant..."

"Yes, sir?"

"The man said I shouldn't be calling you. Carl Benlow said I should anyway, but please keep this quiet."

"No problem. I'll see you soon."

Ethan hung up the phone and again paced around the room. He still didn't know if he should call Sally. He looked at his watch. It was one o'clock, another three hours before classes let out. She would probably be furious at him later for not calling her immediately, but he decided to wait until the authorities arrived. They would know what to do. His thoughts were interrupted by the ringing of the phone. He grabbed it immediately.

"Yes?"

"Mr. Ward?"

"Yes. Who's this?"

"This is Sergeant Matthews."

"Oh. Have you found out anything about my daughter?"

"No, I'm sorry, sir, I don't have any news. I did talk to Mr. Russell, though, and he was with friends all evening up until the time he went back to the dormitory, and his roommate vouches for him being there. I'm still working on it though."

"Thank you, Sergeant. I appreciate your letting me know."

He hung up the phone and waited anxiously for the police and FBI to arrive. A short time later the doorbell rang. Ethan looked out the window to see a black SUV and behind it a gray Ford Crown Victoria in the driveway. He walked hurriedly to the door and opened it. There stood three White males and a Black female. The first man held out his hand to Ethan.

"Mr. Ward?"

"Yes."

"I'm Lieutenant Elliott. We talked on the phone."

"Yes."

"And this is SAC Eddie Kidwell, and Agents Ronnie Bush and Pamela Jackson."

Ethan shook their hands and moved aside to let them inside.

"I'm terribly sorry for what you're going through, Mr. Ward," said Agent Kidwell.

"Thank you."

The group went into the dining room and sat around the table. Ethan spent the next couple of minutes telling them about the last few hours. He told them of the call from Candy and his trip to the univeristy, and then the horrible call from the man. Lieutenant Elliott gave him an inquisitive look.

"Mr. Ward," he asked, "isn't your daughter the one who found the pictures of the lynching in her grandfather's belongings?"

"Yes, in my dad's trunk. You don't think this has anything to do with that, do you?"

"I don't know, but your family has received a lot of publicity because of that."

"I know, but I don't think that has anything to do with it."

"Why do you say that?" asked Agent Kidwell. "Do you have any idea of who would want to hurt your daughter or yourself?"

"Yes, I do - the Russell family."

Ethan told them about his relationship with Ted and Ed Russell and Emily's problems with Julius.

"We'll look into that," said Kidwell.

"Well, I just talked to the UT police, and they said that Julius has an alibi for the time since Emily was last seen."

"We'll still talk to him, but, from what you've told me, they seem like a long shot for the kidnapping."

"Why do you say that?"

"For one thing, the amount of time that has passed since you've had any conflict with the men - what did you tell me, twenty years ago?"

"Yes, but what about Ted's son, just by coincidence, meeting Emily? And what about my dad's gravesite being vandalized? I know that Ed did that. I'm certain that they're behind this."

"There's no way that someone would go to UT just to have the chance to meet your daughter. I'm sure that was just a coincidence. And that's a big jump from defacing a gravesite to kidnapping. And, from what you've told me, this Ted and Ed are not too sophisticated. They don't sound like the type of people that could even pull off something like this."

"Well, I don't agree, and I think you need to investigate all three of them."

"It'll be easy to check on Ted Russell since he's in prison. We already know that Julius wasn't involved, so I'll send someone to see where Ed was during the past twenty-four hours."

"And they could've paid someone else to do it. I think you need to talk to all their friends and acquaintances and check their phone records."

"Yes, we'll look into that. Now, when the man called, was there anything familiar about his voice?"

"No, but he was disguising it."

"How so?"

"It was very low and raspy, almost a whisper."

"Anything else you remember about your conversation with him?"

"Only that he seemed to know all about me and my family."

"What did he say?"

"When I told him that I didn't have that kind of money, he said I would just have to contact my father-in-law and my brother-in-law, my brother and my mother. He said my mother should have my dad's life insurance money by now."

"Hmm," said Kidwell, "it does sound like he knows an awful lot about you and your family."

"Yes," said Agent Jackson, "but that could be most anyone in the state."

Agent Kidwell gave her a blank look.

"You've just transferred here from Chicago, sir, but even before his daughter found the photographs, Mr. Ward and his family were quite well known in Tennessee."

"How so?"

She related to him the story of Ethan witnessing the shooting of the deputy when he was young and the subsequent arrest and trial of his father-in-law. She also told him of the death of Ethan's brother-in-law, Robert, and the ensuing investigation. She then informed him that Senator Tommy Bell was Ethan's brother-in-law.

"It sounds like you know my family pretty well," said Ethan.

"It's just from growing up in the area and reading the newspapers."

"I see," said Agent Kidwell. "I wasn't aware of those things. This will make it more complicated."

"Why do you say that?" asked Ethan.

"Being as well known as you and your family are brings all sorts of crazies out of the closet. Plus people will assume that you are very wealthy, which brings up the next issue. What do you plan on doing about the ransom? Do you have that kind of money?"

"No, we don't. I don't know where he came up with that idea. I'd have to talk to my relatives to see how close we can come. But should we pay the ransom?"

"Mr. Ward, I cannot tell you what to do regarding that."

"But what normally happens? Does paying the ransom guarantee she'll be returned safely?"

"I'm sorry, but nothing can guarantee that your daughter will be returned safely. However, will paying the ransom increase the chances? Yes, it will, but to what degree I cannot say."

"Well, if it's going to help get her back, we'll have to pay what we can. I'll contact all my family and relatives to see if they can help. So what should we do next?"

"The first thing I want to do is get a trace set up on your line. We also need to contact the media about the kidnapping so people can be looking for your daughter."

"No, I don't want to do that. He said he didn't want to hear about it on the radio or TV."

"Mr. Ward," said Lieutenant Elliott, "your best chance of getting your daughter back is by alerting the media. Most cases like this are solved by somebody seeing the victim or remembering something the kidnapper said. You should take Agent Kidwell's advice."

"And there's also the chance that it could make him furious and he could do something to Emily," said Ethan. "He was very specific in telling me not to alert the media. I don't want to do anything that will put Emily at risk."

"But even if we don't contact the media directly," said Agent Kidwell, "it will be almost impossible to keep this a secret once we start talking to people. It will only take one person to say something to the media and then everyone will know."

"Then I want to wait until that happens."

Agent Kidwell turned to the others with an irritated look, then back to Ethan.

"Mr. Ward, I have to tell you that this is a mistake. You are reacting with your emotions, which I understand, but it isn't the right thing to do."

"Maybe you're right, but he was very adamant about talking to the media. At least I want to wait until my wife gets home so I can talk to her about it."

"Fine," said Kidwell, "when does she get off?"

Ethan looked at his watch.

"It's a couple more hours. I don't know how I can tell her what's happened."

"I would like to send Agent Jackson to pick her up. Where does she work?"

"She's a teacher. You don't think we should wait until she gets home?"

"No, I don't. We need to talk to her, as well as yourself, to get a list of everyone you know that might somehow be involved in this. And we need to do that as soon as possible."

"Then I can go pick her up. She should hear it from me."

"No, you and I have a lot of things to go over, and we need to get started immediately. Agent Jackson can pick her up. No matter how we do it, it's going to be a shock."

"And once you do that, the whole school will know what's going on, and then there's a chance someone in the media will hear about it."

"That's just what I said. We will be very discrete, but I think it is important we talk to your wife as soon as possible. She may remember something that could be important in helping us figure out who took your daughter."

"Okay."

"Good. Now, here's what we need to do. Agent Jackson, you go pick up Mrs. Ward and bring her here."

"And my son Justin. He goes to high school."

"Okay. Then bring them back here. Then I want you to pick up Agent Bradley and the two of you check up on the Russell family and see if they had anything to do with this. Go over to the prison and talk to Ted Russell and anybody else the warden thinks might be important. Then go to Greeneville and talk to his brother. Agent Bush, you hook up the recorder to the phone and then get a trace put on the line. Then I want you to meet with the officer at UT...what was his name?"

"Matthews," answered Ethan.

"Yes, talk to Officer Matthews and go over anything he's uncovered. Talk to the people Emily was with before she disappeared and see if they saw anything, And, Mr. Ward, you and I and Lieutenant Elliott have a lot of things to go over."

TWENTY-ONE

It was late afternoon when the man returned to the cabin. As much as she hated herself for it, Emily was glad to see him walk through the door. For the past few hours she had begun to imagine him never returning, and her being left there to die alone. He took off his coat and hung it, along with his knapsack, on a peg by the door and then hung his keys next to them. He walked to Emily with a McDonald's cup and bag in his hands and placed them on the small table next to her.

"This is a little cold," he said. "There aren't many fast food restaurants close to here."

"Did you talk to my parents?" she asked.

"I talked to your dad."

"What did he say?"

"I didn't really have a conversation with him. I just told him to get the money and I would call him back tomorrow night."

"Even if we had that kind of money they couldn't get it by then."

"I didn't say that he had to have it by tomorrow - just that I would call him then. Are you doing okay?"

"Why do you ask that? If you really cared about me you would let me go."

"A man's gotta do what a man's gotta do."

"Why do you keep saying that? You talk like someone's making you do this and you don't really want to. Who's making you do this?"

"Life. Life's making me do this, girlie. Now that's enough questions for now."

She stared at him and took the bag and removed the hamburger and fries. They were cold, but as hungry as she was, they still tasted great. She devoured them and then sipped her coke. The man walked to the door and reached into his knapsack and removed something. He returned to Emily with two books, and tossed them on her bed.

"I thought you might like something to keep your mind occupied."

She picked up the books and looked at them. He had given her *Love Story* by Erich Segal, and *The Color Purple* by Alice Walker. She stared at the books and looked back at him.

"This is quite a combination," she said.

"Well, one's about a girl in college, and the other's about a black woman. I thought you might like them."

"Thanks."

She took *Love Story* and lay back on her bed. The light from the nearby window was just enough to allow her to read. The man watched as she began the book, then turned and went back to his bed. He lay down and within a few minutes Emily heard him snoring.

It was a little after three when Sally Ward and her son returned home with Agent Jackson. The Agent had insisted that she drive them rather than have her take her own car. Sally and Justin were greeted by Ethan as they walked through the door. No words were said as the three clung to each other. After a few seconds, Sally pulled away.

"Have you heard anything more?" asked Sally.

"No, honey. The man said he wouldn't call until tomorrow evening."

She removed her coat and threw it on the banister. As she walked into the living room she saw the two strange men sitting at the kitchen table. Ethan introduced Sally and Justin to Lieutenant Elliott and Agent Kidwell. The men arose to say hello. From the kitchen, carrying a glass of water, came Carl Benlow. He went to Sally and Justin and greeted them with a hug.

"I'm so sorry," he said. "But we're going to get her back."

"Thank you, Carl," said Sally.

"Mrs. Ward," said Agent Kidwell, "I need to talk to you and your son."

"Sure. What do you need to know?" she asked as they sat at the table.

"I need to know the names of anyone who you think might have been involved with this."

"Agent Kidwell, I'm sorry, but I don't know of anyone who would want to hurt Emily or anyone else in the family either."

"Let me make it clearer. I need to know the names of anyone who had a relationship with your daughter. Any new acquaintances she might have made in the past few weeks. Anyone who she might have mentioned that she had a disagreement with. Anyone you or your family might have had a disagreement with. Anyone in the past that might have shown too much interest in her. Anything unusual, no matter how insignificant you might think it to be, that she told you about recently."

"But, Agent Kidwell, I thought this was for money. Didn't the man make a demand for half a million dollars? Then how can this be anyone who has a personal interest in Emily or our family?"

"Yes, he did demand a ransom, and you're probably right - it is probably someone not known to you, but we have to look at all possibilities. And the quicker we rule out any relative or acquaintance, the better."

"Oh, okay."

"And honey," said Ethan, "while you're doing that, I'll continue calling our family to see if they can help out with the ransom."

"Okay. How can we possibly raise that kind of money, Ethan?"

"I don't know. I've looked at our finances, and with our savings, the stock we can sell and the IRA's, we have just about ninety thousand."

"And who have you talked to so far?"

"I talked to my mother and my brother. Mom still hasn't gotten the money from Dad's life insurance policy, but she's going to go to the bank and see if she can borrow against it."

"How much is that?"

"Seventy-five thousand, but she doesn't know how much they will give her or even if they will do it."

"And what about Horace?"

"He said they have about twenty-five thousand they can give us."

"Oh, God, this is awful. I hate to call on people for this, but I guess we have no choice."

"Yeah, I know."

Sally looked at her husband for a second, then burst into tears. Justin looked on helplessly as his dad sat next to his mother and hugged her.

"I just can't believe this," said Sally. "It...it's just too much. Why would someone do this?"

"I'm sorry, Mrs. Ward," said Agent Kidwell, but the only answer is that there are a lot of evil, heartless people in the world."

After a minute she wiped her eyes and turned back to Agent Kidwell.

"I'm sorry. I'm fine now. Let's go over what you need."

As Ethan had done earlier, Sally and Justin spent the next twenty minutes providing Agent Kidwell with a list of people for him to check out. When finished, he informed them that he would have one of his people run the names through the National Crime Information Center database to see if any of them had a criminal record.

Ethan went into the kitchen and picked up the phone to continue his calls. His first was to his brother-in-law Tommy. Luckily, the Senator was in his office. Like his mother and brother, Tommy was noticeably shocked and upset at the news.

"Oh, God, Ethan, I'm sorry. This is just too unbelievable."

"Like a nightmare."

"How are you all doing?"

"Not well, Tommy. We just need to get her back."

"What can I do? Rita and I can be over there in a few hours."

"Thanks, but that's not what we need right now."

"Then what?"

"I'm sorry, Tommy, that I have to ask this, but…well, the kidnapper demanded half a million dollars, and as you know, we don't have that kind of money, so we're calling family and…"

"No problem. We'll do whatever we can. I'll talk to my financial planner and see how much we can come up with. How much do you have so far?"

"Only a little over a hundred thousand, but I'm waiting to see if my mom can get a loan on the life insurance."

"Okay, we'll work on it. Ethan, I'm sorry, but I have to ask. What does the FBI say about paying the money?"

"They don't have an answer. They say it's really up to us, and there's no way I can tell this guy we're not going to pay it."

"I would say the same thing if it was Bobby. I guess they don't have a clue who's behind this?"

"No, not as of yet. I think it's the Russell brothers, but the FBI doesn't seem to think they fit the profile. What do you think?"

"I…I'm sorry, Ethan, I really don't know. They're not too sophisticated, but I guess anything's possible."

"I know. Well, I have to call Sally's dad. I really appreciate your help, Tommy. And one other thing - please don't say anything to anyone about this. He was very adamant about not letting the media know."

"I understand. I'll get back to you, and we'll also be praying for Emily."

"Thanks."

Ethan's next call was to his father-in-law. There was no answer. He looked at the clock to see that it was now three-forty-five. Shouldn't he be home by now? He couldn't remember his teaching schedule, but thought his last class ended early in the day. While he hated doing it, he left a message for him to call as soon as possible. It was almost four-thirty when Professor Robertson called back.

"Ethan, you sounded upset in your message. Is everything all right?"

Ethan told him the same thing he had told the others. When he finished he waited for the Professor's response, but there was only silence.

"Professor...Dad...are you there?"

"Yes. I'm sorry, Ethan...I just don't know what to say. I...I just feel sick."

"I know - like all of us."

"How's Sally holding up?"

"As well as can be expected."

"Should I talk to her?"

"She's with the FBI right now."

"Oh. Then how can I help."

He again relayed the information about the ransom.

"I'm sorry, Dad, but we don't have any choice. Is there anyway..."

"It's okay Ethan. Emily's return is all that's important. I can get you about a hundred and fifty thousand in a couple of days."

"Really. I didn't know you had that kind of money lying around."

"Oh, I do all right, I guess."

"And you can get it in a couple of days?"

"Well, it's almost all in stock, so it shouldn't take that long - a day or two I imagine."

"Thanks, Professor. You don't know how much we appreciate this."

"Sure, Son. And as soon as I get it, I'll come over. In the meantime, please have Sally call me when she thinks she can talk."

"Sure."

After a few minutes, Sally and Justin had provided Agent Kidwell with all the names they could think of. Justin excused himself to go into the kitchen to get himself something to drink. He and his father stood at the kitchen window, staring silently at birds pecking for food in the back yard. Sally arose from the table to join them, but Agent Kidwell turned to her with another question.

"Mrs. Ward, I have to ask your opinion. Your husband feels that the Russell family is behind this. What do you think?"

"I don't know. It's true that Ethan has had problems with the Russell boys most of his life, and I'm sure he told you about Emily's problem with Julius, but I don't know if that means they would do something like this. From the tone of your voice, though, it sounds like you don't agree with him."

"Well, no, it just doesn't seem like the kind of thing they would do, but then I've been wrong before. Either way, I've got one of my men looking into that right now. And, the other thing I've told Mr. Ward is that we need to alert the media about this as soon as possible, but he refuses. I really think that is something that needs to be done."

"Why doesn't he want to do it?"

"He said the man warned him not to say anything to the TV or radio stations. He's scared that if the kidnapper hears something that he might harm your daughter."

"Well, is that a reasonable assumption?"

"My belief is that he has already made up his mind what he plans on doing with her, but again, I have no way of being certain. To answer your question, yes, there is a chance that alerting the media could put your daughter in further jeopardy, but I think the good greatly outweighs the bad. I really think you and your husband need to talk about this."

"And what do you believe, Carl?" she asked of their friend who had been sitting by quietly.

"I agree with Agent Kidwell, Sally, but like he said, only you two can make that decision."

"I'll talk to him about it."

At five-thirty Carl turned to Justin with a suggestion. "Son, why don't you and I run out and pick up a couple of pizzas?"

"Thanks, Mr. Benlow, but I need to stay here in case my parents need me for something."

"Well, I think they can spare you for a while, and it's important for everyone to eat to keep up their strength."

Justin looked to his mother, who nodded for him to go with Carl. The two put on their coats and walked out the door. They returned within the hour with pizza, salads, and sodas. Ethan and Sally both said they weren't hungry.

"Look, I know how difficult this is for all of you," said Agent Kidwell, "but it's important, for Emily's sake, that you all take care of yourselves. You need to eat."

The two of them took a slice of pizza and began eating. Ethan turned to his son, who had spent the past couple of hours in silence.

"That goes for you, too, Justin," said Ethan.

"Dad, I don't..."

"I know, son. Just eat a few bites."

Justin took a slice of pizza and leaned against the kitchen counter as he ate. Ethan finished his pizza and walked into the living room and sat on the couch. He was soon joined by Carl.

"Agent Kidwell told me that he has a doctor he calls in cases like this who will prescribe sleeping pills without any questions. I think it's important you take him up on the offer. Like he said, it's important, for Emily's sake that you all take care of yourselves."

"Okay," answered Ethan.

"We'll get through this," said Carl as he patted Ethan on the knee.

"You think we'll get her back?"

"Yes, I do."

"I hope you're right."

The two men sat silently for a moment before Ethan turned to Carl with a question.

"I guess this puts the issue of the lynching on the back burner, but I should ask - have you uncovered anything else?'

"No, I'm sorry, son. I really thought I would've been able to identify the men or at least the victim by now, but I really don't have anything more than when we talked yesterday."

"Nobody else had any more information on the Pratt boys?"

"Nope. Sorry. But on a good note, it seems that tempers have calmed since the meeting last night. At least when I talked to the Sheriff this afternoon there were no new incidents."

"Gosh, that was last night? It seems like years ago."

"I know."

"Well, anyway, I guess we can worry about identifying the men in the pictures when we get our daughter back."

"Of course."

"So, do you have an opinion on who might have taken Emily?" asked Ethan.

"I think we'll find out that it's someone unknown to you, but I do believe it was brought about by the recent publicity you've received."

"Really? Why?"

"Like Agent Jackson said, your family is quite well known throughout the state, and the recent publicity from the photographs has made you even more famous. I think someone just read about you in the paper and realized that you had a little money and decided to take advantage of it. The papers also mentioned that Emily was a freshman at UT so they knew where they could find her."

"But we don't have a lot of money, Carl."

"I'm not talking about just you and Sally, but the rest of the family - mainly Tommy and the professor."

"But how many people really know that we're even related?"

"From all the publicity you and your family have received over the years? I would guess thousands - no, tens of thousands."

"I guess you're right.

"So you don't think this has anything to do with the lynching?'

"No. Oh I know more than anyone how much pain this has caused for both blacks and whites, but I don't see how anyone could blame Emily. She just found the photographs. And if it was related to that, I think the kidnapper would have said something."

"I guess you're right. Anyway, I guess it doesn't matter why it happened - just that we get her back."

"And we're going to do everything possible to make sure that happens."

TWENTY-TWO

Tuesday, Nov. 15TH

Agent Bush returned to the Ward house a little after nine the next morning. Agent Kidwell and Lieutenant Elliott were in the living room discussing details of the investigation, while Carl Benlow sat with Sally and Ethan at the kitchen table drinking coffee.

"I got the trace put on the line," reported Bush as he handed Agent Kidwell a piece of paper. "Here's the number to call at the telephone central office when the call comes in."

"Thanks. Any luck at the UT campus?"

"No, I'm afraid not. I met with Sergeant Matthews and he had already talked to a lot of Miss Ward's friends, and no one had any new information. I went back to the restaurant where she was last seen and talked to a number of people, but no one remembered seeing anyone or anything suspicious. Sorry, boss."

"So, you confirmed that Julius Russell was with other people all evening?" asked Ethan.

"Yes, sir, I did," answered Agent Bush. "He and eight to ten other guys were playing basketball in the gym until it closed at ten. They then went to a pub and stayed until after midnight."

"What about after that?"

"Well, one of the men with him was his roommate, and they went back to the dorm together."

"But he could have gone back out after he went to sleep," said Ethan.

"Yes, sir," said Agent Bush, "but your daughter's roommate told Sergeant Matthews that she went back to their room a little after ten, and your daughter wasn't there so we put the time of her disappearance between nine-fifteen and ten-fifteen."

Agent Kidwell looked at Ethan, but said nothing. He then turned back to Agent Bush.

"Okay, I want you to go back to the office and pull information on any abduction or attempted abduction of a young girl in the region. Go back a couple of years, and look particularly for anyone with wealthy or famous parents."

"Yes, sir."

"And call me on my mobile phone and let me know what you find."

"Yes, sir," he answered, then turned and left.

At ten forty-five the phone rang. Ethan quickly answered, hoping against hope that it would be his daughter.

"Mr. Ward?" came the woman's voice.

"Yes."

"This is Candy, Emily's roommate."

"Oh, hi, Candy."

"Hi. I've not heard anything from anybody, and I just wondered if Emily's okay."

Ethan thought quickly. He didn't want the news of Emily's kidnapping broadcast over the TV. In this situation, a small lie was acceptable.

"Yes, Candy, I'm sorry we haven't called. Emily is fine. She just had to get away for a few days."

"Oh. I guess I can understand that with everything she's been through in the past few weeks. I 'm just surprised she didn't tell me though."

"Yes, I know. We didn't even know what she was doing until last night. Again, I'm sorry. But hopefully she'll be back in a few days."

"Okay. Thanks for letting me know."

"And thank you for everything, Candy."

Ethan hung up the phone, upset with himself that he had to lie to her. Still it was better than her talking to the media and the kidnapper hearing about it on the six o'clock news."

It was a little before eleven when Agent Kidwell received a call on his mobile phone from Agent Jackson. He talked to her for a few minutes, then told her to call him back if they had any further news, and hung up the phone. He then turned to the others.

"Agent Jackson and Agent Bradley met late last night with Ted Russell and his cellmate at Brushy Mountain Prison in Petros. They still have to talk to the warden and other prisoners, and pull visitor logs and phone records, but their initial impression was that he had nothing to do with this."

"Of course he would say that, but he and his brother are the ones behind this," said Ethan angrily.

"Mr. Ward," said Agent Kidwell firmly, "Mr. Russell was visibly upset when they began questioning him. He had to be restrained by two guards and one of my people. He told them that he didn't even know that his son had met your daughter and that he had no knowledge of Miss Ward being kidnapped. His exact words were that he never wanted to see or hear from the Ward family again."

"And they believed him? He can say anything. That doesn't mean that..."

"Mr. Ward, my people are very experienced at interviewing suspects. Yes, they believed that he was telling the truth. But, as I said, they are still going to investigate the matter further."

"Good. And what about his brother Ed?"

"They're going to Greeneville to talk to him as soon as they finish at the prison. They should be there later this morning."

"You don't have someone else that can go over there sooner?"

"Mr. Ward, I know how upsetting this is, but right now, besides Lieutenant Elliott, Mr. Benlow, and myself, I have three Agents working on this, as well as a couple of others helping out behind the scenes. I think that is more than enough resources."

Ethan looked disappointed but said nothing more.

"Look, Mr. Ward," said Agent Kidwell as he walked to the dining room, "I know how difficult and emotional this is, but I think you are making a big mistake by not letting us release information to the press."

"We can do that tonight after I talk to him."

"What difference will it make to wait until after you've talked to him?"

"It's common knowledge that once a kidnapper spends time with their victim they began to feel empathy with them, right?"

"It's possible, but I wouldn't say it's common. So what you're saying is that you want to wait in the hopes that he'll feel closer to your daughter so that he won't harm her when he hears about the kidnapping on the radio or TV?"

"Yes. That's not reasonable?"

"I don't know how to answer that, Mr. Ward. I can only tell you that my opinion is that we need to go to the media immediately. I doubt if him spending time with your daughter will affect how he reacts."

"But then you don't know Emily. She's a very sweet and charming girl. Besides, when he calls I'll tell him that we had already reported her missing to the UT Police before he called, so if the media picks it up it was from them and not us telling them. And after Agent Jackson talks to Ed Russell, we may find that they took her just like I said."

"Okay, I guess I understand your wanting to tell him that you haven't talked to the media, but I wouldn't count on Mr. Russell confessing."

Ethan nodded his understanding and turned and walked away. Soon Justin came down the stairs and walked to the refrigerator and poured himself a glass of orange juice.

"Hi, honey," said his mother. "Did you sleep okay?"

"I guess."

His mother walked to him and gave him a hug.

"I know this is tough, honey, but you are being awfully quiet. Are you doing okay?"

"I guess, Mom. I just wish there was something I could do. Everybody else is doing something, but there's nothing I can do to help."

"Have you been praying for Emily?"

"Yes."

"Then that's the most important thing. And you provided Agent Kidwell with a list of friends and acquaintances they can check out. And you went and got the food, which I know doesn't seem like much, but it helped. But if we think of something else you can do we'll let you know."

"Why does God let things like this happen, Mom?"

"Well, because He gave people free will and let them do whatever they want."

"Well, I think that was a mistake. I think if He's so smart and knows everything, then He knew all the evil things people would do, so He shouldn't have given them free will."

"I know, honey, but then we would be nothing but robots."

"Well, people can't sin in heaven, right?"

"Yes, that's true."

"Then we'll be no more than robots when we get to heaven."

Sally looked at her husband for help. He only smiled and waited for her answer.

"But the difference is, honey, that we made a decision to get to heaven. Nobody made a decision to be born. So, if God took away our ability to make bad decisions and sin, He would really be taking away our free will."

"And it would be worth it."

Sally walked to her son and hugged him.

"I'm sorry, sweetie, but I don't have all the answers. Now you need to eat something to keep your strength up."

Ethan contacted his stockbroker and told him to sell all the shares of stock that they owned and deposit the money into their account. He then called their financial planner and instructed her to close their IRAs and deposit the money. Both told him that it would take a few days. He requested that they hurry the process as much as possible, and to not tell anyone what he was doing.

It was almost noontime when Ethan's mother called. He quickly brought her up to date on the situation. She then informed him that she had gone to the bank and had taken out a loan against her insurance policy.

"They gave me fifty thousand, Ethan."

"That's great, Mom. I really appreciate your doing that."

"Honey, you know I would do anything for you or the kids. There is one little problem, though."

"What's that?"

"I'm sure that Mr. Swank at the bank could figure out what's going on - especially when he saw how nervous I was and that I wanted the money in twenty dollar bills."

"But he's going to do it, though?"

"Yes, but he said I would have to come back tomorrow to give him time to get it ready. I didn't think fifty thousand was a lot of money for a bank, but I guess they don't have that kind of money in twenty dollar bills lying around. He asked me what was going on, but I told him nothing and begged him to not say anything to anyone."

"And he agreed?"

"Yes, but I'm sure he could figure it out," answered his mother, and then began sobbing. "I just can't believe this is happening, Ethan."

"I know, Mom. I'm sorry. We just have to get through this."

"Okay. I'll be by in the morning after I get the money from the bank."

"Thanks, Mom. You don't know how much we appreciate this."

After hanging up with his mother, Ethan called his brother and had the same conversation. Horace informed him that he would be by the following day with the twenty-six thousand. Soon afterward, Ethan's father-in-law and brother-in-law, Tommy, both called to tell him they were still working on getting the money and would call back later in the day.

It was a little after three when Agent Jackson again called Agent Kidwell on his mobile phone.

"Did you uncover anything new at the prison?" asked Agent Kidwell.

"No, sir, not really. We checked the visitor log for Ted Russell and saw nothing unusual. He rarely gets visitors. His son had not been there in a couple of months. His wife, or ex-wife - we're not really sure about the relationship - comes in about once a month, but that has been the same for the past year. His brother Ed was there in August, and except for a minister from Jefferson City, that's it."

"What about phone logs?"

"Nothing unusual there either. He only makes a few calls a month, and they were to the people we just mentioned. We also talked to the warden and he feels Russell knows nothing about the kidnapping."

"Fine. Where are you now?"

"We just arrived at Ed Russell's house, but he's not home. His wife informed us that he usually doesn't get home from work until a little before four, so it's probably quicker to wait here than to try and track him down."

"What does he do?"

"He's a construction worker. His wife says that he hasn't been out of town for weeks, and that we can verify that with a lot of other people if we want. We'll talk to his boss after we talk to him."

"Okay, that seems like a good plan. Let me know what you find out after talking to him and his boss. Then you and Agent Bradley go back into the office and help Agent Bush. He's checking on any other abductions in the past couple of years. And I know it's a long shot, but I want you two to go over the list of names given us by Mr. and Mrs. Ward to see if you can come up with anything."

"Yes, sir."

Agent Kidwell hung up the phone and informed the others that they were still waiting to talk to Ed Russell.

"When they talk to him they should also ask him about my father's grave," said Ethan.

"I don't think we need to go into that right now, Mr. Ward," said Agent Kidwell.

"I know. I just wanted to say it."

"I understand."

It was five o'clock when Agent Jackson called back to say that they had completed their interview with Ed Russell.

"What was the result?" asked Agent Kidwell.

"Well, sir, he gave us a list of people who could verify that he has not been out of town the past few days. We have called three of them, including his boss, but I don't think it's worth continuing. I know Mr. Ward feels that they are the most likely suspects, but I don't think they have anything to do with it."

"I agree, but we have to cover all bases. Hold on a second."

Agent Kidwell turned to the others and informed them of Agents Jackson and Bradley's findings.

"If they were going to do this then they would have paid somebody else to actually do the abduction," said Ethan. "I think you need to look into that."

Agent Kidwell looked at him for a second and then returned to his phone call.

"Agent Jackson, when you get back into the office please pull Ed Russell's phone records and check NCIC for criminal background on anyone he's talked to."

"Yes, sir."

"Good job."

Agent Kidwell looked at Ethan for a second, but said nothing. After a few minutes, Carl Benlow arose from the couch and walked to Ethan.

"Son, can we take a walk?"

"I guess," answered Ethan.

The two men went outside and walked down the sidewalk.

"I guess you're going to tell me that I'm acting irrationally?" asked

Ethan.

"Something like that."

"So, you really think that the Russell boys had nothing to do with this?'

"It certainly appears that way. Do you still think so?'

"I don't know if I think so any more, Carl, or if I just hope so. If it's them then it should be easy to solve and get Emily back. If it's not them then things don't look so good."

"I understand, son, but you have to look at the facts, and the facts just don't support that they were the ones that took her. Now Agent Kidwell said he would have Ed Russell's phone records pulled, but after that I think you need to let it drop."

"Okay."

"And the other thing is releasing the information to the media. I really think you need to let them go ahead with that."

"I already said I would after he calls tonight. You think I need to do it now?"

"Yes, I do."

Ethan looked at his watch.

"Okay, if he doesn't call by seven o'clock, I'll tell Agent Kidwell to contact the media. That way it will be on the eleven o'clock news, and hopefully I'll have had time to talk to the kidnapper first."

"I guess that's okay," said Benlow.

The two men returned to the house. A short while later Tommy called to inform Ethan that they would be able to come up with a hundred and ten thousand dollars.

"Man, that's a lot of money," said Ethan. "I hate like hell to ask this of you."

"You don't have any choice, so don't worry about it. I know you would do the same for us."

"Yes, but it's still....never mind. We just really appreciate it. Maybe something will happen that we won't need it."

"Like what?"

"Like maybe once he gets to know Emily he'll just let her go."

Anything is possible. I should have the money by tomorrow, so we'll come by sometime tomorrow night."

"Thanks, Tommy. You're great."

"No problem, Ace. And we're praying for you."

After hanging up from Tommy, Ethan dialed his father-in-law's number. He answered on the second ring.

"Robertson here."

"Hi, Professor."

"Hey, Ethan. Great minds think alike. I was just getting ready to call you."

"I guess I saved you a dime, huh?"

"Yeah. Anything new?'

"No, sorry. He's supposed to call again this evening. And we're going to announce it to the press after that. I sure hope I'm making the right decision."

"That's probably the right thing to do. Ethan, I talked to my financial planner, and I can only get about one hundred and forty thousand. I should have it sometime tomorrow."

"Wow, that's a lot of money. Thanks, Dad. I really appreciate it."

"No problem. Can I talk to Sally?"

Ethan called Sally to the phone. She wiped her eyes as she talked to her father. Ethan looked at the clock. It was almost five-thirty, and although the kidnapper had not given him a time when he would call, Ethan expected it would be between six and eight o'clock. Soon Sally hung up from her father, and the group sat nervously awaiting the phone to ring.

TWENTY-THREE

Emily watched the man as he arose from his bed and put on his shoes. She knew, from earlier conversations that it was almost time for him to go call her parents again. While she hated making the recording, if doing so would make her become free sooner, she would not argue with him again. He picked up the recorder and walked to her bed.

"It's about that time, girl," he said.

He handed her the recorder and his note with the words he wanted her to say. She looked at the paper for a second then turned back to him.

"You know, my parents are not stupid."

"What do you mean?"

"They're going to know that this is a recording. It's not going to work."

"I guess we'll see about that. Now you're not going to give me a hard time, are you?'

"No, you already told me that I'm not getting out of here unless I do this. I just want to let you know that they're going to know it's a recording and will want to talk to me."

"And I guess you think I should take you with me, huh? Then somebody sees us and where does that leave me?"

"Hopefully in jail where you belong."

He did not respond but pointed to the recorder. She stared at him for a second, and then recorded the message and shoved the machine back toward him.

"Anything I can bring you back?" he asked.

"You're kidding, right?'

"No. Haven't I been good to you?"

"Except for abducting me and chaining me to the floor, you mean?"

"Yes."

"Then I guess so."

"So, do you want anything?'

"Yes, some fresh clothes."

"No, I'm not going into a store to buy a teenage girl's clothes. The water works, you know. You can take a shower."

"Right. With cold water, and the shower is filthy. I'd rather stay in my dirty clothes."

"Okay. I'll bring you something to eat. What would you like?"

"How about steamed lobster, or maybe some caviar?"

The man looked at her and grinned. It was the first time she'd seem him smile.

"I'll work on that. And maybe I'll bring you some new books or magazines."

"Thanks."

With that he turned and walked out of the house, locking the door behind him. As he left, Emily again tried to understand why he was doing this. On more than one occasion he had stated that he had no choice but to kidnap her, and in reality, he had treated her very well. He had brought her food to eat and books to read. He had placed the kerosene heater on her side of the room so that she would remain warm. And he had, on numerous times, promised her that she would not be hurt. He was a strange and confusing man. She also wondered where he went when he left the house. At least two or three times a day he would leave and be gone for anywhere from thirty minutes to a couple of hours. On some occasions she knew that he must be roaming the woods near the house since she did not hear the engine on the van start. But other times he would drive away and not return for a while. And he would usually return with something for them to eat, or a book or magazine for her to read. Perhaps he just went into a nearby town and purchased a few things and then returned. Or perhaps he just drove around because he felt guilty about seeing her held captive. She still could not figure out if she had seen the man before. Although he looked familiar, she had racked her brain trying to remember where she had seen him, but it was to no avail. Finally, she quit trying. If what he said was true, she would understand everything in a few days.

After a few minutes she turned to the hook in the floor, which secured her chain. She had been trying for two days to loosen it but to no avail. If she could find a small metal rod to put through the eye of the hook, perhaps she could turn it. The sun was going down, and the room began to grow dark. She took the flashlight he had given her and, for the fourth or fifth time, looked under the bed for a piece of metal she could use. After a few seconds, she threw herself back on the bed and shined the light around the room. Once more she began to fear that something would happen to the man, and that she would never be found and would die a slow and lonely death. She closed her eyes and said a prayer. After a few seconds she wiped the tears from her eyes, opened her book, and attempted to take her mind off her situation.

It was seven-fifteen when the Wards' phone rang. As Ethan hurried to answer it, Agent Kidwell reminded him to try and keep the man on the phone as long as possible so they could trace the call. Agent Kidwell held up his hand to Ethan, then brought it down as both men picked up a phone at the same time - Ethan's to talk to the kidnapper, and Agent Kidwell's to record the call.

"Hello," said Ethan.

"Mr. Ward?" came the low, raspy reply.

Ethan nodded to Lieutenant Elliott who dialed the phone company on Agent Kidwell's mobile phone to have the trace started.

"I want to talk to my daughter," said Ethan.

"Very well."

After a few seconds Emily's voice came on the line.

"I'm fine, Mom, Dad. Please just do what the man asks so that I can come home. I miss you."

"Emily...," said Ethan, then realized he was talking to dead air.

"So, now you talked to her," said the man.

"I want to talk to her in person - not a recording. I'm not a fool. You could have made that recording anytime. Now I want to talk to her and make sure she's okay, or we don't have anything else to say."

"Your daughter is fine, Mr. Ward. Now, did you get the money?"

"We're working on it. Now, you listen to me - I talk to my daughter in person or you're not getting one cent."

"You can talk to her before you deliver the money. I can assure you, she's fine. I hope you understand, I can't risk bringing her out in public. Now again, did you get the money?"

"It takes time to get together that kind of money, but I have everyone in my family working on it. We should have it in the next couple of days."

"All half a million?"

"It's probably going to be a little over four hundred thousand. That's all we can raise."

"Mr. Ward, you don't follow instructions very well, do you?"

"I swear, that's all we have. I've talked to everyone in my family, and they're withdrawing every penny they have. And you said we can't let anyone else know about it, so I can't go to the public for help. There's no more money."

"And it's all in non consecutive twenty dollar bills?"

"Yes, but that takes time too."

"Very well, but no more negotiations. And you haven't called in the police or FBI have you?"

"No, of course not. But I have to tell you, we had already reported Emily missing to the UT police when you called the first time. And all of the people at the banks want to know why we're withdrawing so much money in twenty dollar bills. I don't know how long it's going to be until the TV or newspaper figures out what's going on."

"Well, you're a newspaper man. I'm sure you can come up with a creative story to tell them. I guess you'll just have to put them off for another couple of days."

"Fine, but I just want you to know if some reporter gets hold of this, it didn't come from us. Now when can we get our daughter back?"

"I guess that depends on when you have the money. You said it will take a couple of days, so I'll call you the same time on Thursday."

"Wait!"

"What?"

"How do we know that Emily is okay?"

"You can talk to her Thursday before we discuss how you will get me the money."

"And please give Emily a message for us."

"What?"

"Just tell her that we love her and miss her."

"Fine. Now, this call's over."

With that the phone went dead. Ethan stared at the receiver for a second then placed it back on the hook. He looked to Agent Kidwell for a response.

"You did fine, Mr. Ward."

"Do you think that was long enough to get a trace?'

"We should know in a few minutes. He didn't seem too upset about the money."

"No, not as much as I thought he would be."

"From this conversation, did his voice sound familiar?'

"No, but then, as you heard, he did a good job of disguising it. From listening to him, was there anything that you found unusual?"

"Well, he didn't seem as heartless as most kidnappers."

"Really?"

"Yes. He didn't even get angry when you told him that you had already reported your daughter missing to the UT police."

"That's a good sign."

"Yes, and he made reference to you being a newspaper man."

"Does that mean anything?"

"Probably not. We've already discussed that half the people in the state are familiar with you and your family. However, it seems like sort of a personal remark to me. And he seemed a little sarcastic. You can't think of anyone through your job that you might have made angry recently?"

"No, not really, but I'll think about it."

"So, what do we do now?" asked Sally.

"Well, while we're waiting to hear from the phone company, I think, like we talked about, we need to discuss how we're going to get information to the media."

"Excuse me," said Justin, who had been standing by listening to his father's phone conversation.

"Yes?" said Ethan.

"Well, I've been thinking about this, and I think I may have a plan."

"How's that?" asked Agent Kidwell.

"Well, Dad, since you don't want the kidnapper to think that you went to the media, how about having a reporter talk to Emily's roommate, Candy. She can say that she's concerned that Emily hasn't been at school the past couple of days, but then the reporter can say that he tried to talk to us about it, but we have no comment."

"Hmm," said Agent Kidwell, "that sounds like a good plan. What do you all think?"

"I like it," said Ethan. "And we can also have him say that reliable sources report that we've withdrawn a large sum of money from our bank account but that we deny it. That way, if the kidnapper hears any of this he'll think that we had nothing to do with it."

"I think that's a great idea," answered Sally.

"It sounds good to me," said Ethan. "Then we get the message out, and if the kidnapper hears about it he can't get mad at us since we've refused to talk to the reporter."

"And I have a reporter that will work with us and say whatever we want him to."

"Someone we can trust?" asked Sally.

"Absolutely. I've worked with him in the past, and he's one-hundred percent trust worthy. That's a great plan, Justin. I wish I'd thought of it."

"Thanks."

Sally hugged her son while Ethan patted him on the back.

"This sounds good, Justin" said Ethan. "You all can draft up exactly what you want them to say, and I'll contact Candy."

For the next few minutes Sally and Justin sat with Agent Kidwell, Lieutenant Elliott, and Carl Benlow drafting a script to be read by Candy and the reporter. Ethan went to the kitchen and called his daughter's dorm room. Candy answered on the first ring. Ethan explained to her that he had had to lie to her the previous day, and told her everything that had transpired.

"Oh, my God," said Candy. "I'm so sorry."

"Me too, Candy. But if you can help, there's something we need you to do."

"Sure. What?"

He told her of their plan, which she agreed to immediately.

"And, above all, Candy, this has to look like the family is not involved at all."

"I understand."

Ethan told her that the reporter would be calling her soon and thanked her for her help.

"She's lucky to have such a good friend," said Ethan, with a crack in his voice.

Ten minutes after Ethan finished talking to Candy, Agent Kidwell's mobile phone rang.

"Kidwell," he said.

The others listened intently as he responded to the caller. Soon he hung up the phone and turned to them.

"They traced the call to the Middlesboro, Kentucky area, but he hung up too soon to get a phone number."

"That means he's got Emily in Middlesboro?" asked Justin.

"Well, yes and no. From what the guy at the phone company told me, the call was traced from here to the long distance center in Lexington, and from there to a group of lines that go to Middlesboro. Unfortunately, those same lines also serve the surrounding counties."

"How many counties?" asked Carl Benlow.

"Four total."

"And that's pretty rough country up there. A lot of very isolated places," said Carl.

"I know," said Agent Kidwell, "but it's a lot more than we had before. Let me call the reporter and get him in contact with Candy to set up the interview, then I'll talk to my people and have them start searching in Kentucky."

"Does Candy have a picture of Emily?" asked Justin.

The others stared at each other blankly

"Uh, I guess we kind of overlooked that," said Agent Kidwell. "I guess it's a pretty good thing we have you around."

"I'll take her one," said Justin.

"Honey, I don't think..." began Sally.

"It's okay," said Ethan. "This was his idea, so he should do it."

Sally nodded and hugged her son.

"You just be careful," she said.

TWENTY-FOUR

At eleven o'clock, the group gathered around the Wards' television set to watch the news. It was not long before reporter Hugh Lawton came on with a breaking story.

"Has a local UT coed been kidnapped?" he began. "Eighteen-year-old freshman, Emily Ward, has not been seen by her roommate or classmates since Sunday evening, and although her family denies anything has happened to her, questions remain. Let's go to Miss Ward's roommate, Candy Wells for her comments."

The scene shifted to Candy, in front of the dormitory, being interviewed by Hugh Lawton.

"Miss Wells, when is the last time you saw your roommate?"

"Uh, Sunday evening, when she left a restaurant alone to go back to the room."

"And no one on campus has seen or heard from her since?"

"No, sir, and she's not been in any of her classes."

"Did you report this to the authorities?"

"Yes, the campus police, but they can't locate her either."
"And have you talked to her family?"

"Yes, and they say she's fine and will be back in a few days, but I don't believe it. She's not the kind to do something like this - leaving without telling anyone, or taking any of her belongings."

"I see."

Lawton turned back toward the camera.

"We also tried to contact Emily's parents, Ethan and Sally Ward, but they would not talk to us. And local police and FBI officials tell us that they have no open case on Miss Ward's disappearance. And if the Ward name sounds familiar, it's because Emily is the young woman who recently found the pictures of the man being lynched among her recently deceased grandfather's belongings. If that has anything to do with her disappearance, we can only guess. But if this was just the case of a student not attending classes for a few days, there would be no story here. But there's one other strange occurrence. Reliable sources tell us that Mr. and Mrs. Ward just today withdrew a large sum of money from their bank account - and it was taken in twenty-dollar bills. Can that be for a ransom? We think there's more to this story, but right now the family is not talking, and that's all we know. But in case Miss Ward has been kidnapped, here is a picture of her. If anyone has seen this girl in the past two days, please call your local police and let them know. Hugh Lawton, reporting."

The camera focused in on the picture of Emily that Justin had given to Candy. As the news changed to the local weather, Sally turned off the TV.

"The only problem with that," said Ethan, "is that it won't be shown in Kentucky."

"Yes, tomorrow we need to work on getting this information released to all the surrounding areas, but we don't want them to say that it's coming from us, or that we know what area he's in."

"Why?" asked Justin. "Don't we want people to know where he's taken Emily so they can be on the lookout for her?"

"Yes, but we don't want him to hear on the evening news that we're closing in on him, or he'll take her and move to someplace else."

"Then how are you going to get the information to the people in Kentucky to be on the lookout for them?"

"That's what my agents are doing now. They'll be hitting every hotel and motel, restaurant, gas station, and convenience store in the area."

"But the local news could pick it up and broadcast that they're looking for her there."

"That's true, but hopefully by then we'll have located them."

"This sure is confusing," said Justin.

"Yes, it's a bit of a cat and mouse game," answered Agent Kidwell.

After the news, the Ward family and their guests retired for the night. As was the case the night before, Carl Benlow was given the guest bedroom, and Agent Kidwell and Lieutenant Elliott slept on the couches. No mention was made of anyone using Emily's bedroom.

Wednesday, Nov. 16TH

Ethan's mother called before breakfast to tell him that she had gotten the money from the bank and would be coming over in a couple of hours. Because of the amount of money she was carrying, Carl Benlow volunteered to come over and drive her back, but she declined, saying she wanted to be there as soon as possible. She also informed him that she had just heard from Horace, who told her there was an unexpected delay in getting the money, and that it might take another day or two. She arrived at the Ward house a little after nine o'clock. Ethan opened the door and introduced his mother to Agent Kidwell and Lieutenant Elliott. Sally came into the room and hugged her mother-in-law.

"I'm so sorry, Sally," said Hilda.

"Me too, Hilda. Thank you so much for coming and bringing the money."

The two women clung to each other, sobbing. Soon Hilda pulled away.

"I feel like some type of spy lugging this bag around with the money," said Hilda.

"We need to take the money and start writing down the serial numbers," said Agent Kidwell as he took the bag from Mrs. Ward.

"I think that's a good job for Justin," said Sally. "He wants to help, and this will give him something to do."

"That's a good idea," said Agent Kidwell. "That'll be a lot of work, so we'll have to help him, but that's a good idea letting him be in charge of that."

Carl Benlow came into the room with a cup of coffee and handed it to Hilda.

"With cream and sugar, right Hilda?"

"You're a good man, Carl," she said as she took the coffee and gave him a kiss on the cheek. "And with a good memory, too."

"Well, there's a couple of things old age hasn't robbed me of yet. And, Hilda, I moved my stuff out of the guest room so you can move in there."

"You didn't have to do that."

"Sure I did. I should be camping down here with the other men anyway."

"Well," she answered, "my granddaughter will be home soon, and we can all go back to our own beds."

———————

It was a little before noon when Agent Jackson called to check in with her boss.

"Good morning, sir," said Agent Jackson.

"Good morning, Agent Jackson. How's it going there?"

"Okay, but I really don't have any news to report. We've divided this up so one agent has each county."

"That makes sense."

"Yes. This is not a highly populated area, but there's still probably over a hundred places we need to check out in each county. Any chance we can get more help?"

"I'm sorry, but we're spread pretty thin as it is. We're still working on the bank robbery from last week you know."

"Okay, but it may take us two or three days to talk to everyone up here."

"I understand. Just do the best you can."

After he had hung up, Carl turned to Agent Kidwell.

"I'm not doing much around here but getting in the way. Maybe I should go up there and help out."

"Sure, I'd be glad to get the help."

Agent Kidwell provided him with the phone numbers for his agent's mobile phones, and with instructions on what to say and do. He nodded his understanding, and went to tell the others he was leaving for Kentucky.

As they were eating lunch the phone rang. Praying that it might be her daughter, Sally answered it.

"Hi, honey," said her father.

"Hi, Daddy."

"Anything new?"

Sally had talked to him earlier and informed him of Candy's interview on the TV and of the phone company tracing the call to Kentucky.

"Hilda got here a little while ago, and Carl Benlow just left for Kentucky to help out the FBI Agents up there. Justin is writing down the serial numbers on the money that Hilda brought. Other than that we're just sitting around praying."

"Well, that's important too."

"Right. How's it going there?"

"Well, I have the money and am leaving now. I should be there before five."

"That's great, Dad. We really appreciate what you're doing."

"No problem, honey. See you soon."

Shortly after one o'clock Ethan again called his bank and financial planner. He was told that the money should be available for withdrawal sometime the following afternoon.

"Look, Mr. Ward," said the banker, "I saw the news last night about your daughter and, with you withdrawing this money, it doesn't take a genius to figure out what's going on. Is there anything I can do to help?"

"If you can get me the money like we talked about, that will be great. Thank you."

"Okay, I understand."

Shortly after talking to him, the phone rang. Sally picked it up and said a few words and hung up. She then turned to the others.

"That was Rita. She said they are also having a delay in getting the money. She said Tommy thought it would be late tomorrow or maybe even Friday morning."

The others said nothing but nodded their understanding. Agent Kidwell placed a call to his agents to check on the status of the search, while the others gathered around the table copying serial numbers off the twenty-dollar bills his mother had brought. Their thoughts were interrupted by the ringing of the doorbell. Ethan walked hurriedly to answer it. Thinking it might be a reporter and wondering how he would respond, Ethan was surprised at the two people standing there.

"Uh, Rachel...Mrs. Mills?"

"Hi, Ethan," said Rachel solemnly. "We just heard about Emily this morning."

"Oh. I appreciate your coming over, but you really didn't have to do that."

"You don't understand," said Rachel with her mother by her side, wiping tears from her eyes. "We think we know who kidnapped your daughter."

"You what! Who?"

"My father."

PART FOUR

TWENTY-FIVE

Ethan stood in shock as Rachel and her mother walked by him into the room. In a daze, he turned to the others and repeated what Rachel had just told him.

"Rachel says she thinks she knows who kidnapped Emily,"

The others rose and walked toward the two women who stood clinging to each other.

"What?" asked Sally, her eyes open wide.

"She says she thinks it was her father," said Ethan.

Sally's hand came to her mouth as Rachel and her mother began to sob. Ethan's mother put her arms around Sally.

"Let's move into the dining room where we can all sit down," said Lieutenant Elliott.

Ethan ushered the two women to the dining room table. The others quickly gathered around.

"Do you women want some water?" asked Lieutenant Elliott.

"That would be nice of you," said Rachel.

The Lieutenant hurried to the kitchen and returned with two glasses of water. Justin, who had remained at the table, looked in confusion at the two women, then back at his dad.

"I'm sorry," said Agent Kidwell, "but who are you ladies?"

Ethan introduced the women to Agent Kidwell and Lieutenant

Elliott.

"Oh, now I recognize you," said Agent Kidwell, "you're the actress and country singer. I'm sorry, it took me a minute."

"That's okay," answered Rachel.

"And you two are friends?" he asked of Ethan.

"Yes, very old friends."

"Okay," continued Agent Kidwell, "if what you say is true, we don't have a lot of time to waste. What can you tell us about the kidnapping?"

Rachel looked at her mother who, was holding her glass of water like a shield. Her hand shook as she took a sip of water.

"Mom, do you feel up to talking?"

"I guess I have to."

The others looked at Mrs. Mills, waiting for her to begin.

"I'm...I'm Charlotte Mills - of course, Ethan and his family know that. I know it'll take a few minutes, but I think I have to go back in time to tell you how we got to this point."

"That's fine, Mrs. Mills," said Agent Kidwell. "Just try to make it as quick as possible."

"Okay," she said, and then took another sip of water. "The story actually goes back to the summer of 46 when I was a young woman just out of high school."

Agent Kidwell and Lieutenant Elliott gave each other a confused look, each wondering what something that happened so long ago could have to do with Emily's kidnapping. They said nothing as Mrs. Mills continued.

"Like Ethan, I grew up in Greeneville. My mother had passed away a few years earlier, and it was just my father and me. I was selling Avon - using my father's truck while he was at work - and, one day it stalled on a country road. While I was sitting there with the hood up wondering what to do, a young man - a young black man - not much older than me, came along and asked if I needed any help. Well, he did something to the truck, I don't know what, and it started. I asked him if he needed a ride. He was kind of hesitant, but finally accepted.

I gave him a ride into town, although he made me stop before we got too close so no one would see us together. Well, I found out his name was Billy - Billy Sewell - and he was about the handsomest young man I'd ever seen. I found out that he had just moved there a few months before, and was working for a farmer delivering eggs and milk and butter. He had just gotten out of the army and didn't really have much family. He lived with his aunt, but they didn't get along too well. Well, anyway, we started spending time together, and, to make a long story short, we fell in love."

"This was the young man in the pictures Miss Ward found, right?" asked Lieutenant Elliott.

"I'm getting to that. Well, we slipped around, seeing each other for a while. In Tennessee in 1946 a white girl didn't date a black man - it just wasn't done. And I'd been dating Gerald - Rachel's father - since I was sixteen and everyone expected us to get married, but I realized, after meeting Billy, that I really didn't love Gerald. I didn't know what to do. Then one day Billy gave me an ultimatum. He played the trumpet, and a friend who had moved to New York sent him a letter saying he had a job for him playing at the nightclub where he worked. He asked me to go away with him. I told him that I loved him, but I didn't think I could leave my dad. He said he would make it easy. He was leaving in a couple of days, and said if I wanted to go with him I should be on the bus. He told me if I wasn't there, he would understand. Well, I couldn't decide what to do. Finally, at the last minute, I went to the bus station to ask Billy not to go, but the bus had already left. I was heart broken, but decided that was the way it was meant to be. Eventually I got over it, or at least thought I did, and married Gerald. I never saw or heard from Billy again."

"And, like Lieutenant Elliott asked, Mrs. Mills, was Billy the young man in the pictures?" asked Agent Kidwell.

"The pictures were not too clear, and it's been over forty years," she said as she wiped her eyes, "but yes, I'm sure it was him."

"And you never went to Billy's aunt to ask about him?" asked Ethan.

"I...I thought he had moved to New York. A few weeks later I did go by her house, but she had moved away."

"And you said he had no other family?" asked Sally.

"No. He grew up in Georgia, but his father was killed when he was young, and his mother died of kidney failure while he was overseas, so when he got out of the army he came to stay with is aunt, but that didn't work out."

"Okay, let's get back to the matter at hand," said Agent Kidwell. "When the pictures of the lynching were put in the paper, did your husband say that he did it?"

"Oh, no. He and I have never discussed the matter at all, but there was a change that came over him after the pictures were printed."

"How so?" asked Lieutenant Elliott.

"He became quiet and withdrawn - even more so than ever. It was like a big cloud hanging over our heads the past few weeks. I didn't want to mention it because I would have to tell him about having the affair, and he would never admit to me that he had helped lynch a young man."

"But I take it that your husband has not been at home the past few days?" asked Agent Kidwell.

"No. Not since Saturday."

"My father is a long-distance trucker," said Rachel, "so it's not unusual for him to be gone for a week at a time."

"But you haven't heard from him since he left?" asked Agent Kidwell.

"No," answered Mrs. Mills, "and that's not unusual either. He practically lives in his truck, and it's kind of hard to make a phone call. But there's a man that sometimes sets up trips for him - Roy Tilson - he's like an agent for different trucking companies. When we heard about Emily being kidnapped this morning, I called him to see if he'd talked to my husband recently, and he told me that Gerald had called him Friday and said he was taking off for a couple of weeks and to not call him."

"I see," said Agent Kidwell. "And why do you think he kidnapped Miss Ward? What would that have to do with everything else?'

"I'm not sure. Maybe he's mad at her for finding the pictures and bringing all of this to a head. Maybe - " she said as she looked up sheepishly at the others, "well, I hate to say this, but maybe he's mad at Ethan because he and Rachel never got married. He always liked Ethan and... I'm sorry."

Ethan and Sally looked at each other and shook their heads. Rachel stared at the table, saying nothing.

"You and Miss Mills used to date?" asked Agent Kidwell.

"Yes, but that was a long time ago, and - I'm sorry, Mrs. Mills - but I just can't believe this could be over that," said Ethan

Mrs. Mills said nothing, but continued to look at the table.

"Does your husband ever visit Middlesboro, Kentucky, Mrs. Mills?" asked Agent Kidwell

"Not that I know of, but then he goes all over the country. Why?"

"We have reason to believe that the kidnapper has taken Miss Ward up there. What kind of car was your husband driving when he left?'

"He wasn't driving a car. He was driving his truck - a big truck - the kind that hauls trailers."

"Do you have a description and the license number?"

"Here's a picture of the truck," said Rachel, removing pictures from her purse. "You can see the license plate. We thought you might need it. There's also a picture of my dad."

"Very thoughtful. Thank you," said Agent Kidwell as he examined the pictures.

There was a short silence in which Ethan pondered if he should ask the next question. Then he decided he had to know.

"Mrs. Mills, assuming it was your husband in the photographs, do you have any idea who the other men might have been?"

"No, Ethan, I'm sorry, but I have no idea. I - I can't even tell from the pictures if it is Gerald or not."

"Did Mr. Mills hang out with the Pratt boys back then?"

"Not that I know of."

"And," he continued slowly, "were your husband and my father good friends back then?"

"Well, they knew each other, Ethan, but then Greeneville is a small town - even smaller in 1946 - so everybody knew everybody else. But I don't think they really spent much time together."

"So you have no idea how the pictures came to be in Mr. Ward's possession, Mrs. Mills?" asked Lieutenant Elliott.

"No, I'm afraid not. I've told you all everything I know. So what do we do next?"

"That's a good question," said Agent Kidwell. "Right now I have to talk to Lieutenant Elliott and my people and decide how to handle this. Will you be in town for the next couple of days?"

"We were planning on going back home, but I guess we can stay at a motel until you decide if you need us."

"I would appreciate that - at least for tonight. Please give us a call and let us know where you're staying."

"Okay."

"And thanks to both of you for coming here," continued Agent Kidwell. "I know how difficult this was for you. We really appreciate it."

The two women got up and headed for the door. While Agent Kidwell and Lieutenant Elliott continued to talk, Ethan, Sally, and Mrs. Ward arose to see them out. As they got to the door, Rachel turned to the others.

"All I can say is that I'm sorry."

"You're not responsible," said Sally.

"I know, but...okay, thanks."

Hilda put her arms around Mrs. Mills, who began to sob.

"Everything will work out okay," said Hilda. "Just have faith."

Mrs. Mills nodded her head. The two women turned and walked out the door.

"Well, I need to go lie down for a few minutes," said Hilda. "That took a lot of energy out of me."

Ethan and Sally stood at the door, looking at the two women as they got in their car and drove away. After a few second, Sally turned to Ethan.

"So, do you think that was good news or bad news?"

"Good news, I think. Everything else aside, if it really is him, he's always been a decent man.'

"A decent man doesn't kidnap a young girl and hold her for ransom," answered Sally. "Or, for that matter, lynch a young man because he's seeing his girlfriend."

"I guess you're right. Maybe I really didn't know him at all. This reminds me of the Bible verse that talks about the sins of the fathers being passed unto the third and fourth generations."

"What do you mean?"

"Well, if Mr. Mills is behind this - Emily's kidnapping as well as the lynching - it's probably a result of the racism and anger that he grew up with. And, if my father was involved in the lynching, forty years later his granddaughter is paying for it."

"So, are you saying that God is punishing Emily for what her grandfather did?'

"No, I don't think God meant it like that. But I think, since He created mankind, He knows how the things a person does will impact future generations."

"That makes sense, but it doesn't help us get our daughter back. What do we do now?"

"I guess we need to see what Agent Kidwell and Lieutenant Elliott recommend."

Just as he finished his sentence, Agent Kidwell came to talk to them.

"So, what did you two think of what they had to say?"

"What do you mean?" asked Ethan.

"Do you think Mr. Mills is the one behind this?"

"Well, it makes sense," answered Ethan. "Especially if he really was one of the men who committed the lynching."

"But, you realize we have no proof of anything she said."

"You think she's imagining things?" asked Sally.

"I really don't know. I'm sure she believes everything she told us, but she has no proof that her husband was involved in the lynching, or is the one who has taken your daughter. He's never confessed to her about the lynching, and, it's entirely possible that he just wanted to get away for a few days."

"So, I'm confused. Are you saying you don't believe Mr. Mills was the one who took Emily?" asked Ethan.

"Actually, I'm playing a bit of a devil's advocate. I think there's a very good chance he's behind this, but I believe that we have to continue looking at other possibilities as well. That's what Lieutenant Elliott and I were discussing - what do we do with this information?"

"That's what I was about to ask you," stated Ethan.

"Well, let me ask you - what kind of man is Mr. Mills? Does he have a bad temper? Is he easily depressed? Is he unstable? Do you think he's capable of hurting someone?"

"We were just discussing that. I always liked him. He's always been pretty quiet and withdrawn, but he was always nice and polite to me. No, I've never seen him lose his temper, but then he never showed much emotion of any kind when I was around."

"Then what do you two think of releasing the photograph of him to the press?"

The two looked at each other for a few seconds, then Sally turned back to Agent Kidwell.

"Well, I think we need to do it," she said. "I think it's time that we go public with this anyway. There's already a chance that the kidnapper, whoever he might be, saw or heard about last night's TV report, so I don't think it will do any harm now, and could help."

"Ethan?" he asked.

"I guess my wife's right. We should go ahead with it."

"Good, then I'll get the picture and a statement to the media."

"We also need to get copies to the agents in Kentucky," said Lieutenant Elliott. "And, since I'm just waiting around here, I can take them."

"You can't just fax them?"

"We can, but it's not as clear. Besides, I don't think there's much I can do around here, and they need as much help as they can get up there."

"Thanks," said Agent Kidwell. "That's a good idea."

"I have a suggestion," said Sally.

"What's that?" asked Agent Kidwell.

"I think it would be a good idea for me to go on TV and beg the kidnapper to return our daughter. If he has any conscience left, it might help."

"It's worthwhile," said Agent Kidwell. "And for added impact I think you should have your son with you. Mr. Ward, what do you think of that?"

"Whatever you say," answered Ethan. "My intuitions haven't been too good on this."

"Then, Mrs. Ward, you and your son follow Lieutenant Elliott to have copies of the picture made, then you go to the studio and meet with Hugh Lawton while Lieutenant Elliott takes the copies of the pictures to Kentucky. I'll call Hugh and tell him you're coming."

"You don't think I should go with Sally and Justin?" asked Ethan.

"No, I think you should stay here in case the kidnapper calls."

"But he said he wouldn't call until tomorrow."

"That means nothing. He could call at any time - especially if he saw the news or reads about it in the paper."

"Oh. That makes sense. I guess I'll just wait here. Are you going to have the police look for Mr. Mill's truck?"

"Yes, I'll call them in a minute, but I don't think it's going to do any good."

"Why?"

"If he really is behind this he would have dumped the truck and stolen another vehicle - probably a van."

"Why would he do that? His truck has a sleeping compartment."

"The truck would be too easy to recognize, and it's really not a good vehicle for a kidnapping. It would be hard to get into a remote area with it which is probably where he's taken her. And it has no bathroom so he would have to keep taking her out of the vehicle, which is a risk. And the two of them in the vehicle for any amount of time would be very uncomfortable and stressful. No, he's probably left it somewhere and stolen a van and then painted over the windows. But we still need to search for it, but we also need to have the police look for any van stolen in the past week."

"Looks like you've thought of everything."

"I wish - but I do have a little experience in these situations."

Ethan said goodbye to his wife and son and watched as they got in the van and followed Lieutenant Elliott's car. He returned to the house and sat in the living room listening to Agent Kidwell talk to the police and other Agents who were trying to find his daughter. He looked at his watch. It was not yet three o'clock. It would be another hour or so before his father-in-law arrived. He couldn't remember when he had felt so helpless.

TWENTY-SIX

Emily Ward finished her sponge bath and put on the new sweat suit her captor had brought her. She then brushed her teeth and returned to her bed. Since the previous day, the man had only made her wear the shackle at night - she assumed so that she could not attack him while he was asleep. She was elated when, the day before, he left the cabin leaving her unchained. She immediately tried the door, which, of course, was locked. She then went to each window which she found, like the one over her bed, had steel bars. Remembering something she had once read in a book, she returned to the door and tried to remove the pins in the hinges. They were too big and rusty to be removed, and she could find no tool with which to try and pry them loose. After a while she returned to her bed, resigned to the fact that the only way she would leave the cabin was when her captor, or the police, released her.

Since her captor still refused to tell her his name, the previous day she began calling him 'Mr. Smith.' He seemed not to mind - at least if he did he didn't complain. She still couldn't figure him out. He was as distant as ever, but had treated her well. He had brought her a couple of changes of clothes and plenty of food to eat. He had even brought her toiletries - a toothbrush, toothpaste, deodorant and such. Before leaving he had informed her that the following day he would take her with him when he went to call her parents. Then, if everything went as planned, she should be free in the next day or so.

She lay in bed thinking of everything that had happened in the past few days and wondering why God had allowed it. She wondered what she had done to deserve this. She thought of all the good and evil in the world and why it had to be so. After a few minutes she picked up the note pad Mr. Smith had given her and began to write down words that had been going through her mind. She wrote:

CHOICES

Darkness falls, a child calls,
Through the stillness of the night.

An outstretched palm, but the people rush on,
In search of an eternal light.

A heart cries out, in fear and doubt,
But who will answer the call?

Of the many who've died, and more who've cried,
Over the misery and suffering it saw.

Evening falls, two lovers are enthralled,
All that's heard is a tender sigh.

A fiery red rose, in the garden grows,
And awaits a passing butterfly.

A bursting heart sings, of the wonderful things,
That has filled it with joy and love.

Of crickets at night, of flickering twilight,
And the coos of turtledoves.

A child is born, his life is scorn,
It's one of suffering and woe.

His life he lives alone, with no wife nor a home,
Nor a child, his heritage to sow.

He is mocked and criticized, and on a cross he dies,
From his wound the blood does flow.

A life swept away, like the darkness with the day,
Forever leaving his brothers below.

A Savior arrives, in the still of the night,
Bringing with Him peace and love.

The people did listen, to His words of wisdom,
Brought from His Father above.

His life was more adorned, than any ever born,
And when He died, the people did cry.

His life He freely gave, the pathway He paved,
To His heavenly home in the sky.

The plan is laid, two choices can be made,
The answer must come from within.

A life of love, with our savior above,
Or the eternal darkness of sin.

The decision it is known, we must face alone,
The most important we ever shall make.

But no harder for us, than God's most loved,
For in His pain all our sins He did take.

She finished her poem and closed the notebook. When Mr. Smith returned, she hoped to talk to him about the decisions he had made that had brought them to this point.

Gerald Mills loved the woods. As a young boy growing up in Greeneville he often spent hours in the woods with just his dog and his rifle. Sometimes he would pretend he was a World War I soldier on a secret mission. Other times, he would find a fallen tree and climb upon it, making believe it was an airplane and that he was the captain. And, even though he always carried his rifle, he rarely shot anything. When younger, he had once shot a rabbit, but upon seeing its bloody carcass, decided he could never be a hunter.

The air was crisp and fresh this autumn afternoon. He walked the woods near the cabin to be alone and to go over in his mind, for the tenth time, what he had to do in the next couple of days. Tomorrow night he would take the girl with him to call Ethan. After Ethan had talked to his daughter, he would give him instructions for dropping off the money. He knew by now that the police and FBI would be involved. And while he had purposely not listened to any news reports, he was certain that his wife had already figured out that he was responsible for the kidnapping. As much as it tore him apart to never see his wife and daughter again, it would be better than spending his remaining ten or twenty years in a prison cell. For, as much as he would like, he would never be able to convince his wife, or the authorities, that he was not responsible for the hanging of Billy Sewell,

While he knew that the police and FBI figured him to be just a poor dumb truck driver, and that all of Rachel's intelligence and talents must have come from her mother, he would soon prove them wrong. If he said so himself, his plan for delivering the money was brilliant. He would instruct Ethan to take one of the mobile telephones from the FBI and board a southbound train at Whitley City, Kentucky. Then, at just the right time, he would call him on the mobile phone, and tell him to throw the money off the train. And the location would be accessible to only him on his motorcycle. Even if the FBI was following the train, he had chosen a spot where the track was far from any road. And by the time they got to the drop off point he would be long gone. Since he had already visited the area, he had his trail through the woods planned. Within 30 minutes he would be back at the van, many miles away from the drop site. When he was a couple of hours away, he would call and give them the site where Emily was being held. It would take a few days, but he would eventually reach Colorado. With a new beard and glasses, he would not be too recognizable, and would find a cheap hotel room to rent up in the Rockies. Then, when springtime arrived, he would head down to Mexico. It would be a lonely existence, and he would certainly miss his wife and daughter, but it would be better than spending the rest of his life in a cell for a crime he didn't commit.

Shortly after his wife and son left for the TV studio, Ethan's father-in-law arrived. Ethan was watching out the window as his car pulled up. He walked out to greet him. Professor Robertson hugged Ethan and handed him the satchel with the money inside.

"Thanks, Dad. You'll never know how much we appreciate this."

"No problem. Anything new?"

"You might say that. Let's go inside."

Ethan took Professor Robertson inside and introduced him to Agent Kidwell who was sitting at the dining room table. They then went into the kitchen where Ethan poured a glass of lemonade for the Professor. The two then sat at the kitchen table.

"So, what's going on?" asked the Professor.

Ethan told him about their visit from Rachel and her mother. Professor Robertson shook his head as he recanted their story. He also told him about Sally and Justin leaving for the TV studio.

"That's unbelievable," said the Professor finally.

"Isn't it?"

"Do you think it's really him?"

"I hate to say it, but yes, I do. It all makes sense."

"And what does the FBI think?"

"Agent Kidwell says he thinks it's probably Mr. Mills, but he still wants to consider other possibilities as well."

"I guess that makes sense. I guess he has to cover all his bases. What do you think of him?"

"We don't agree on a lot of things, but he seems to know what he's doing. He's had a lot more experience at this than we have."

"Of course."

The two men sat silently for a moment before the Professor turned to Ethan.

"I've met Rachel on a couple of occasions, but never her parents. What's he like? Can you believe he would really do something like this?"

"Well, as I was telling Agent Kidwell, he's a quiet type, but he was always polite and nice to me. I remember a time when I was a junior in high school and we had a football game - a bowl game over in Oneida - and Mr. Mills gave me and two other players a ride...."

Ethan stopped, his eyes growing wide.

"What is it?" asked Professor Robertson.

"Oh, my God. I just realized where he's holding her!"

Ethan jumped up from his chair and ran into the dinning room, Professor Robertson following close behind. Agent Kidwell was on the phone, but upon seeing the look on Ethan's face, said that he would call the other person back.

"What is it, Mr. Ward?"

"I just realized where Mr. Mills is holding Emily. I can't believe I didn't think of this before."

"What are you talking about?"

"When I was seventeen, we had a football game up in Oneida - that's in Scott County, about an hour north of here."

"Yes, I know where it is."

"Anyway, I remember when we had just gotten into Scott County,

Mr. Mills pointed out an area where he went hunting. He said a friend had a cabin down there and he would sometimes go there to get away for a couple of days. That's got to be where he's taken Emily."

"Okay, let's think about this. The reason you didn't think of this before was because it was a comment he made twenty years ago."

"I know, but it makes sense."

"Mr. Ward," said Agent Kidwell slowly, "I know you're excited about this, but you need to stop and think about what you're saying."

"What do you mean?"

"First of all, we still don't know for sure that Mr. Mills is the one who has your daughter."

"I know, but even you said it's highly likely. You said..."

"I know. Okay, let's assume it is him. The one thing we know for certain is that the kidnapper called from Kentucky. Now that's about an hour from Scott County. How do you explain that?"

"I don't know, but I feel certain that that's where he's keeping her. We need to get someone over there immediately."

"Are you as certain about this as you were that the Russell family was behind the kidnapping?"

Ethan did not respond, but gave him an angry look.

"Okay, I apologize for that remark, but my point is that you are too emotionally involved in this to be objective. You want me to send my agents to scour an area based on a comment someone made twenty years ago. And even if I pulled them out of Kentucky, how could we find the cabin? You never saw the cabin, right?"

"No, I never actually saw it."

"Would you even know the area he was talking about? What exactly did he say?"

"We were driving along - I remember we had just gotten into Scott County - and he pointed down a dirt road and said that he had a friend that had a cabin a mile or so down the road and that he went hunting there sometimes."

"Do you really think you could find the road he was pointing to?"

Ethan thought for a moment about his question.

"I...I think so."

"Just as I thought."

"Well, maybe Mrs. Mills or Rachel knows where the cabin is or who owns it."

"The only problem with that is they haven't called in yet, so we have no way to get in touch with them."

"But, I think, if I went up there, I could find it."

"Look, Mr. Ward, I have to do what I think is right in order to get your daughter back, and right now I need my people to keep doing what they are doing. And besides, it will be dark in another hour or two, and by then it will totally impossible for us to even locate the cabin. But tomorrow morning I'll have one of my agents meet you and you and he can try and find the cabin."

Ethan stared at him for a moment and opened his mouth to say something, but then turned and walked out of the room. Professor Robertson followed him as he went outside onto the front porch.

"Can you believe him?" said Ethan angrily.

The Professor said nothing.

"So what do you think? Do you think I'm being crazy?"

"Son, I don't know what to tell you. I understand that you want to do something - and you could be right - but I also understand Agent Kidwell's position. Do you really think you could even find the cabin?"

"I don't know, but I'm going to try."

"You're what?"

"I'm going over there to try to find it."

"On your own?"

"Yes."

"Ethan, I don't think..."

"Dad, I have to do this. I know it's a long shot, but what if I'm right and something happens to her? I could never forgive myself. It's less than an hour's drive, so despite what Agent Kidwell says, there's plenty of daylight."

The Professor stared at him for a second, then turned and looked toward the house. Shaking his head, he turned back toward Ethan.

"Well, since I know I won't be able to talk you out of this, I'll go with you."

"I don't want you to do that. Sally and Justin will be home soon, and you should be here for them. Besides, I'm not going to do anything but get close enough to see if I can see the cabin and if there's a car there. If I see anything at all suspicious I'll call the Scott County Sheriff's office or Agent Kidwell."

"I really think I should go with you, Ethan."

"It's better that you stay here. They're also going to need help writing down all the serial numbers on the money. Besides, I'm sure Agent Kidwell is right and I'm way off target on this, but it's something I have to do. I'll be back in a couple of hours."

TWENTY-SEVEN

Emily looked up from her notebook to see 'Mr. Smith' walk through the door. He hung his hat and coat on the peg and nodded to her

"How was your walk?" she asked.

"Fine."

"What do you do out there in the woods?"

"Just walk - and think. What are you writing?"

"A poem. You want to see?"

"I don't guess it would hurt."

He walked over to the bed and took the notebook from her. Emily watched as he read her poem. She tried to gauge his reaction, but could see no expression in his eyes. He finished it and handed it back to her.

"Covered a lot of territory there, didn't you?"

"What do you mean?"

"Good, evil, life, choices, eternity. Seems like you covered it all."

"I guess, but like the title says, it's really about the choices we make and how they affect your life. Do you ever worry about the decisions you make?"

He looked at her for a second.

"I guess we all make bad decisions along with some good ones."

"And do you ever worry about going to heaven or hell?"

He thought of his many conversations with his wife, Charlotte, and daughter, Rachel, about his soul.

"I've been through this many times before, girlie. You're not going to try and save me too, are you?"

"Well, you know, Jesus said nobody gets to the Father except through Him."

"Yeah, I know, but I ain't sure I believe that."

"Just because you don't believe it doesn't mean it's not true. And what if it is? Kind of late to find out He was telling the truth once you die."

He looked at her for a second, saying nothing. He walked to the door and removed his hat and coat from the peg, then turned back toward her.

"I'm going out to get something to eat. What do you want me to bring you?"

Emily thought about continuing the conversation for a moment, but decided to let it go.

"Maybe I can go with you?"

"You know I can't do that, girl."

"Emily. My name is Emily."

"Okay, Emily. You know I can't do that."

"You're going to have to take me with you tomorrow to talk to my dad."

"Then we'll wait until then."

"Are you going to tape my hands and legs again when we go out?"

"You know the answer to that. Now what do you want to eat?"

"What if I promise to not try and escape? Will you not tape my hands and legs then?"

"We'll talk about that tomorrow. Now, for the last time, what do you want to eat?'

"Can you get me a roast beef sandwich from Subway on whole wheat with oil and vinegar and olives and red peppers?"

"I don't know if there's one nearby, but...okay, but you better write it down."

Emily wrote her request in the notebook, then tore out the page and held it up. He walked back to her, took the page, then turned to walk away. He had only taken a couple of steps when they looked up to see the door open and a man walk in. Emily stared at him for a second, then her heart leaped as she recognized the man. It was her grandfather's Doctor, Merle Anderson.

"Doctor Anderson," she shouted, "Oh, thank God. How did you..."

She stopped as she saw the strange look in his eyes. It was not one of compassion, but one of anger, and it seemed to be directed toward her.

"What are you doing here?" asked Gerald Mills.

"It's my cabin, remember? And you're an idiot for pulling something like this!" said Doctor Anderson.

"It was only a matter of time until they figured it out. I had no choice."

"Sure you did. You could have kept your mouth shut and done nothing and everything would have been fine."

"My wife would have gone to the police. I couldn't wait."

"And this is your answer?" he asked, pointing to Emily. "Holding her for ransom? How stupid is that?"

"Well, I needed money, and we don't all have your financial resources, Doc. How did you know?"

"It's on the news that she's been kidnapped. When I couldn't get in touch with you or your family it didn't take long for me to figure it out. Although I really hoped you wouldn't be dumb enough to bring her here. And they probably already traced the calls."

"I'm not quite as dumb as you think. I drove into Kentucky to make the calls, so I hope they did trace them. It'll keep them busy."

Emily's hope turned to terror as she listened to the two men talking. She quickly realized that Doctor Anderson was not there to free her but to protect his own interests. She pulled the covers up to her neck as she watched and listened to the two men.

"And everything would have been fine if you hadn't come along," said Gerald. "I'm picking up the money in a day or so, so I'd be gone and the girl would be free."

"And everybody would know your identity."

"What difference does that make? I'll be out of the country, and they couldn't tie any of this to you."

"And what about my cabin? You think they wouldn't wonder why you happened to pick my cabin?"

"So what? That doesn't mean anything. Just because I've been to your cabin doesn't mean you had anything to do with the lynching."

Emily gasped at the mention of the lynching. Now it all made sense. She had been selected because she had found her grandfather's pictures of the lynching.

"Well, the question is, 'what do we do now?'" asked Gerald.

"There's only one thing to do," answered Doctor Anderson, turning toward Emily. "She can't be allowed to identify us."

Gerald looked at Emily, shaking under the covers, and then turned back to Doctor Anderson.

"No, we're not going to hurt her," he said.

"I don't like it either, but there's no other choice," he said as he moved toward the bed. "You're the one responsible for this."

"I'm not going to let you do that," answered Gerald as he moved between the Doctor and Emily, pulling a knife from his pocket.

Quickly Doctor Anderson reached into his coat and pulled out a handgun and pointed it toward Gerald.

"We're in this together, Gerald, but I'm not letting her send me to prison and ruin everything I've worked for all my life. Now, move out of the way."

Gerald looked down at Emily who was sobbing and trying to protect herself with a pillow. He turned back to Doctor Anderson and held up the knife.

"It's not going to happen. You strong-armed me into killing one young man, and it's not going to happen again."

Gerald moved forward toward Doctor Anderson with the knife in his hand. Emily watched in horror as the Doctor fired one shot into Gerald. He grabbed his stomach, dropped the knife, and fell to the floor in front of her bed. Doctor Anderson looked down at Gerald, then back to Emily.

———————————

Less than a half hour after leaving his house north of Knoxville, Ethan Ward took the highway 63 exit off of I 75 and headed towards Oneida. Unfortunately, the road quickly became unfamiliar to him. It had been many years since he had traveled the area, but the one thing he remembered was how narrow and horrible the road was. It had wound around the Tennessee hills like a snake, sometimes doubling back on itself. The maximum speed was usually about thirty-five to forty miles per hour. But this road was wide and straight. He looked around to see if perhaps he had somehow made a wrong turn, but then soon realized what had happened. They had replaced old highway 63 with a new road. He looked to his left and could see the old road beneath him. As he drove along he noticed that, from time to time, the old road crossed the new one. With that knowledge, he drove on, waiting until he got to Scott County to find his way to the old road and hopefully to the cabin.

A short time later, he saw the sign welcoming him to Scott County. He quickly began looking for an exit to the old road. One came up within a mile, which he quickly took. Unfortunately, he soon discovered that within a couple of hundred yards, it came back into the new road. He drove on, searching his memory for something that looked familiar. Again he soon came upon another exit to the old road to the right. He quickly turned down it and was pleased to find that it lead away from the new road. He slowed down, searching for a familiar landmark that would help jog his memory. He shortly found it. There was an older white house by the road with a statue of a deer in the front yard. Although it had been twenty years, it now came back to him. He remembered that they had just passed the house when Mr. Mills had pointed down a road toward the cabin. Ethan slowed the car to a crawl, and within a few seconds, saw a gravel road to his right. He quickly exited and continued down the road and began a steep incline. Soon the gravel road became dirt, and twisted around through the woods. There had been only one house on the road near the entrance to the highway. If anyone wanted a secluded place to hunt, or to kidnap someone, this would be the place for it.

He drove on for another mile or so, keeping his speed around ten miles per hour to keep the noise down. He was glad, at his wife's insistence, he had gotten his muffler replaced the month before. In another minute or so the road made a sharp turn to the left. After coming around the curve he saw what he was looking for - a cabin, only a hundred or so feet in front on him. In front of the cabin sat a black Lincoln Towncar, and a white van. While the Lincoln looked familiar to him, he couldn't place it. And if Gerald Mills really had kidnapped his daughter and brought her here, why was there another car in front of the cabin? He brought the car to a stop and rolled down the window, trying to decide what to do next. He decided to keep to his original plan and find a phone and call the Scott County Sheriff's department. He would wait for them on the highway. He was about to back up when he heard a pop, which sounded like a gun shot, then a woman scream. There was no doubt - it was his daughter's voice. He opened the door and ran to the cabin.

Merle Anderson stood looking down at Gerald Mills, shaking his head. He then turned back to Emily, shivering and holding the pillow in front of her for protection.

"Please don't hurt me," she begged. "I...I won't tell anybody, I promise."

"Now we both know better than that, don't we?"

He started to move in her direction when the door opened. He turned quickly to see Ethan Ward rush in. Ethan looked at Gerald Mills lying on the floor, and Doctor Anderson with the gun in his hand. He then saw his daughter on the bed.

"Oh, Daddy!" she cried. "Oh, God, please help me."

Emily threw off the covers and jumped from the bed, as Doctor

Anderson pointed the gun at her.

"Stop. Don't move!" he shouted.

Emily froze in her steps as her father ran toward her. Doctor Anderson moved back from the bed and let the two hug.

"He killed him, Daddy!" she cried. "He just shot him."

"I know, honey."

"And he was going to shoot me. He's going to shoot us, Daddy"

Ethan looked at the Doctor with fire in his eyes.

"Who's with you?" asked Doctor Anderson as he walked to the door and stared outside.

"It's just me."

"That's good," he said as he turned back to them.

"I guess I understand your comments about the Pratt boys doing the lynching a little better now."

"Yeah, and it would have worked too, if Gerald hadn't of been such an idiot."

"So, what do you do now?"

"Sorry, Ethan, but I really don't have much choice."

"Oh, God, Daddy. What will we do?"

Ethan hugged his daughter and whispered in her ear.

"It'll be okay, honey. I promise you."

"There should be a shovel in the closet over there," said Doctor Anderson with a wave of his gun. "Go get it."

Ethan moved toward the closet.

"No, I want your daughter to get it."

Ethan released his daughter and nodded for her to follow the Doctor's instructions. Emily walked slowly to the closet and opened the door and removed a shovel. She turned back to Doctor Anderson.

"What now?" she asked as she wiped the tears from her eyes.

"You and your father and I are going around back of the cabin and take a little walk."

He again waved the gun at Ethan, who walked to Emily and put his arm around her. The two headed for the door, with Doctor Anderson following a few feet behind.

"And don't try to run," he instructed as they turned right and walked along front of the cabin.

Emily dropped the shovel, which Ethan picked up and dragged behind them. They walked around behind the cabin where he directed them to a path which led into the woods. Suddenly, Emily turned back to the man with fire in her eyes.

"I can't believe you're doing this!" she yelled. "You're going to go to hell for this."

"Probably," he answered. "If it'll make you feel any better, I really don't enjoy doing this, but then I see people die almost every day. It's just part of the natural process. Now keep walking."

"I just have one question," said Ethan.

"What's that?"

"What role did my father have in the lynching?"

"I guess I owe you that much, huh. Of course, you're not going to like the answer. You see..."

"Mister," came a voice from behind Doctor Anderson, "I got a .38 pointed at your backside, and at this distance I can't miss. So if I were you I'd put down that gun nice and easy and then put your hands up."

Ethan saw the look in the Doctor's eyes and knew what his response would be. As he spun around with the gun in his hand, Ethan grabbed Emily and pulled her to the ground. He got off one shot before being hit with two bullets. Emily looked up to see her Grandfather Robertson walk to Doctor Anderson and kick his handgun away. He then walked to his son-in-law and granddaughter and helped them up.

"Oh, Gramps, thank you," cried Emily. "I love you."

"I love you too, honey," he said as he pulled her close.

"What took you so long?" asked Ethan.

"Well, I had to make sure you two weren't in the line of fire."

"Oh, I guess that makes sense. I'm sure glad you insisted on coming along."

"And I'm sure glad I brought my gun with me, or we'd all be in trouble."

"Right," said Ethan as he looked down at Doctor Anderson and shook his head.

"Surely you're not feeling sorry for him, are you?"

"No, but he was just about to tell me if my dad was involved in the lynching. Now I guess I'll never know."

"I'm sorry, I couldn't hear what you were saying, and I had to take the opportunity when I could."

"Daddy," said Emily, "I think the other man is still alive."

"Mr. Mills is still alive?"

"Mr. Mills? You mean that's Rachel's father?" asked Emily.

"Yes, honey, I'm afraid so. You think he's alive?"

"Yes. Well, when I walked past him I saw him move. He tried to protect me, Daddy. That's why the other man shot him. He wouldn't let him kill me."

"Okay, let's go check on him," said Ethan.

"No, you take Emily and go for help," said the Professor. "I'll check on Mr. Mills. She doesn't need to be around here any more."

"You're right. Thanks."

Emily and Ethan each hugged the Professor again and then got in Ethan's car and drove back down the road. They waved to the Professor as he walked back into the cabin.

TWENTY-EIGHT

Oneida, Tennessee is located in Northeast Tennessee on the Cumberland Plateau. It sits in the foothills of the Appalachian Mountains, just south of the Kentucky state line, seventy miles north of Knoxville. While the area was first settled in the late 18th century, having been incorporated in 1913, Oneida is a relatively new town in Tennessee's history. With an abundance of natural resources in the area, many of Oneida's residents are employed in the logging, coal, or oil industries. A large number of residents also make their livelihood in the farming industry, while others work at the small factories in the town. The people, while being patriotic Americans and Tennesseans, are also fiercely independent. Hunting and fishing are major pastimes for most Oneidians. Most residents are enthusiastic sport fans, supporting the local Oneida High Indians teams as well as the University of Tennessee Volunteers. The love of the UT sports teams is so intense that the Oneida High School teams copied the Orange and White colors of the Volunteers.

Scott County Hospital in Oncida sits on a hill on U.S. highway 27 at the north end of town. While it serves all of Scott County with a population of less than 20,000, as the only major medical facility in a radius of forty miles, it has seen more than its share of human suffering. From gunshot wounds to stabbings and beatings - heart attacks and strokes - in its thirty year history it has seen almost every known type of injury and illness. Tonight, however, was an exceptionally busy one. The emergency room was already full when they received a call from the Sheriff that three more victims were on their way. Emily Ward was examined by one of the emergency room doctors and found to be suffering from extreme stress and exhaustion. She was transferred to a room and put on an IV and given a tranquilizer to help calm her nerves. Gerald Mills was stabilized and X-rayed to determine the location of the bullet, and was taken into surgery. The bullet was successfully removed and the bleeding was stopped, and he too was transferred into a room, with an Oneida police officer guarding the door.

There was nothing to be done for Doctor Merle Anderson, who was pronounced dead on arrival at the hospital. The cause of death was listed as massive internal injuries from two gunshot wounds. His body was processed and sent to the morgue to await the medical examiner.

The Scott County Sheriff took statements from Ethan Ward and Professor Robertson, who told them he would need to talk to Agent Kidwell to verify their story. Ethan called his home number. Sally answered on the first ring.

"Hello," answered Sally.

"She's okay, honey," said Ethan.

"Oh my God," she began to cry. "She's okay?"

"Yes, she's fine. We're at the hospital. They gave her something to make her sleep, but she's doing fine."

"Where are you?"

"In Oneida - the Scott County Hospital."

"What happened?"

"It's a long story. I'll tell you about it later."

"And was it Mr. Mills?"

"Yes, and he's here too. He's been shot, but he's doing okay."

"Shot - did you...?"

"No, no. Like I said, it's a long story. I'll tell you about it later. Emily should be released in the morning so your dad and I will stay here until then."

"We're coming over."

"Sally, it's dark and it's getting late and you all will be upset. I think you should wait until the morning. Emily's sleeping anyway, so..."

"Ethan, I want to see my daughter."

"I know but I think..."

"We're coming over."

Ethan looked up at the Sheriff who was waiting patiently nearby.

"Look, the Sheriff needs to talk to Agent Kidwell to verify our story. Maybe after he's finished talking he can drive you and Justin. I would imagine he needs to come over anyway."

"Okay."

"And then someone should call Rachel and her mother. They shouldn't have to hear it on the news."

"Okay. I hate to do it, but I guess it has to be done. One way or another, we'll see you in a little while," she said.

"Okay, honey. See you soon."

Ethan handed the phone to the Sheriff and listened while he talked to Agent Kidwell. After he hung up he turned to them and told them that no charges would be brought against Professor Robertson. He then told them they could go to Emily's room.

As they entered her room, they found Emily sleeping soundly. Ethan stood by her bed, while his father-in-law seated himself in a nearby chair.

"There's a recliner here so you can lay back and relax if you want, Dad."

"No, thanks, Ethan, I'm fine. You take it."

After a few minutes, Ethan seated himself in a chair next to his father-in-law. He glanced out the window, then back at his daughter. The two men sat silently watching her as she slept. Soon a nurse came in and took her blood pressure and pulse.

"How is she?" asked Professor Robertson.

"She's fine," she responded as she turned and started to walk away, then turned back to them. "Look, I heard what you all have been through, and I just want to say how sorry I am. If there's anything we can do, just let us know."

"Thanks, nurse," said Ethan.

"And, we shouldn't have anyone else in the other bed tonight, so if one of you wants to use it just go ahead."

"Thanks," said the Professor. "We might take you up on that."

It was a little after nine when Sally and Justin and Ethan's mother arrived at the hospital. Sally went to her daughter's bed and kissed her on the cheek. Emily awoke long enough to smile and say hello, then went back to sleep.

"She's doing okay?" she asked.

"She's fine. They just want to keep her overnight, so she should be released after the doctor checks on her in the morning. Did Agent Kidwell drive you here?"

"Yes. He's down with the Sheriff now. He told us everything that happened after he got off the phone with him. Dad, I'm so sorry."

"Me, too, honey, but there really was no choice in the matter."

Sally went to her father and gave him a hug, while Justin and his grandmother stood by the bed watching Emily. The family was gathered around the bed when Agent Kidwell came to the door. Ethan motioned him into the room.

"So, that's Emily?" whispered Agent Kidwell.

"Yep. Pretty cute, huh?" answered her grandfather.

"Yes, she is," he responded with a smile. Then, turning to Ethan asked, "Can I talk to you in the hall?"

The two men left and walked out of the room.

"Is there something wrong?" asked Ethan.

"No, I just wanted to apologize."

"For what?"

"For not listening to what you were saying."

"You mean for not following my wild, crazy hunch?"

"Which turned out to be right."

"I know, Agent Kidwell, but you were doing what you thought was right. If I'd been in your place I would have done the same thing."

"Thanks. Anyway, I'm glad things turned out all right."

"What's going to happen to Mr. Mills?"

"As soon as he's able to travel I'll take him back to Knoxville to face kidnapping charges. Then it's up to a judge and jury. The Oneida police have a man guarding his room, and I'll have a man here soon to help out. And Carl Benlow said to tell you he'll be over in the morning to see you."

"And what about Rachel and her mother? Are they here?"

"I haven't seen them, but we called them from my car. They probably haven't had time to get here yet."

"Okay. Thanks for everything."

"My pleasure."

The two men shook hands and Agent Kidwell walked away. Ethan walked back into the room to see the rest of his family huddled together at the foot of the bed.

"What's this - a conspiracy?" he asked.

"No, we were just saying it's getting late and wondering what we should do for the night," answered his mother.

"Well, the nurse told me earlier that there's a nice motel just a mile or so north of here - Tobe's Motel, I think she said. You all can stay there and I'll stay in the room with Emily."

"I'm not leaving my daughter," said Sally.

"Then we'll both stay."

"Sounds fine to me," said Mrs. Ward. "I'm too old to be sleeping in a hospital room unless I have to."

"Me, too," added Professor Robertson. "Justin, you coming with us?"

"Shouldn't somebody stand guard by the room?"

"There's no need for that," said Ethan as he put his hand on his son's arm. "There's no danger, now, and besides, there's a policeman right down the hall. Just go to the motel and get some sleep."

"Okay. I guess we need to get a ride since your car is still over at the cabin."

"No, one of the deputies brought it over," he answered, handing his son the keys. "Now, you all have a good night's sleep."

Ethan and Sally hugged their family, who then turned and left the room.

"You can have the bed and I'll take the chair," said Ethan.

"No, I'll take the chair. I'm smaller so it'll be easier for me, and, besides, I can better keep an eye on her."

"I'd argue with you, but I know it wouldn't do any good. I'm exhausted, so I'm going to try and get some sleep."

He kissed his wife and took off his shoes and lay down on the bed. Sally took the extra blanket the nurse had left, reclined her chair, and feel asleep watching her daughter.

———————

Ethan awoke by seven the next morning, and quietly went to the bathroom so as to not wake his wife and daughter. When he came out, Sally was sitting on Emily's bed stroking her hair.

"So, how you doing this morning, sweetie?" he asked as he walked to Emily's bed.

"Fine, Daddy. Thank you for coming to find me."

"Sure, honey."

"You sure are a smart Daddy."

"Or maybe just lucky."

"Where's gramps?"

"He and your grandmother and Justin are at the motel," answered Sally.

"He saved our lives, Mom."

"I know, honey. I heard all about it."

"You sure you're feeling okay, honey?" asked Ethan again.

"I feel fine, Daddy. Right now I'm starving."

"Breakfast should be here in a few minutes, sweetie."

"Do I get to go home today?"

"As soon as the doctor comes and checks on you," answered Sally.

As the three were talking, Sally looked up to see Rachel standing nervously at the door. Sally waved her in but Rachel shook her head. Ethan walked over to greet her. They moved outside the room to talk.

"I'm sorry, I don't think Emily needs to talk to me."

"It's okay," said Ethan.

"Well, we'll just talk out here. How is she?"

"She's fine."

"Oh, I'm so sorry, Ethan," she said as she began to cry.

"It's okay, Rachel. You're not responsible for what anyone else does, no matter who it is."

"I know but...anyway, my dad says he would like to talk to you."

Ethan looked at her for a second then turned his eyes away. After a few seconds he looked back at her.

"Rachel, I'm sorry, but I don't have anything to say to him. Tell him..."

"Ethan, he said it's about your dad. He said he knows you need to know about what happened."

Ethan's heart began to race. With everything that had happened since last night, he had forgotten about the lynching and what involvement his father had. As much as he disliked the idea of talking to the man who had kidnapped his daughter, he knew he had to have answers.

"Okay, tell him I'll be down in a few minutes."

She nodded her understanding, wiped a tear from her eye, and walked back toward her father's room.

Ethan went back into the room long enough to tell his wife and daughter he was going for a walk. He then walked nervously down the hall toward Gerald Mill's room. He was stopped at the door by an Oneida police officer who informed him that anyone going into the room had to be searched.

"I'm sorry," he said. "Chief's orders."

"It's okay," answered Ethan as he raised his arms to allow the officer to do his duty.

"Okay. You can go in," he said when finished.

Mrs. Mills was sitting in a chair by the window, reading her Bible when Ethan walked in. Seeing Ethan, she closed her Bible and put it on the windowsill and arose and walked toward him. Without speaking, she gave him a sad smile, then put her hand on his arm as she walked past him and out of the room. Ethan hesitated for a moment, then walked to the foot of Gerald Mill's bed. As he walked past the curtain dividing the room, he saw Mr. Mills lying in bed, his eyes closed, his arm handcuffed to the bed rail. Ethan cleared his throat and waited for him to look up. Getting no response, he made a louder sound. Mr. Mills opened his eyes and looked at Ethan.

"Hello, Ethan," he said.

Ethan said nothing, but stood staring at the man.

"Why don't you have a seat?" he asked, pointing to the chair.

"I'm fine here."

"Well, my voice is pretty weak, so I would appreciate it if you would come closer."

Ethan stared at him a moment, then moved closer and sat in the chair.

"I appreciate your coming."

"You have information about my father?"

"I wouldn't have hurt her, you know? I never would have hurt her."

"You *did* hurt her."

"I guess," he said with a sad look in his eyes. "But I would have never physically hurt her. Merle Anderson was going to shoot her, you know. I couldn't let that happen."

"If you're looking for me to say thank you after what you put us through, you're in for a long wait."

"Okay. I understand. So you want to know about your father?"

"Yes," answered Ethan, remembering Dr. Anderson's warning that he wouldn't like what he heard.

"I understand Charlotte told you a lot of what happened back then?"

"Yes."

"Well, she has some of the story, but not all. And I'm sorry if this goes on too long, but I think you need to know the whole truth. I just hope my voice holds out."

Ethan said nothing, but nodded.

"Charlotte and I started dating when I came back from the war that Spring. I guess a lot of us soldiers came back about that time, including your dad. Anyway, we dated for a few months, and I thought everything was okay. Then she started acting kind of strange and distant. I asked her what was wrong, but she said nothing. I mentioned it to my brother George, and without me knowing it, he began spying on her."

Ethan remembered Rachel's Uncle George, whom he had only met on a couple of occasions, but greatly disliked. Rachel had said that he gave her the creeps, always making suggestive comments or racial slurs. As a teenager, she had shed few tears when he had died.

"A few days later he came to me and told me why Charlotte was acting so funny. He said she'd been seeing a colored boy. Well, I told him I didn't believe it. I guess I was afraid of what would happen if it was true. I'd be made fun of and harassed by my friends for losing my girl to a colored boy. But I guess what was scarier was that she really didn't love me. So anyway, I just tried to ignore it. After a couple of weeks, though, George decided to take matters into his own hands. He went and got Doc Anderson - well, he was just Merle then - and your grandpa, and they went to visit this boy, Billy."

"My grandpa!" repeated Ethan with surprise.

"Yes, I'm sorry, son, but you need to know the truth."

Ethan was shocked, but then, as he thought about it, not surprised. He recalled what an evil man his grandfather had been.

"So George and Merle and Walter got in their pickup and went to pay Billy a visit. He lived out in the country with his aunt, and she was working, so no one else knew about it. I reckon they pretty much terrorized the boy until he confessed that he was seeing Charlotte. Then my brother came and got me and said he wanted to show me something, although he wouldn't tell me what it was. We also went by your dad's house and picked him up. George told him your grandpa needed to see him, but he couldn't tell him why, so he followed us in his truck. George also told him to bring the new camera he had just bought.

"Where was my mother?"

"I don't know, but she wasn't home. Your dad had taken her somewhere, I guess. Anyway, we went back to Billy's house, where he confessed to me. He said he was leaving town that afternoon on the Greyhound and wouldn't ever be back, and begged us to let him go. Well, Merle said he would let him go, but he was going to teach him a lesson first, so they tied him up and put him in the back of the truck and took him into the woods."

"And you and my dad just went along with this?"

"Well, son, we didn't know what they were planning on doing. And, besides, this was my older brother who had always intimidated me, and your dad was even more scared of your grandfather than I was of my brother."

"I understand he was pretty much an SOB?"

"Your grandpa wasn't exactly the nicest man I ever met, Ethan. Sorry. Anyway, when we got to the woods, they tied him to a tree and used a whip on him. I was sick to my stomach, and I knew your dad was too, but we tried not to show it."

Ethan visualized his father watching as his grandfather used the whip on the young man. It made his stomach churn. He also imagined the terror the young man must have felt, being captured and beaten by three white men.

"After a few minutes, I said that I thought he had had enough, and your dad said we should let him go. But by then, the others had had a few beers and were out for blood. Even though your dad and I objected, before we knew it they had hung him from the tree."

"Oh, God."

"I know, Ethan. It's something that stays with me every day of my life. I know Buster and I should have tried harder to stop it, but we were still young, and it's hard to stand up to your big brother or your father."

"So then you took the pictures?"

"Yeah. Merle and George had white sheets and so everyone put them on to take pictures. They wanted to send a message to any other colored boys who decided to date white women."

"Who took the pictures?"

"Your dad took some and then I took some. They wanted us to all be in one of the pictures, which I don't understand, since we were wearing sheets."

"So what happened to the pictures then? Where did they get them developed?"

"In your grandpa's basement. He had just bought equipment to develop pictures - it's not that complicated, I understand."

"And how did my dad end up with the pictures?'

"I didn't know he had them. But I know that they were planning on sending the pictures to the newspaper, but after they sobered up they decided that wasn't such a good idea. Your dad told them that the FBI might get involved for something like that, so your grandpa told him to destroy them. I guess he decided he should keep one set in case he ever decided to do something about it."

"That makes sense."

"And the rest you know, son. I'm sorry, but at least you know your dad's heart wasn't in it, and it was something that bothered him the rest of his life."

"You talked about it?"

"Not much - only probably a couple of times over the past forty years. As guilty as we felt, we couldn't do anything without sending ourselves to jail."

"And, obviously, the Pratt boys had nothing to do with this?"

"No, that was just Merle's way of throwing you off the track."

"Just as I thought. I guess that explains it all. I appreciate you telling me what happened."

"It's the least I can do."

Ethan started to walk away, then turned back.

"Mr. Mills, I believe everything you've told me, but that still doesn't explain why you would kidnap Emily. I would like to know."

Gerald Mills closed his eyes and rolled his head, then looked back at Ethan.

"I guess I just went crazy, Ethan. I don't know any other way to explain it. Like I said, I knew from the beginning that I would never hurt her, but it seemed like a way out of my predicament. And I guess I was depressed and scared and desperate. For forty years I've lived with a woman who didn't love me - who settled for me. And I've lived with the guilt of what we had done, and couldn't tell anybody. I was the star of our senior class - the Valedictorian - I bet you didn't know that?"

"No, I didn't."

"I was supposed to do great things. Then the war came along, and when I came back - well you know what happened there. And for forty years I've lived with all of these issues. When Rachel became a star, everyone would joke and say they knew where she must have gotten all her talent. Since I'm just a dumb truck driver, she couldn't have gotten anything useful from me. And then, when they put the pictures in the paper, I knew that Charlotte would figure it out and go to the police, and beside the disgrace, I would spend the rest of my life in a small cell. I just went crazy. There's no other way to describe it. I'm sorry."

Ethan nodded his understanding, and with nothing more to say, turned and walked away.

"Ethan," called Mr. Mills.

"Yes?"

"Tell Emily how sorry I am, and that I'll think more about what she said in her poem. She's a smart girl."

"I'll tell her."

Ethan went back to Emily's room and related what Gerald Mills had told him. Neither Sally nor Emily said anything. When he finished, he looked at Emily who was staring out the window - tears rolling down her cheek.

"Are you okay, honey?" asked Ethan.

"I don't know, Daddy. It's just - well, I understand now what Grandpa was trying to tell me the last time I talked to him."

"Really? What did he say?" asked Ethan.

"He apologized for being such a bigot when he was younger, and hoped I would forgive him if I ever heard anything bad that he did."

"You never told us that, honey," said Sally.

"I just thought he was a little delirious from the medication. Anyway, now I'll never be able to tell him I forgive him and that I still love him."

"It's okay, sweetie," said Ethan. "He knows."

———————

It was a little after ten when the doctor came into Emily's room, and after a quick exam, told her she was free to go. As they were waiting for Emily to change into the clothes her mother had brought her, Justin gave an inquisitive look to the others.

"Yes?" asked Ethan.

"Um, I'm just wondering how we're all going to fit into your Mustang?"

"Oh, good thinking," answered Ethan.

"Did Agent Kidwell already leave?" asked Professor Robertson?"

"I think so," said Emily. "Oh, well, I guess somebody will just have to hitchhike home."

"Did I hear somebody say they needed a ride home?" asked Carl Benlow as he entered the room.

The others laughed and greeted him.

"So, you think some of us might get a ride with you?" asked Hilda.

"For a price," he answered.

"What's that?"

"You got to buy one of my duck decoys. Business has been bad this week since I've been spending all my time at the Ward house."

Ethan and the Professor laughed and slapped him on the back as Emily emerged from the bathroom and hugged Carl.

"You doing okay, honey?"

"I'm doing fine, Mr. Benlow. Thank you."

"When are they going to release you?"

"They just did. I'm a free woman."

"That sounds good," said Carl. "Well, if everybody's ready to go, then let's load up."

The group walked as quietly as possible down the corridor toward the entrance. As they passed Gerald Mill's room, the police officer nodded. As they looked into the room they saw Rachel and her mother sitting at the foot of the bed, staring ahead blankly. Without speaking, Sally turned and walked into the room. The police officer put his arm out to stop her, then took her purse and let her pass. She went into the room and, without speaking, hugged Rachel and then her mother, and turned and walked away. Rachel, with tears in her eyes, waved goodbye.

A cold drizzle had just begun as Ethan and his son climbed into his Mustang. They waited as the rest of the family got in Carl's car and pulled in front of them. They drove slowly down the hill from the hospital, then turned right onto U.S. Highway 27, and headed for home. As they drove away, Ethan watched in the rear view mirror as the hospital faded in the distance.

TWENTY-NINE

December 17ᵗʰ, 1988

Snow began falling at sunrise in Greeneville, and although it only came in flurries, by mid-morning an inch or so covered the area. It was a fine, dry snow, and with the temperature in the upper thirties and no wind, it was still a pleasant day in East Tennessee. Ethan Ward and Tommy Bell sat on the bench, looking out over the rolling hills of the cemetery where both of their fathers were buried.

"You've been here every year on your dad's birthday, right?" asked Ethan.

"I've only missed once. We had the ice storm a few years back and I couldn't get out of Nashville."

"Oh yeah, I remember. I'm sure he forgives you for that."

"Let's hope."

"Too bad your mother couldn't come. I hope she gets over the flu soon."

"I'm sure she'll be fine in a couple of days."

When Tommy had told Ethan that he was visiting his father's gravesite, Ethan offered to accompany him and also visit his father's grave. The two men had stopped and bought flowers and placed them on the graves, and now sat in the falling snow.

"Guess the flowers won't last too long this time of year," said Tommy.

"No, but it's the thought that counts," said Ethan, then added, "so, Mr. Senator, you changed your mind about running for another term?"

"No, I'm afraid not. I think this is it for me."

"So what are you going to do?"

"Probably just move back here, if I can talk Rita into it. Or maybe we can talk my mother into moving in with us, although she's pretty set in her ways. Either way, it'll give me more time to spend with my family. My mom's not getting any younger, you know. So what's in your future?"

"Nothing exciting, I hope. Just continue at my job, and go watch Justin's football games. Emily said she might try out for the ladies' basketball team this fall. I hope that's all the future holds for us. I can stand a big taste of boredom for a while."

"Sounds good."

The two sat silently for a while, enjoying the brisk winter air. Soon the silence was broken by the sound of an approaching car. They looked up to see the familiar sight of Rachel's BMW. She parked behind Tommy's car, and got out and walked toward the two friends.

"Good morning," said the two men in unison.

"Hi, guys."

"Strange seeing you here," said Tommy.

"Well, I called Ethan's mother and she said you two were coming over here."

Ethan and Tommy moved apart and let Rachel sit between them.

"What's new?" asked Ethan.

"Well, I just talked to my dad's attorney, and the Knoxville district attorney made them an offer."

"What's that?"

"Well, first I need to call Emily and thank her for her statement. After what she had been through, it was very nice of her to say anything nice about my dad."

"Well, as she says," said Ethan, "he did save her from Doctor Anderson."

"I know, but - well, anyway, based on her statement, they offered him ten years, and he will be eligible for parole in five years."

"That's not too bad," said Tommy.

"Yes, and at least he should have a few years of a normal life left when he gets out."

"What about the lynching?"

"Well, Carol Duncan hasn't finished her investigation, but, based on feedback she has given us so far, she believes everything my father has told her. And Dad's information did lead them to Billy Sewell's body - or remains. And they found a distant relative of his in North Carolina, so he'll be getting a decent burial."

"But they still might bring charges against him in that case?" asked Ethan.

"I guess, but hopefully they can run concurrently. And I know that somebody should pay for what happened to him, but the three men that were really responsible went unpunished."

"Life is not fair," said Tommy. "And unfortunately it never will be."

"That's true, but your father and mine paid for it every day of their lives, Rachel," said Ethan.

Rachel said nothing, but nodded her agreement.

"How's your mother?" asked Tommy.

"I guess as well as can be expected. She's also living with the guilt that her affair with Billy cost him his life."

"She's not responsible," said Tommy. "All they did was fall in love. Tell her that...."

"I know, Tommy. And you're right, but it's just something that will take time. Anyway, let's change the subject. I have some good news."

"What's that?" asked Ethan.

"My husband and I are getting back together."

"That is good news," said Tommy. "When did this happen?"

"Well, we've been talking and trying to work things out. I went over

to see him last weekend, and we are going to give it another chance. Only this time we will put our marriage first and not our careers."

"That's great," said Ethan. "Guess that means that we won't be hearing any new songs from you for a while?"

"No, probably not. And maybe we'll start a family - if I'm not too old, that is."

"No, of course not," said Tommy. "Now, if you were as old as Ethan, there might be a problem."

"Right," laughed Ethan. "I'm the oldest by what - four months?"

The three friends continued talking for a while before Rachel arose to leave.

"Well, anyway, that's all my news. Guess I'll leave you two alone."

"We were just getting ready to go, too," said Tommy as he and Ethan arose.

Tommy and Ethan hugged Rachel who then turned and walked to her car. She waved goodbye as she drove away.

"Well, Ace," said Tommy, "you ready to go?"

"As long as you're driving. I'm too old to drive in weather like this."

EPILOGUE

January 21st, 1989

Ethan Ward answered the door and greeted their guest. After taking his coat and hanging it in the closet, he led him toward the kitchen, where he introduced him to his wife.

"Mr. Ross, this is my wife Sally. Honey, this is Terry Ross."

"Pleased to meet you, Mrs. Ward," said their visitor.

"It's nice to meet you, Mr. Ross. Pretty cold out there, huh?"

"It's bitter."

"And do you normally work on Saturdays?" she asked.

"Well, you know - whatever it takes to get the job done. I just appreciate you two taking the time to talk to me."

"No problem. Would you like some coffee or a cup of tea?"

"A cup of tea would be nice, thank you."

"That sounds good. I think I'll join you. Honey, what would you like?" she asked, turning to Ethan.

"Well, since you're asking, a cup of hot chocolate would be good."

Sally went into the kitchen while Ethan directed their guest to the table in the breakfast area.

"So, does Emily come by and visit on weekends?"

"Usually. She's going to the Lady Vols basketball game this afternoon, so she's coming by for dinner."

"And, if I'm not being too nosey, what does Justin normally do on weekends?"

"Well, last night he spent the night at a friend's house. Most weekends he spends hanging out with friends - after he finishes his homework, that is."

"I know he's a great football player, but he didn't also want to play basketball?"

"I think he wanted a break from all the practices and the coaches yelling all the time. And he likes his free time as much as he likes sports."

The two men continued chatting until Sally returned with the drinks. After placing the cups on the table, she sat next to her husband.

"Well," said Mr. Ross, "I really appreciate your doing this interview with me. So, The Tennessean didn't have any problem with you being interviewed by another newspaper, Mr. Ward?"

"Oh, no. They figure the more publicity, the better. I'm more surprised the News-Sentinel would want to interview an editor from another newspaper."

"Well, like you said, the more publicity the better. But, to be honest, it was really my idea. I had to convince them that it would make a good story."

"We're flattered, Mr. Ross," said Sally, "but I'm still not sure why you would want to do a story on our lives. Other than the fact that we are a racially mixed couple - which is not as big news as it was twenty years ago - we're just average people."

"I'm sorry, but I can't agree with you there, Mrs. Ward. If any two people have had interesting and exciting lives, it would be you and your husband."

"I guess we have had more than our share of adventure, although it was never something we planned or wanted," said Ethan. "But I'm curious - how do you know so much about us, and why did you want to do a story on our lives?"

Mr. Ross gave them a sly smile.

"Actually, it feels as if I have been stalking you most of your life

- unintentionally, of course."

"What do you mean?" asked Ethan.

"Well, I'm only a few years younger than you, and I grew up in Morristown. As a kid I remember hearing about you witnessing the shooting of Deputy Pratt. Then, when I was thirteen, my parents moved to Chattanooga about the same time as Professor Robertson's trial began, so we followed that. Then, in 1977, I got my first job at a little newspaper near Nashville, so I remember reading about what happened with your brother-in-law Robert Simpson. And now, here I am in Knoxville and your daughter was kidnapped."

"Wow," said Sally, "I guess that is quite a set of coincidences."

"Yes, so hopefully you can see why I wanted to do a story on the two of you. I think it will make interesting reading for our subscribers, plus, I get to know you better."

"This is very flattering of you, Mr. Ross. So, what all do you need to know?"

For the next forty-five minutes, Mr. Ross listened to Ethan and Sally as they recanted the past twenty-five years of their lives. Soon, after they had brought him up to their current lives, he asked one final question.

"So, if there is one lesson you have learned from life that you would like to pass on to others," he asked, "what would that be?"

"Hmm," said Ethan, "that is a very good question. I'll have to think about it for a minute."

"And you, Mrs. Ward?"

"Oh, that's easy. Love conquers all."

"Really? That simple, huh?"

"Actually, I don't think it's that simple. Let me ask you a question, Mr. Ross. What's the difference between Jesus and Satan?"

"Between Jesus and Satan?" he repeated wide eyed. "That's quite a question. I guess the obvious answer - based on your statement - is that Jesus loves everybody and Satan hates everybody, right?"

"Well, close. I've spent a lot of time thinking about this and...well, to me the answer is that Satan did love, but only himself, while Jesus loved everybody. I believe that God gave everybody the ability and the need to love and be loved, but some people turn it inward, like Satan, while Jesus instructed us to love each other as we loved ourselves. Wouldn't the world be a wonderful place if everybody really did that?"

"Yes, it would, but we both know it never will happen."

"Of course not, but it's a nice thought."

Sally and Mr. Ross turned to Ethan, awaiting his answer.

"Well, honey?" she asked.

"Okay. I was just thinking of something a professor in college told me many years ago. I didn't think much about it when he said it, but I've thought about it from time to time, and I now realize how true it is."

"What's that?" asked Mr. Ross.

"He said 'Live the examined life'"

"Live the examined life?" repeated Mr. Ross. "What does that mean - that you have to analyze everything that you do all the time?"

"Sort of."

"That seems like it would be awfully stressful to me."

"Perhaps, but...well, let me give you an example. We were just talking about the day that I saw Deputy Pratt get shot. I remember that day - I had just finished lunch and I asked my mother if I could go to my friend Billy Caldwell's house. If I had not gone, or if I'd left an hour later, I would have not been there, Sally's father and his friend would have not picked me up, the Deputy would have not been shot, and - not only my life, but a lot of other people's lives would have been changed."

"I guess that makes sense," said Mr. Ross.

"So, if a little decision like that," continued Ethan, "can have such an impact on so many people's lives, just think what a difference other, more important decisions can make. Somebody offers a kid a cigarette and he takes it and becomes hooked and dies from lung cancer. A young boy starts hanging out with the wrong crowd and they talk him into helping them rob a liquor store. A teenage girl lets her boyfriend talk her into having sex and she gets pregnant. If people realize in advance the impact such decisions can have, perhaps that knowledge can help change their decisions and therefore their his lives. God gave us laws and rules to live by for a reason - not to make lives more difficult, but to protect us from things that are harmful. Yes, it might be tough to go through life thinking of every decision you make, but I think it would be worth it."

"Well," said Mr. Ross, "not only have you two given me a great story, but you've given me a lot to think about. I really appreciate your time."

Their guest arose from the table and shook Ethan and Sally's hands. They walked him to the door, where Ethan removed his coat from the closet and handed it to him.

"Thank you both for the interview," he said.

"Thank you," they both responded.

"When do you think the story will run?'

"Hopefully within the week. I'll let you know when I have a definite date."

The two said goodbye to their guest and watched as he got in his car and drove away. They returned to the table where they finished their drinks.

"That was nice of him to do that," said Sally.

"Yeah, he seems like a nice man. So, what do you want to do the rest of the day, Mrs. Ward?"

"Oh, something exciting."

"Like what?"

"How about a hot game of checkers."

"Sounds good to me. Loser has to fix lunch."

"You're on."

Ethan arose from the table, kissed his wife, walked to the closet and returned with the checkerboard. They sipped their drinks as they enjoyed a quiet morning at home.

Author's Comments: *The Third Generation* deals with decisions people make and how they come back to haunt future generations. Part of the story concerns racial issues in the town of Greeneville, Tennessee in the 1940's. Please note that, to the best of my knowledge and research, no such occurrence ever took place in Greeneville. Greeneville has always been a peaceful town void of racial turmoil. This story is entirely fictional and resemblance to any actual event or person is purely coincidental.

Larry Buttram

Other books by Larry Buttram

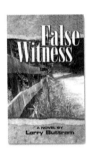

FALSE WITNESS

It is the summer of 1963 in rural East Tennessee. Ethan Ward, thirteen, is enjoying his summer vacation. On a trip to a friend's house--on a hot and dusty country road--he sees two black strangers shoot and kill a Deputy Sheriff. They escape leaving him the only witness. The men are never caught, and for years Ethan lives in fear of their return. Then, in a chance meeting six years later, he learns that things are not always what they appear, and that good and evil aren't divided along the color line.

HONOR THY SISTER

It is 1978 in Murfreesboro, Tennessee, and Sally Ward, with a caring husband, two young children, and a fulfilling job as a teacher, is content with her life. Then, her wayward sister, Merita, moves back home, and her world is torn apart. Merita, or Rita as she now likes to be called, apologizes for her past behavior, and for abandoning the family. Sally accepts her apology, and is happy to have her sister back in her life. Then, when disaster strikes, Sally must decide if she believes her sister was an innocent victim, or was the cause of the tragedy.

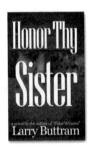